DEAD ON DELIVERY

An utterly gripping British crime thriller

STEVE PARKER

Detective Ray Paterson Book 8

JOFFE BOOKS

Joffe Books, London
www.joffebooks.com

First published in Great Britain in 2022

This paperback edition was first published
in Great Britain in 2022

Cover art by Stuart Bache

ISBN: 978-1-80405-280-8

CHAPTER ONE

The newly married Mrs Clocks was in no mood for her husband's jokes. She let him know this by the look on her face and the fact that she had him up against the wall by his throat in their hotel room.

He'd seen her angry before. The first time was when they initially set eyes on each other and he'd made one distasteful remark too many about the parts of a dead girl in a freezer. She'd punched him in the side of the head hard enough for him to slip into unconsciousness for a second or two.

He knew from that moment that she was the girl for him.

'What's the one thing I asked from you?' she screamed at him.

'Errghh . . . Lynds! Lynds! I can't . . . I can't breathe,' he squeaked. 'I can't fuckin' breathe!'

'What? What did you say?'

He gripped the hand around his throat. 'Can't . . . breathe.' He felt the blood flushing his face and a vein swelling on his temple. Tears welled in his eyes.

'I asked you if you had any kids and you said no, and suddenly a son turns up out of the blue? You lying piece of shit!'

Clocks held up one finger as he felt himself fading. 'Lemme . . . explain. Again. Lemme . . .'

She eased off the pressure, let him go and turned away. 'You bastard!'

Clocks sucked in a huge lungful of air then spent the next few seconds trying to regulate his breathing. Slowly, his face returned to normal. 'Will you just . . . let me explain meself?'

She sat herself down heavily onto the corner of the bed. 'Go on, then. Get on with it.'

'Look, I don't know anything about 'im. I really don't. I swear to you. I'da told you if I did, but I didn't.'

'So what the fuck is he doing showing up now?'

Clocks shook his head. 'I honestly don't know. All I know is, 'e turned up at the weddin' late and told Ray 'e was me son. Never seen 'im before in me life. Truly.'

'Who's his mum?'

'No idea. If 'e is me son, an' I ain't sayin' 'e is, then it must've been some ol' slapper from the estate I lived on when I was younger.'

'Which old slapper?'

'I don't know. I just said.'

'Was there a lot of old slappers on your estate, then?'

Clocks looked up at the ceiling. 'I'm not gonna lie. There was a fair few, yeah. We didn't 'ave PlayStations an' the like. Just bike sheds and . . . well, there wasn't much else to do, so . . . we made our own entertainment, y'know?'

'So what you're telling me is that there could be more little bastard Clockses running around that you don't know about?' Lyndsey, her face locked into a deep frown, gave him daggers.

'What? No! Of course not.'

'Could be though, right?'

'No, sweetie. An' look, we don't even know if 'e's on the level, do we?'

'So why would he show up out of the blue?'

'I said I *don't know*!'

Lyndsey launched herself off the bed and stood nose to nose with him. 'Don't take that tone with me, John. Just don't!'

'Alright, alright. I'm sorry. Sorry. I know you're upset.'

'Why the fuck did Ray have to tell you? He should have kept it to himself.'

'He 'ad to, didn't 'e? The man was worried that the kid would come up to me and introduce 'imself. Ray wanted to give me an 'eads up, that's all. He'd already squared 'im up about sayin' anything to you. I 'ad to tell you, gel. It's only right.'

Lyndsey dropped back onto the bed. She cast her eyes to the floor and nodded. 'I s'pose so.'

'Look. I know it's a shock an' a shit way to start married life. I geddit. But we can work through this. You know I love yer more than anythin'. You know that.'

She looked up at him. 'It's not your fault. Well, it is, but it isn't. You know what I mean?'

'Yeah, yeah. Course I do. No worries. I'm sorry.'

'I'll get over it. Just a shock.'

'I know, Lynds, but we 'ave to try an' move past it. I'll set up a meet with 'im. Find out what the game is.'

Lyndsey gave him a slight nod and a weak grin.

'So,' he said. 'We good?'

'Yeah, we're good, you idiot. C'mere.'

Clocks sat on the edge of the bed next to her. They held each other tightly for a few moments. Lyndsey whispered, 'I love you' in his ear.

He hugged her tighter. 'I love you too, sweetie. More than anything. I'm so sorry.'

'Yeah, I know,' she whispered. 'I'll deal with it. Look, I've got something to tell you too.'

Clocks froze. 'What?'

'I think I'm going to take up Wol's offer to join his squad.'

Wallace Young, ex-commissioner of the Metropolitan Police, the only commissioner to still think and act like a police officer and not a politician, was the most powerful ally

Clocks had. They'd got off to a shaky start, but he quickly took a shine to Clocks and his partner, Detective Superintendent Ray Paterson, and their way of policing: unconventional, tough and totally uncompromising. He'd once said that they reminded him of himself when he was a youngster in the job.

Clocks let go of Lyndsey and pushed her back so he could see her face. 'Oh, Christ. You serious? Why the fuck didn't you say so before?'

She glared at him. 'John, don't start.'

'No! I'm gonna start. Now you 'old up a minute. I know Wol offered you a job, but this ain't any ol' job, is it? This is contract killing work, fer fuck's sake. That ain't you. You do the job, the whole police thing, to do right by people. You're a copper, not the Jackal!'

'Who? Who's "the Jackal"?'

Clocks shook his head. 'An assassin. Tried to take out a French president years ago.'

'Which one?'

'I dunno. The one with the big 'ooter . . . de Goal or somethin'. It don't bloody matter which one, does it? The point is, you'll be killin' people for money!'

'I do that now, don't I?'

'Yeah, alright, funny girl. The difference is, you do it for the right reasons. To protect people. Innocent people. The public. You do it to keep us safe from terrorists, villains, any mad fucker that wants us all dead. You do it because it's the right thing to do. You're on the right side of the equation.' He took a deep breath, stood up and walked over to the kettle. He picked it up and tested its weight. There was enough in there for one cup. 'Seein' as 'ow we've slaughtered the minibar, I'm gonna 'ave a cuppa. You want one?'

'No.'

He flicked the switch on the kettle. 'So, come on then . . . 'ow come you've decided to join up with an ex-police commissioner an' 'is little band of cut-throats?'

Lyndsey sighed. 'Honestly, I'm not sure. But I don't want to just keep working for the Met. I'm tired of all the rules and regs that stop us doing our job properly. I'm tired of having to be investigated as a criminal when I shoot someone who had to be shot. I'm tired of the suspensions that go with it, and I'm tired of being accused of everything under the sun just for doing my job. I feel there's less and less support from the senior management. I'm just fucking tired, John.'

Clocks nodded as he put a teabag in the mug. 'I know.' His voice softened. 'So, what's yer play, then? What about us? I mean, Christ, we only got married a little while ago.'

'What d'you mean, "What about us?" This won't make any difference to us, John.'

He whirled around, disappointment on his face. 'Course it will. If you're gonna take off swannin' about all over the world, 'ow are we gonna make a go of it?'

'Like any other couple where one partner works away. Like the army, the navy. Like those guys. It won't make any difference if we work at it. And you have to work at a marriage, love.'

'I know, but I thought we'd 'ave about twenny odd years before we started 'avin' to do that.'

'We'll be fine. Trust me.'

Clocks sighed deeply. 'I do trust you. But I'm worried for you. You do know he doesn't just want you for your admin skills an' dinner-makin' abilities, don't yer? There's gonna come a time when you'll 'ave to top someone. Then what? Then you'll be a murderer.'

She dropped her head and looked into her lap. 'Depends how you look at it. And let's face it, this world would be better off without some people. You know that.'

He poured out the kettle and watched the steaming water fill the mug, beige liquid swirling as the teabag and milk melded together. 'Yeah, okay. Fair point. You're right, but why not leave it to the White Ghost? Let 'im do that shit. It's what 'e's good at.'

'And so am I, John. You know that.'

'Yeah. Okay. Okay. But if you end up toppin' someone, 'ow you gonna come back to the Met? You'll be wanted.'

5

'Only if they know it's me.'

Clocks shrugged. 'It's risky. Very risky. You could walk into work an' get yer collar felt before you know it. I don't like it.'

Lyndsey nodded. 'I know. And I'm sorry. But I'll be careful. You know I will.'

'Alrighty, then. Your mind's made up and I know there's no point trying to change it. Guess you gotta do what you gotta do. Just be careful.'

'I will. Of course, I will.'

'When you going?'

'Soon. Not sure exactly when.'

'Wow. Lots of surprises all round today.'

'Yeah, I guess,' she said.

'But me an' you. We're good, yeah? About the son thing? It's not going to be a problem for us, is it?' he said. 'I genuinely didn't know about 'im'.

She shook her head. 'I know you didn't and of course we're good, you dick. But, be warned. If any more bastard kids come crawling out of the woodwork with your name on them, I'll cut your bollocks off and use 'em as stress balls. Got it?'

Clocks smiled. She still loved him.

CHAPTER TWO

DAY 1

PC Matthew Kelder pressed down hard on the accelerator. The engine surged, the front wheels seemed to lift and he felt himself pushed back hard into the driver's seat. He stole a quick glance to his left: his partner, PC Chris Welch, had one hand gripped tightly around the grab handle while he snatched up the radio mic with the other.

'Mike Delta . . . Mike Delta from Mike One,' Chris announced. 'Chase message.'

PC Welch, the radio operator of Mike One, the division's high-speed pursuit vehicle, sat himself back in his seat as the driver gunned the engine, following a motorbike that had failed to stop for them. Perhaps the rider was just another young idiot who didn't want to be stopped and questioned for a traffic infringement, but the fact that he'd chosen to ignore the blues and twos suggested to Matthew that there was likely more to it than that. Either way, the motorcyclist had made a big mistake. There was no way Matthew was going to allow any distance to be put between them.

'Your location, Mike One?'

Good. Susan Tallis was on shift. The young civilian station controller was keen and excitable, but she always managed to stay in control, and Matthew had never known her to put a foot wrong.

'We're on Old Jamaica Road, toward Abbey Street,' said PC Welch. We're behind a motorcycle. Rider has failed to stop. We've just passed Marine Street on our left.'

'Registration?'

'Negative. It's part obscured. Can't see it properly. That's why we wanted to stop him.'

'Understood. Description, please.'

'Male, wearing black leathers. Livery shows Sprinter courier company. Bike looks to be a black Kawasaki of some kind. Could be a Honda, I dunno.'

'Any unit to assist Mike One? Fail to stop . . . Old Jamaica Road toward Abbey Street?'

The airwaves crackled with responses.

'Mike Delta Four Five.'

'Mike Delta Two.'

'Mike Delta Four Five . . . Mike Delta Two . . .' confirmed Susan Tallis. *'Thank you. Anyone else?'*

'Mike Delta from Papa Seven. We're at the top end of Jamaica Road. Happy to help.' Papa Seven, the pursuit vehicle from Deptford Division, bordering Rotherhithe, was obviously fishing for work on a quiet morning.

'Papa Seven from Mike Delta,' said PC Welch. 'Thank you for the offer. Please stay that end of the ground in case suspect heads your way.'

A disappointed voice answered, *'All received, Mike Delta.'*

'Suspect has picked up speed,' said Welch. 'Turned left into Abbey Street — failed to give way. Forced a vehicle to brake sharply.'

'Thank you, Mike One,' said Susan Tallis.

'Mike Delta Four Five just leaving the Arnold's Estate. I'm coming out into Druid Street.'

'Thank you, Four Five.'

'Still got eyes on but losing him in traffic,' said Welch. 'Druid Street toward Tower Bridge Road.'

'Thank you, Mike One,' said Tallis. *'Four Five . . . Suspect headed your way.'*

'Received,' said the driver of Four Five.

The airways were silent for a few moments while Matthew strained to keep eyes on the motorbike that was weaving through the traffic ahead of them.

'Mike Delta from Four Five. I see him. Traffic heavy. He's on the outside. Standby.'

Traffic began a panicked move to the left as Mike One, still with its siren blaring and lights flashing, pushed its way through the heavy throng of morning rush hour traffic. The motorbike was a good two hundred yards ahead of them and getting further as Mike One lost speed against the building traffic. Any motorcycle had the advantage of outmanoeuvring a car on any given day, but trying to catch one in heavy traffic was nigh on impossible.

But then Matthew saw Mike Delta Four Five shoot out into the road and block the bike's path. Its brake light came on and the back wheel wobbled as the rider took evasive action.

The bike stopped.

Matthew pushed Mike One closer.

The driver of Four Five jumped out and ran around the front of his car.

The rider waited.

As the driver of Four Five drew level with the bonnet, the bike revved, turned hard right and shot off into Sweeney Crescent, from where Four Five had just come.

'Mike Delta,' said PC Welch. 'Our boy's evaded Four Five. Now in Sweeney Crescent toward Jamaica Road.'

'All received,' said Susan Tallis. *'Any units near Jamaica Road?'*

There was no reply.

The driver of Four Five jumped back in his car and spun it around to take up the chase.

Matthew saw a gap in the traffic ahead. He floored the car and mounted the pavement, screeching Mike One into Sweeney Crescent. He stayed quiet and calm as he came up behind Four Five.

'Four Five,' said Welch into the radio. 'Move aside.'

Four Five did as he was told and allowed the bigger, faster car to overtake him.

'Standby,' said Welch. Silence filled the airways until he continued: 'Our boy's left into Jamaica Road. Left into Jamaica Road. Do we have any black rats on bikes nearby?'

'Christine's onto traffic branch now,' said Tallis. *'India Nine has offered assistance.'*

'We'll take it,' said Welch. 'Traffic's bad. Eyes in the sky would be good.'

'Understood, Mike One.'

'He's followed the road into Tanner Street. Going back on himself. Now back on Druid Street. Picking up speed.'

'Speed estimate?'

'Fifty. Sixty, at least. He's all over the road! Standby. Standby. He's gonna lose it!'

Matthew shared his partner's fears, but the rider somehow managed to stay upright.

'Nope,' said Welch. 'He's on the pavement toward Tower Bridge Road.'

Silence.

'Coming up to junction with Tower Bridge Road. Amber light showing. Not slowing down. No brakes. Red light! Red light! He's not gonna stop!'

Matthew felt as if his stomach was falling through the floor of the car as he witnessed what happened next.

'Oh, shit!' Welch shouted. 'RTA! RTA! He's been wiped out by a car. Urgent ambulance required, Mike Delta!'

'Understood, Mike One. Standby. All units make your way to Tower Bridge Road, junction with Druid Street. Assist the crew of Mike One with a serious RTA.'

Matthew screeched the car to a halt, partly blocking both northbound and southbound traffic.

Welch jumped out of the car and ran to the motor-cyclist. Within ten seconds he was pulling open the man's jacket and then pumping his chest. Even from where he sat, Matthew knew it was futile. Welch would know it too, but it wasn't their remit to certify death, and if he did nothing the Twitter and Facebook mob would accuse him of just standing around letting a man die.

Matthew pulled open the door of the car that had hit the motorcyclist and spoke to the driver, a smartly dressed woman in her fifties. She was rooted to her seat, hands still gripping the steering wheel, staring blankly toward Tower Bridge. He was joined by a few passers-by, who surrounded the car, telling the woman that it was alright, it was an accident and the rider would be fine. Anything to reassure her.

Matthew left her with the members of the public. He knew his job right now was to secure the scene for when the traffic investigators arrived. They would expect the road cordoned off, even though it was in the middle of rush hour traffic on one of the busiest roads in and out of London. The resulting jam was going to be horrendous.

He walked to the back of the car to get some tape when something lying in the road caught his eye. What he saw didn't quite register at first.

Then he felt his stomach churn.

CHAPTER THREE

Detective Superintendent Ray Paterson could feel the sweat trickle down his back as the heat of the day began to rise. It was shaping up to be a stinker of a day in more ways than one. It was less than a five-minute walk from his office in Tower Bridge Police Station to the scene of the accident, but it seemed longer. A lot longer. From the second he'd picked up the phone and shouted to Detective Inspector Johnny Clocks that they had a call-out, the older man hadn't stopped whining.

'You serious, guv? I don't understand,' Clocks had said as he pulled his jacket off the back of his chair.

'Me neither, John. But Inspector Norris wants us to attend, so we attend. It's a couple of minutes' walk. Not going to hurt, is it? Anyway, the exercise will do you good.'

'Never mind the exercise, I just don't understand why we've been called. You know No-Nuts Norris 'as just got 'is panic on again, don't cha? Bloke can't take a shit without callin' for someone to 'elp wipe 'is arse, can 'e?'

'True enough. But we won't know if he really needs our help until we get *our* arses out of the office and across the road, will we?'

Clocks shook his head. 'Still think we should wait and let the 'elmets deal with it all first and then call us if necessary. Me bloody tea'll get cold.'

Detective Constable Tommy Gunn, new to Paterson's team, looked up at them with a little sideways smile and hope in his eyes. 'Want any help, guv?'

'No thanks, Tom. You're alright. Hold the fort down until we get back, will you?'

'Course, guv.' Gunn returned to typing up a report that he'd started a week before. Writing reports wasn't his strong suit.

'You're not going to need your coat, Clocksy.'

'I'm going out to represent the Metropolitan Police Service, sir. I need to look smart and efficient at all times.'

'Don't take the piss,' said Paterson.

Clocks laughed. 'Fair enough, guv.' He slung the jacket on his desk and followed Paterson.

* * *

Ahead of him, Paterson could see the traffic beginning to build northbound along Tower Bridge Road, and he knew the same would be happening for the westbound traffic along Druid Street. He checked his watch: 8.17 a.m. Not the best of times for this to happen. In the distance, a couple of uniformed police officers struggled to contain the scene and hold back the traffic. Help was on its way. Blue lights flashing, siren blaring and on the wrong side of the road, the message car, Mike Delta Six, was seconds away. Two more police officers to help. More would be behind them.

Mike Delta Six parked in front of the northbound traffic and prevented any chance of it moving any further. The radio operator jumped out and, putting on a reflective tabard, headed across the road to stop the westbound vehicles from moving.

'Fuck me, it's 'ot, ain't it?' said Clocks as he and Paterson cut through the traffic that had been lucky enough to clear the junction before everything went tits up behind them. Now they were just stuck in good old regular London traffic.

Paterson ignored him as he scanned the scene looking for Inspector Norris. 'John, can you see No-Nuts anywhere?'

'Nope. Probably gone home sick by now, I'da thought.'

Paterson chuckled. 'Doesn't matter. I can see him.'

The two detectives made their way toward Norris, pushing through the crowd that was already gathering. Many of them had their phones out and were busily recording everything around them. Nothing quite like a little bit of excitement to start the day, and with the added bonus of a few more likes on Twitter and Instagram.

A uniformed police officer blocked their way. 'Can you stand back, please, sir.' Her voice was uncertain. Paterson took her in: nineteen if she was a day, uniform neatly pressed, shiny shoes, flushed face. A newbie. Very new. Things had changed since he joined up — more so for Clocks. In their time it was sixteen weeks training at Hendon before you went out on the streets. Hendon training centre had since been sold off to property developers, and these days you signed up and got your training through a baptism of fire. Stupid and dangerous.

'Jump out the way, babe,' said Clocks. 'Let's 'ave a butchers at what's goin' on.'

'Sir!' she shouted. Clocks stopped dead. 'Please. You can't go this way. There's been an . . . incident. Step back, please.'

Clocks grinned. 'An incident? What? Where?' He craned his head past her. 'I'll go and 'ave a little look, see what's 'appened an' I'll come right back an' tell yer.'

'Sir. *Please*. Step back.'

'Come on, love. Don't be like that. Just a little peek. Is anyone dead? Any bits 'anging out of anyone?' He moved forward.

'Sir! Step back or I'll be forced to arrest you.'

Paterson shook his head.

'What?' said Clocks. 'Nick me? What for?'

The young woman flushed even more.

'Pretty sure you can't nick me for just walking along the street, can you? What powers are you relying on for that, officer? What act and section? Hmm? You don't know, do you? Neither do I, so there you go. Carry on. Don't be threatenin' me with false arrest.'

Paterson had seen this before. Clocks liked to overload people with questions. One question after another, rapid-fire. It clogged up the thought process and created confusion, and sure enough, the young officer wore an expression of total bewilderment at Clocks's onslaught.

'John, that's enough,' said Paterson. 'Pack it in.' He reached inside his jacket for his warrant card and showed her his ID, which only served to confuse her further. She stared at his card for longer than was necessary, desperate to escape the confusion and embarrassment that had swallowed her whole.

'It's okay, officer. I'm Detective Superintendent Paterson.' He put his ID back in his pocket, breaking the spell over the young girl. 'And the country's favourite arsehole here is Inspector Clocks. We're from the murder squad over at Tower Bridge. Inspector Norris called for us.'

Clocks had already walked past her and was heading for Norris.

'He's just playing with you. It's his idea of fun. Sorry about that.' Paterson smiled at her as he walked past.

Clocks was hovering around Inspector Norris, who had his back to him and was talking to a woman. Paterson took a moment to take everything in. On the ground was a motorcycle, its front wheel pointing up to the sky, and there were fragments of plastic strewn all over the road. A strong smell of petrol stung his nostrils.

Scattered across the road were several large plastic boxes, their lids open and their contents warming up in the early morning sun. Some fifteen feet away from the bike, a car stood silent. The driver's door was open and, if he had to guess, the woman Norris was talking to was the driver. One or the other had jumped a red light and the motorcycle courier lying on the ground, his left leg bent at an awkward angle and his head at another, turned out to be the loser of this particular meeting of metal and plastic.

A uniformed PC stood by the dead man in a futile attempt to obstruct people taking photos with their phones. It was a battle he wasn't going to win. This man's body would soon be all over social media.

Paterson walked back to the crowd and targeted a young man in a light summer jacket who was craning his neck to get a better view with his phone.

'Detective Superintendent Paterson,' he said as he stood himself in front of the man's phone. 'Time to do something useful. Give me your jacket, please.'

The young man looked at Paterson. 'What?'

'Your jacket. You've just volunteered it.'

'Have I? What for?'

'To give this man some form of dignity from people like you. Used to be a time when people would see if there was anything they could do to help victims of accidents, not try to take photos that they could share with their pathetic little imaginary "friends".'

'But he's dead. Can't help him now, can I?'

'That's where your jacket and this poor sod's dignity comes in, son. That could be a member of your family lying there. Think how you'd feel if it was.' Paterson glared at him. The young man nodded and pulled off his jacket. He handed it to Paterson. 'Thank you,' said Paterson.

Paterson laid the coat over the courier. Although he was still wearing his crash helmet and couldn't properly be identified in photos, Paterson still felt that covering him was the respectful thing to do.

Inspector Norris had escorted the driver of the car to Mike One and sat her down on the back seat. Paterson could see that she was in a bad way; she had tear-streaked cheeks, was shaking violently and had a vacant look in her eyes.

Shock had taken a firm grip of her. In the distance, the wail of an ambulance signified its approach.

Inspector Norris left her with a uniformed officer and turned around only to bump into Johnny Clocks. 'Jesus, John! I never saw you.'

'I know. Very few people do when I've got me ninja on. Could've killed you if I wanted. You need to be a bit more vigilant, No-Nuts, me ol' son.'

Norris brushed past him. 'Where's Paterson?'

'Nestled comfortably between the thighs of some dusky maiden on a golden beach somewhere, I should think.'

Norris shook his head. 'Clocks, why are you such a dick?'

Clocks shrugged. 'Gives me somethin' to do when I'm bored. Speakin' of bored, why 'ave you called out the Met's two greatest murder 'tecs, livin' or dead, to a bleedin' road accident? This is one for the traffic boys, innit?'

'So you think you're above investigating a road traffic accident, do you?'

'Er, yeah. That's for the rats. Their bread an' butter, doin' this. We don't ask them to investigate murders, do we? I take it you've called them?'

'I have. The nearest unit is in Catford.'

'Oh, cosmic. They'll be ages, then.'

Norris nodded. Rush hour traffic from Catford to Bermondsey was going to be a bitch, blue lights and sirens or not.

'Morning, Inspector,' said Paterson as he joined them.

'Morning, sir. Thanks for coming.'

'No problem. I take it we're here because of the bits of meat lying all over the road, yes?'

'Yessir,' said Norris.

Clocks perked up. 'Meat? What d'you mean, *meat*?' He spun around to take a better look at the scene he had breezed through in his haste to annoy Inspector Norris.

'So, what have we got?' Paterson watched Johnny Clocks as he walked away.

'Obviously, a fatal RTA. Car v. Motorcycle. The rider is — was — a courier. From what I can make of it, he was on his way to Guy's hospital on a run with transplant organs. According to the driver and a few other witnesses, the rider went straight through a red light and got collected by a car.'

'In rush hour traffic? She looks to be on the wrong side of the road. She overtaking?'

'So the witnesses say. Probably late for a meeting. Maybe just fed up sitting in traffic. Who knows? She's too shook up to give a coherent statement. Anyway, she went straight into the side of him and sent him flying across the road. Dead as a doornail by the time he stopped.'

'Okay. Bad day for him. Why are we here?'

'Well, this is where it gets interesting. Once we arrived and ascertained he was dead, we did a quick search of him. All he had on him was a set of keys and his wallet. We found his driving licence. Stuart Glossop, aged forty-two. Lived over in Devon Mansions. He also had a folded-up delivery notice.'

'And?'

'Well, with these boxes, it's usually one organ to each box. So, one organ, one box. By my count there are more organs than boxes. A lot more.'

CHAPTER FOUR

Paterson and Inspector Norris walked back over the scene, careful to avoid disturbing any of the wreckage from the collision. Everything was evidence now: bits of glass, twisted metal, broken plastic. Everything would reveal something. Clocks was scratching his head when Paterson joined him.

'What d'you think that is, guv?' he said.

Paterson peered down at a piece of meat and shrugged. 'Not sure. You?'

'Dunno. Liver?'

'Liver is a different shape,' said Norris.

Clocks looked up. 'Really? What shape is it, then?'

'Usually tapered. That's bean-shaped. Smaller too. It's a kidney.'

Clocks wrinkled his nose. 'Thank you, Dr Norris.'

'Not a doctor, John.' He pointed to an open white box lying on the floor. 'I just read the label.'

'Eh? Oh, yeah. Nice one, Sherlock. Shoulda seen that, shouldn't I?'

'It's what I would have hoped for from a detective of your reputation,' said Norris, his voice thick with sarcasm.

Paterson pointed to another box that was lying on its side, partially opened. 'Let's see what's in this one.'

'I 'ope it's an 'ead,' said Clocks. 'I've always wanted to open a box with an 'ead in it.'

'A head?' said Norris. 'Who puts a head in a box?'

'Mafia. Triads. Albanians. Quite popular, from what I understand. Maybe someone pissed off another someone and they're posting 'im back to 'is missus in bits. Just a thought.'

Norris shook his head. 'Things you think of.'

'Open it, then,' said Paterson.

Clocks looked up at Norris. 'Got any rubbers on you, No-Nuts?'

'Rubbers?'

'Yeah. Rubbers. Gloves. Rubber gloves. What'd you think I was gonna do? Fuck whatever's in 'ere?'

'Wouldn't surprise me in the slightest.' Norris dug around in one of the pouches attached to his belt.

'Nor me,' said Paterson.

'Well, hardy-fuckin'-har. Ain't you two a pair of comedians?'

'You would though, wouldn't you?' said Norris.

'Probably,' said Clocks.

Norris smiled and handed Clocks a pair of rubber gloves.

Clocks carefully lifted the box upright then opened the lid. Inside was a white plastic tray with a large number of little glass jars, each packed in plastic, gathered at one side of the box. 'The fuck's this?' he said.

Paterson and Norris took a look. Norris shook his head.

'What's the label say, John?' said Paterson.

Clocks took a quick look on the opposite side of the box. 'Says "Corneas". What's a cornea when it's at 'ome?'

'It's the clear outer layer that covers your eyeball,' said Paterson. 'Bit like a window.'

'Really? Who makes them, then? One of the big double glazin' firms?'

Paterson rubbed his face. 'No, John. They're not literal windows. They're not made of glass, are they?'

'I dunno. Can do all sorts of things these days with a bit of technology, can't they? I read somewhere they're making meat with one of those 3D printer things. I dunno 'ow they make meat out of plastic. Surely it'd melt in the oven, wouldn't it?' He shook his head. 'I'm not eatin' meat made out of melted plastic.'

'These come from donors,' Paterson said. 'Dead people. The corneas are cut off their eyes and packed up for transplant onto someone with defective eyesight.'

'Cut off their eyes? Fuck that! Wouldn't let anyone near my eyes with a scalpel. That ain't 'appening.'

'What? You'd be dead, John. It wouldn't matter, would it?'

'Would to me. Fuck puttin' a scalpel near my mince pies, matey boy.'

'Sir,' said Norris. 'Why do you indulge him? He can't really be that thick, can he?'

'Oi! I ain't thick, No-Nuts. I just don't want anyone near me eyes with a Stanley knife, whether I'm dead or alive.'

'Yes, I know. But as the guv said, it wouldn't make any difference . . .'

'You see!' said Paterson. 'You get sucked in. We all do. He's got this annoying way with him. It's almost a compulsion he triggers in people. It's a bit like that need, that pull, you have inside to help a disabled person when they're struggling with something.'

Clocks was grinning. 'So . . . a box of eyes, then. This should see us through the week.'

Paterson and Norris shook their heads.

'I've been thinkin', guv . . . If the driver 'ad turned a different *cornea* this might never 'ave 'appened. Geddit? Cornea. Corner. Turned a different corner. George Michael song.'

Paterson pulled out his notebook and flipped it open.

'What you doin'?' said Clocks.

'Writing that one down. Stunningly funny, John. Best play on words I've ever heard.'

'Alright. No need for that, is there? Just tryin' to lighten the day. No point in being miserable about it. I just thought if we're goin' to make jokes about eyes, the cornea the better.'

Paterson laughed. 'Yeah, that one was pretty good, actually. Now, when you've finished your audition, we've got work to do.'

'I take it you 'ave a cunnin' plan?' said Clocks.

'The courier firm this guy worked for . . . Let's see what they can tell us.'

CHAPTER FIVE

'Morning.' Paterson stepped inside the Sprinter Couriers office. Clocks followed him in.

A fat, middle-aged man who looked like he could use a good wash and a shave looked up at him. 'Can I help you, squire?'

'Would be nice if you could.' Paterson held out his warrant card for the scruff to see it.

The man peered at it over the top of his blue-framed glasses and sniffed. 'What can I do for you, *officers*?'

'Are you in charge?' said Paterson.

'I am at the moment. Why?'

'Because I want to talk to whoever is in charge — the owner or whatever. Is that you?'

'Nah. I don't own it, but I'm in charge. Boss is on his holidays. Won't be back for a fortnight.'

'Then you'll have to do.' Paterson pulled out his notebook. 'Can you tell me if you have a courier by the name of . . . Stuart Glossop?'

The scruff narrowed his eyes. 'Why d'you wanna know?'

'Part of an enquiry, fellah,' said Clocks. 'Nothing to worry about.'

'I'm not worried, mate. But I don't have to tell you who we've got working for us.'

Clocks pulled himself upright. ''Ere we go. Always one, ain't there?'

'Always one what, mate?'

'An uncooperative little bunny, such as yerself. That rarely works out well.'

'What? What'd you say? You threatening me?'

Clocks smiled. 'Nah. I don't do threats, mate. I do promises. At the moment, I've done neither, but I'm more than 'appy to revise the situation if need be.'

'He can't talk to me like that,' said the scruff. 'I know my rights.'

Paterson sighed. 'Well, sir, you do indeed seem like the sort of gentleman that knows his rights. Most likely due to occupational hazards, I'd guess. But just to be clear, you'd be amazed at how easy it is for us to violate those rights if we want or need to. Now, we didn't come here for you or anybody you might be involved with or any little dodgy things you may have going on in here. So, again, let's all be nice. Dial this back a bit and start again. Do you have a Stuart Glossop working for you, yes or no?'

'No.'

'Are you sure?'

'Yes.

'Are you?' Paterson felt his hackles rise a bit. 'I'm asking because he just got wiped out in an accident in Tower Bridge Road. Dead. So, if you do know him, I need to know. Have another think for me.'

The scruffy man shook his head. 'Nothing to think about, mate. Never heard of him. He don't work for us.'

'D'you know all your riders?' said Clocks.

'Yep. Haven't got too many.'

'D'you do 'ospital runs? Y'know . . . boxes full of human bits an' bobs an' that.'

'You mean medical runs?'

'Yeah.'

'Nope.'

'Well, the man we scraped off the road earlier was on a bike with your firm's livery all over it, so how d'you explain that?' said Clocks.

'Can't,' said the scruff.

'Well,' said Paterson, 'we'll need to take a look at your employee records. Just to be sure.'

The scruff pulled himself up straight. 'Nah. Can't do that.'

'Look, mate,' said Clocks, we're not tryin' to find out 'ow much you put through the books. We're not the bleedin' tax man. We're murder squad.'

'Murder squad? Why didn't you say so?'

'Would it 'ave made a difference?'

'Nah. Not to me. Data protection an' all that. Can't just hand it over.'

'Not askin' you to 'and it over, mate. Askin' you to give us a look, that's all.'

'Can't do that.'

'Why not?'

'Data protection.'

Clocks rubbed the back of his neck. 'So, you want us to go get a court order, that what you're sayin'? Or make a data request, yeah?'

'Yeah,' said the scruff.

'That'll take ages.'

'Better get started then, officer.'

Clocks rolled his eyes. 'Why does everybody 'ave to be a dick these days? We're tryin' to be reasonable, fellah, without 'avin' to go to a lot of trouble to get you to answer a simple question.'

'Law of the land, mate. I don't make the rules.' The scruff smirked at them both.

'You're right about that,' said Paterson. 'And you're right to abide by the law and you're right to expect us to abide by it. Trouble is, we rarely do. Now, you can either give us a quick peek at your employee records as I asked for or all you'll do is create a situation that you'll regret. Maybe not today. Maybe not tomorrow. But you will regret it down the road, and when it comes, this situation, it will be fucking heavy. It really is up to you.'

The scruff eyed Paterson up and down. 'That sounded like a threat.' His tone was a little less cocky.

'Excellent. It was supposed to. I'm glad we're getting somewhere. So, now we've worked out who the dominant species are . . . your employee records, please.'

The man stared at Paterson for a moment, then nodded. 'Back room. They're on a computer. This way.'

He led them into a small room that housed a desk with a few pens dotted around, a computer and two rickety old chairs. The place stank of mould.

The man sat himself down and logged on to the computer. 'What was his name again?'

'Glossop. Stuart. With a "U",' said Paterson.

The man typed in the name two-fingered. 'Nope. Nothing. Told you.'

Paterson took a look at the screen. The man had spelled the name right. 'Okay. Thanks. I appreciate that. Wasn't too hard, was it?'

The man gave Paterson a sullen look. 'I'm gonna complain.'

'Not a problem,' said Paterson. 'Nip along to Tower Bridge Police Station, go to the front counter and you'll see a ticket machine. Grab yourself a ticket and take a seat. Better take a sleeping bag too. There's a lot of people in front of you.'

Clocks grinned and flashed his eyebrows at the man before he and Paterson walked out of the office and into the heat.

'Where to now, Ray?'

'Glossop's address. Must be something we can find.'

CHAPTER SIX

Inside the entrance to Devon Mansions, Paterson looked at the sign taped to the lift door. Clocks's shoulders sank.

'Oh, leave off! Fuckin' lift's broken. Great. I s'pose our bloke Glossop lives on the top floor? Be about right.'

Paterson looked at another sign, this one screwed to the wall and setting out which flats were on which floor. 'Near enough, Clocksy. Let's get moving, then.'

'Can't *you* go?'

'What?'

'Can't *you* go? I've got a dodgy back.'

'You never mentioned it earlier.'

'I never 'ad to climb fifteen flights of stairs earlier.'

'There's nothing wrong with your back. Don't try that one with me.'

'There is. I've got a special chair in the office. For dodgy backs.'

'You swiped that out of the crime squad's office, and it wasn't because you had a bad back, was it? You said you liked the colour and the spinny wheels.'

Clocks sniffed. 'Ah. You remember that, then.'

'I do. Now, let's get a move on.'

'I'm gettin' pins an' needles in the top of me legs just thinkin' about it.'

'Then don't think about it.'

'That's not possible, mate. If I say, "Don't think of a pink elephant," you 'ave to think of a pink elephant to understand what I'm sayin'.'

'John, I rarely understand what you're saying. Wait here, then, you old sod.'

'Oi! Not so much of the old. I'm still in me prime. Just with a dodgy back.'

'I doubt you ever had a prime, John. I'll see you in a minute.'

'I'll come with you.'

Paterson, one foot on the bottom step, stopped. 'What? What about your dodgy back?'

'It's better now. Thanks for askin'.'

'I can't do this. I'm off. Stay if you want. Come if you want. You're doing my brain in.'

Clocks smiled. 'I know.'

* * *

With considerable ease, Paterson took the stone stairs two at a time, leaving Clocks at least one flight behind him.

'Slow down, Ray! Jesus!'

'Come on, John! Nearly there! I thought you were supposed to be going to the gym a bit more these days!'

'Nah, fuck that. My old Uncle Dennis used to say that if you're fairly fit, yer don't need to go to the gym, and if you're not fit, they're no good for yer. Give you an 'eart attack.'

'Is this the Uncle Dennis I met at your wedding? The one you said was a kiddie fiddler?'

'That's 'im.'

'Only he wasn't a kiddie fiddler at all, was he? You decided to call him that one day because he offered you and your friends some sweets.'

'Yep. Fuckin' perv.'

'But he wasn't a perv, was he? He was just being nice to you all.'

'Was 'e? You don't know. You weren't there, were yer?'

'You're so full of shit, John, you make a backed-up toilet look clean.'

Clocks grinned.

'One more flight to go! Come on, you can do it!' said Paterson.

Clocks, hand on the metal railing, breathed heavily as he hauled himself up the stairs. 'Why the fuck don't they mend the lifts in this block?'

'No idea. Cutbacks maybe. Labour shortage. Don't know.'

'Fuckin' councils. Nothin's changed 'as it?'

Paterson reached the front door, feeling as fresh as he had before they climbed the stairs. 'Let me know when you're ready.'

Clocks shook his head and sucked in a lungful of air. 'Wait a minute. I'm done in. Me legs are on fire.'

Paterson rolled his eyes at his friend. 'You've got to do something to get in shape. You've got a son to think of now. He might want a game of football in the park with his old dad.'

'Funny bastard. I still don't think 'e's my son. An' even if 'e was, 'e's in 'is bleedin' twenties. Can't see 'im wantin' to play footie in the park.'

'You never know. Ready?'

'Go on, then.'

Paterson rang the bell to the flat. No answer. He knocked several times before taking a peek through the letterbox.

'See anythin'?' said Clocks.

'Nothing. Looks like there's a kitchen off to the left. Living room to the right, I'm guessing. Couple of other rooms. Looks reasonably tidy.'

Paterson stood up. 'Try the neighbour, John.'

Clocks rang the doorbell of the flat opposite then knocked loudly. 'Nope. Probably at work.'

'Give me the key?' said Paterson.

'Key? I ain't got no key. Thought you 'ad it.'

'I haven't got it. I thought you had it. I asked you to grab them.'

'Did yer? I don't remember that.'

'I did.'

'Still don't remember you sayin' anythin'. You talk too quiet, that's yer problem.'

'I'm not gonna argue with you. Let's go back and get them from Norris.'

'What? Fuck off! I'm not climbing back up these stairs again. Get out the way.' He pushed past Paterson.

'John . . .'

Clocks stood back and took a kick at the door. It rattled but held. Two more kicks and it flew inwards, bouncing back off the wall. 'Tch. Fancy going off to work an' leavin' yer front door unlocked. Bloody stupid thing to do, that is.'

'Well done, John. Now we have an insecure premises on our hands.'

'Stop moanin' you ol' woman. We'll get a probationer to stand on the door until the council come out and fix it. It's an emergency, so it'll only be about three weeks.'

Paterson stepped inside the hallway and made a quick recce of the room. He'd been right: the kitchen was to the left, the living room to the right.

The flat was almost bare, and their voices made a slight echo sound.

'I think the geezer's been burgled before we got 'ere,' said Clocks. 'Fuck all in it. No telly, no carpets, a skinny little mattress on the floor. That's it. You think 'e was movin' in or out?'

'I think he's a minimalist.'

Clocks wrinkled his nose. 'A what?'

'A minimalist.'

'Why'd you think that?'

'Place is virtually bare but very neat with what there is. They're people that don't want to own much in life. Not big fans of material possessions. They generally tend to prefer experiences to things.'

'That's a bit weird, innit?'

'Not really. It just means that he has only what he *needs*, not what the adverts or society tells him he needs.'

'Soppy bastard. Everyone *needs* a telly.'

Paterson ignored him. He spotted a small pile of paperback books stacked up neatly on the floor next to the futon bed. On the top was a small red notebook. Paterson picked it up and flicked through it.

'Anything?' said Clocks.

Paterson shook his head. 'Could be. A couple of names . . . Lee Burkhan and Tony Dare. That's it name-wise.'

'No phone numbers?'

'Nope. Nothing.' Paterson flicked to the back of the book. 'Hold on, there's a set of dates and . . . I think they're box numbers. They look similar to the medical transport box numbers we just saw.'

Clocks looked over Paterson's shoulder. 'Could be. Makes sense.'

'Looking at this, it seems that Mr Glossop's done something like fifteen runs in the last two months.'

'Does it say from where to where?'

'No. Nothing. Let's keep looking.'

Paterson headed back into the kitchen. On the countertop was an electric kettle, a cup and a box of Earl Grey tea bags. The drawers showed enough cutlery for just two people, neatly separated from each other. There were two plates, two small cereal bowls and a few pots and pans. On the window sill was a small potted plant, its earth slightly damp.

'Oi, oi!' said Clocks from another room. ''Ere we go.'

Paterson wandered out of the kitchen to join Clocks in a little room that was being used as makeshift office. A small table sat under the window, and on it was a neatly positioned laptop, a small colour printer, a mouse and a pair of headphones.

'What you got there?' said Paterson.

'A laptop,' Clocks beamed.

'And?'

'That's it. A laptop.' Clocks's face fell a little bit.

Paterson nodded slowly. 'Hmm. Did you get into it?'

'No.'

Paterson nodded slowly again.

'What's that mean?' Clocks's voice was slightly agitated.

'What's what mean?'

'The 'ead business. What's with the slow nod?'

'Nothing.'

'It's not nothin'. It means, *Oh, you're a clever little bunny ain'tcha? Finding a whole laptop by yerself. The Met need more detectives like you, Clocks, me ol' son. World'll be a better place if every 'tec was as sharp-eyed an' 'andsome as you.*'

Paterson shook his head. 'What are you drivelling on about now?'

'You know. We both know.'

'How'd you get all of that nonsense from me nodding my head a couple of times?'

'It looked sarcastic.'

'It *looked* sarcastic? How does nodding a head *look* sarcastic?'

Clocks shrugged. 'You know what I mean.'

'I don't have time for this, John. Did you get into it, yes or no?'

'No.'

'Thank you. That's all I needed to know. No drama required.'

Paterson hit the enter key and the computer flashed up a password box. He looked around the desk for a password. Nothing. He looked under the desk. Nothing. Clocks had a ferret around the rest of the sparse room but found nothing.

'It was worth a try,' said Paterson.

'Yeah. I guess we're dealing with a criminal mastermind, Ray. If 'e's gone to the trouble of rememberin' 'is password, then we're no doubt dealing with a highly organised criminal enterprise, is all I can say. I mean, who in their right mind would *memorise* their password?'

Paterson sighed. 'Who's being sarky now?'

'Oh, that would be me. Definitely, definitely me.'

'Well, thank you for your honesty. Now, let's get a uniform here to stand on the door and we'll get this over to the Forensic IT boys and girls. We also need to figure out who this Dare and Burkhan are.'

CHAPTER SEVEN

With two mugs of tea in his hands, Johnny Clocks ambled across the floor to join Paterson at the back of the office. Setting Paterson's mug down, he parked his backside on the corner of the table and waited. Paterson's team were all in attendance, notebooks at the ready.

'Morning everybody,' Paterson said. 'Interesting one for you all today. For those of you who don't know, Clocksy and I were called to the scene of a road traffic accident today. Car v. motorcycle. As you'd probably expect, the motorcyclist lost and died at the scene. The duty inspector, Mr Norris, called us because the rider appeared to be a courier. I say *appeared* because all is not what it seems. I'll come back to that.

'On the ground were a number of human organ transplant boxes. A few of them had burst open on impact and their contents scattered around on the road. Kidneys, livers, corneas, et cetera. Nothing unusual in that per se, but it appears that there were more parts scattered around than was written on the delivery note the rider had on him.

'The rider had a driving licence on him in the name of Stuart Glossop. We still need this confirmed. The licence showed an address in Devon Mansions. Clocksy and I checked it out. Very bare bones. Laptop seized and sent to

Forensic IT. We also found a book with just two names in it and what looks like a schedule of pickups and drop-offs.

'Before we went to the flat, we'd popped along to what we thought was his place of work, and after a discussion with the proprietor learned that Mr Glossop did not work for the company and never has. The livery on the bike was a fake.

'We also sent a photo of the courier's note we found at the scene of the accident to Dusty, and I'm hoping he can enlighten us a bit more. Dusty, the floor is yours.'

Clocks sipped loudly from his cup before handing over the second cup to Paterson.

Ronnie 'Dusty' Doneghan along with Michael 'Monkey' Harris were long-standing members of Paterson's squad of detectives and the ones he and Clocks had the most time for.

'Thanks, guv.' Dusty turned to address the room. 'The note you sent over shows that the courier was heading for Guy's hospital with said boxes. However, there was no name or department on the note, so at the moment we have no idea who they were for. It may be that they were meant for just one person or for different people in different departments. I don't know how the system works. There were barcodes on the boxes themselves, so hopefully the hospital itself will be able to tell us more. Thought I'd start at the top, and I've made you an appointment to see a Dr David Coleman. He's the chief executive and chief medical officer at Guy's. One o'clock this afternoon.'

'Brilliant,' said Paterson. 'Thanks, Dusty. So . . . any theories spring to mind, folks? Nothing's off the table.'

'Organ trafficking,' said Monkey.

'Yep,' said Paterson. 'But let's be careful we don't blind ourselves with the one theory. Any other thoughts, anyone?'

The room fell silent.

'Someone's opening a saveloy factory?' said Clocks. 'They're all stuffed with arse'oles an' elbows, ain't they?'

A few of the squad chuckled.

Paterson ignored him. 'No one? Nope. Okay. For now, organ trafficking it is. So, the obvious questions are . . . where the fuck did these parts come from and what happened to the owners?'

A hand went up: DC Colin 'Tetley' Yorkshire, a man disliked by most of the team for his inability to fit in. Clocks thought he was an incompetent, but Paterson put him straight on that one, pointing out that the man's paperwork was meticulous, as were his thought processes. With that information, Clocks revised his opinion from 'incompetent' to 'just a wanker, then'. Paterson was more comfortable with that.

'Sir,' said Yorkshire, 'before I joined you, I worked for a while on the Human Trafficking squad. What usually happens — but take this as a springboard from which to start and not as gospel in this case — is that refugees are brought over to the UK from whatever country they're from. It used to be that the refugee would have to perform some sort of work to pay off their debt to the person who brought them over. Prostitution, drug running, that sort of thing.'

There was a lot of nodding.

'Well, back then it was financial. Nowadays their fee for safe passage is often a healthy organ. The debt is paid immediately with, say, a kidney, which is then sold on.'

'Fuck me,' said Clocks. 'Times 'ave changed, ain't they?'

Paterson stroked the small beard he'd been growing to hide the scar that ran the full length of his jaw — a present he'd received from the 'Childmaker', when the man determined to remove Paterson's face. 'Okay. Makes sense. So, bear with me, Tetley. Here's a theory . . . Our courier is working for someone who brings in refugees. That someone, or someone on his behalf, whips out an organ and has it sent to somewhere for onward transmission for cash. So, that someone is likely a middleman, yes?'

'Yes, sir,' said Yorkshire.

'Why use a motorbike courier?' said Clocks. 'Surely you'd get more boxes of giblets in a car?'

'Two reasons. One, it's the fastest method. Two, it's the safest bet, sir. We all know that time is of the essence with these sort of things, and a bike is perfect for the London roads.

'So, if by some chance the courier *is* stopped and has to produce paperwork, most coppers don't know what they're looking at. To do any checks on the street will take time, and nobody wants to be the one to delay things when a life could be at stake. If a complaint was made that the copper delayed a vital transplant there would be hell to pay.'

Paterson nodded. 'You make a good point, Tetley. Thank you. D'you still have any contacts in your old team?'

'Yes, sir. One good one. That said, he's moved on to Interpol, so that works well for us.'

'Yeah, okay. Give them a heads-up then drop their details in to me. I'll see if I can clear it with their guv'nor and we'll bring them on board for a bit of advice if we need to. Cheers for that.'

'No problem, sir.' Yorkshire wrote something in his notebook.

'Right,' said Paterson. 'We need to move this along. Dusty, you follow up on the names we found in the book, please. Find out everything you can about this Dare and Burkhan. Monkey, you carry on logging all the evidence for us. Clocksy and I are off to visit Guy's to see if we can shine a light on this delivery. Everyone, back here at six tonight. Let's go to work.'

CHAPTER EIGHT

At exactly 1 p.m., Paterson and Clocks were shown into Dr Coleman's office, a large, bright room on the fifteenth floor of Guy's Tower. Coleman was a portly gentleman that Paterson put in his early sixties. He was sharply dressed with no hint of jewellery save for a silver wedding band. Paterson assumed it would be platinum. For a man of his age he had an impressive head of thick, white hair that was as neatly trimmed as the rest of him. His bright blue eyes shone out of his ruggedly handsome face and finished off a commanding feature set.

'Gentlemen, gentlemen! Please come in, come in! Take a seat, take a seat!' He shook each man's hand then gestured to two chairs that had been set out carefully around a small but tasteful coffee table. Paterson and Clocks introduced themselves. 'Can I get you anything?' Dr Coleman asked.

'Er, a coffee would be nice, please.' Paterson unbuttoned his jacket and sat down.

'I'll 'ave a cuppa tea if there's one goin', fellah. Provided it ain't out the 'ospital canteen, know what I mean?' Clocks shuffled about on his chair until he felt comfortable, then unbuttoned his jacket.

Coleman chortled. 'Oh, I do, I do, officer. I know exactly what you mean. Rest assured it will not be from the canteen. Can I get you anything else? Biscuits, perhaps.'

'Ooh, yeah. Don't suppose you've got any Jammie Dodgers, 'ave yer?'

Paterson rolled his eyes.

'I'll certainly see what I can do.' Coleman stepped outside and had a short, muffled discussion with his personal assistant.

'It's on its way, gentlemen. Jammie Dodgers too. Now, how can I help you both? You're from the murder squad, I understand, yes?'

'That's correct, sir,' said Paterson. He went on to explain the events of the morning, watching carefully for any flicker of recognition at the mention of Glossop's name. There was nothing save the occasional look of surprise and the odd *tch, tch* as Paterson laid out what they knew.

'So, the courier's note suggested that the boxes were headed for Guy's, but we don't know which department or individuals they were meant for. That's where we hoped you might be able to help us.'

'Indeed, gentlemen, indeed. Now, can you tell me . . . did these boxes have barcodes on them at all? Can you tell me that, hmm?'

Paterson took out his phone and showed some pictures of the barcodes he'd snapped at the scene. 'We have these.'

Dr Coleman craned his neck as Paterson flicked through the images.

'Yes, yes, thank you, thank you. Most helpful, most helpful. Let me get someone up here with a handheld.'

'A handheld?' said Paterson.

'Yes, yes. A scanner, a scanner. A barcode reader. That should help us.' Coleman walked out of the office again and had another short, muffled conversation with his assistant.

Clocks gave Paterson a look that suggested that Coleman was a bit of an oddball. He gave the man a broad smile as he re-entered the room.

'Shouldn't be too long, gentlemen. Not too long at all. I've left instructions that this is a matter of urgency.'

'I 'ope you're talkin' about the tea and me Jammie Dodgers,' said Clocks. 'I've not 'ad me breakfast yet. I could eat me own elbows.'

'Oh, I'm sorry,' said Coleman. 'I'll chase them for you.'

A sudden knock at the door preceded a cart being rolled into the room, pushed by short middle-aged man with greying hair and a pot belly. The badge pinned to his jacket read, 'Senior Management Catering Staff'.

'Ah, good, good. Tea and coffee it is, gentlemen, tea and coffee it is.'

The caterer left the room and there was a short, awkward, silence. Paterson cleared his throat. 'Do you happen to know if Guy's uses the same courier firm for all these organ transplants?'

'As far as I know, we use two companies. Two companies, yes. They've proved themselves to be the most reliable and trustworthy of all the couriers we've used. We need that reliability, of course, of course.'

Clocks frowned, and Paterson, knowing his friend as well as he did, could see that he was bursting to ask Coleman why he kept repeating himself. Paterson shook his head slowly and discreetly at Clocks. Clocks grinned.

'Have you ever had problems with organs going missing en route before?' Paterson was keen to say something before Clocks lost all control and embarrassed everyone in the room.

'No, no. Never. No, not at all. Not that I know of. No.' Dr Coleman swept a hand through his hair. Paterson noticed a sudden twitch in the man's eye.

'So, everything is accounted for? You have strong protocols in place to ensure nothing goes wrong?'

'Yes, yes. We can't afford to lose organs, can we? No, no. That just would not do. No, we have very robust practices in place.'

Paterson gave a single nod. 'Good to know.'

Clocks dunked his Jammie Dodger in his tea. ''Ere . . .'

Paterson stiffened and he gave Clocks the death stare.

'What 'appens in a case like today where the courier is wiped out an' the giblets go bouncin' up an' down the road? I take it you can't just give 'em a quick rinse off under the tap before you bung 'em in someone, can yer?'

Dr Coleman gave Clocks a horrified look. Paterson was relieved. Of all the things Clocks could have come out with, this was probably the least offensive.

'What? What? Run them under a tap? A tap? No, no, we most certainly don't run them under a tap. No, no. That would never do.'

'I just wondered. Seems like a waste of good organ if you ask me. I mean, if you give it a good rinse an' get all the grit off, the person gettin' the giblet won't 'ave a scooby it was rollin' around in a puddle 'alf an hour ago, will 'e? Probably just 'appy to get a second 'and kidney or whatever.'

'A scooby?' said Dr Coleman. 'A scooby? What is a scooby, please?'

'Scooby Doo, the cartoon dog detective. Frightened of ghosts.'

Coleman looked lost.

'Scooby Doo . . . *clue*,' said Clocks.

Coleman frowned and shook his head.

'He tells me it's cockney rhyming slang,' said Paterson. 'But I'm not so sure. He has his own language, doctor, taught by a family of wolves. Handed down to him from one generation to the next.'

A sudden rap on the door relieved Coleman from this verbal nightmare. 'Oh, good, good. That must be the barcode reader. Yes, the barcode reader.' He shouted for the person outside to come in.

A small, wiry man in a grey porters coat entered the room. 'You wanted a barcode scanner, sir?'

'Yes, yes. Do come in, come in.'

Paterson handed the man his phone and briefly explained what he wanted. The man scanned the first code. Nothing came up. He scanned the second and again, nothing. He scanned all the codes and all of them returned a negative result.

'Okay, fellah. Thanks. So, I'm right in thinking that these codes don't exist anywhere within your system, yes?'

'Yes, sir,' said the man. 'Correct.'

Paterson sighed. 'Alright. Thank you for your time. I appreciate it.'

The man nodded courteously and left the room.

'Dr Coleman, thank you for your time too. Kind of you to see us at such short notice.'

'It was a pleasure, sir. A pleasure. I'm so sorry that I couldn't have been of any help.'

Paterson and Clocks thanked him, left Coleman's office and headed for the lift.

'What d'you think, John? Straight or bent?'

'Dunno with that one. Could go either way, but Mr Clocks's criminal radar, patent pendin', says straight.'

'Yeah, you're probably right. But did you see the little tic in his eye and the hair sweep when I mentioned losing bits before?'

'I did. But I get the impression 'e was embarrassed at bein' asked the question more than coverin' shit up. I reckon 'e'd be too scared to get into anything too dodgy. Probably fiddles the staff Christmas raffle to snag a bottle of cheap plonk and the odd box of biscuits for 'imself, but I don't 'ave 'im down for dealin' in organs.'

'Fair enough. We'll leave it at that for now.'

They entered the lift and Paterson punched the button for the ground floor.

'Tell you what though, 'e drove me mad the way he kept repeatin' 'imself all the time. Fuck bein' in a meetin' with 'im. You'd be there twice as long than you need to be.'

Paterson grinned. 'Yeah. And sod being the minute taker.'

'Shame really. Good-lookin' geezer, weren't 'e? Bet 'e was *smothered* in crumpet when 'e was a lad.'

Paterson shrugged. 'Bet it wasn't for long, though. Can you imagine listening to him all night long? How was it for you? How was it for you? Any good, any good? Hmm? Did you come, hmm? Did you come? No? No? That will never do, that will never do.'

When the lift doors opened on the ground floor the small crowd waiting for the lift looked askance at Paterson and Clocks as they giggled like a pair of naughty schoolboys.

'Ah!' Clocks wiped a tear from his eye. 'You bastard. Nailed 'im to a tee.'

Paterson, still chuckling, walked out into the heat of the day.

'What now, Ray?'

'I ain't got a scooby, Clocksy. Not a fucking Scooby Doo.'

CHAPTER NINE

Alicia Warren looked out of her Paris office window at the maelstrom of rush hour traffic barrelling its way around the Arc de Triomphe. Cutting and carving each other up, the little cars and buses below went about their business of getting people to their places of work.

Born in Paris as Anaïs Monet, hers was not a happy childhood. A product of the seamier side of the French social system, her mother and father abandoned her to cocaine and heroin from the moment she was born.

At the age of seven, her papa turned her over to a paedophile drug user who infected her with gonorrhoea. From there, her parents kept her around for the income she provided. When she was ten, they were approached by a man who offered them a life-changing opportunity. He had a wealthy client whose child had been in an accident and who was willing to pay good money for a healthy kidney. A deal was struck, and assuming she was just being whored out again, she was taken to a filthy room somewhere in a Paris backstreet. She woke up to find herself alone with a crudely stitched wound in her side.

When her father arrived to pick her up, he was so enraged to find that their 'saviour' had taken off without paying that he took it out on Alicia, beating her black and blue in the process of sexually abusing her.

This was a step too far even for the drug-addled neighbours, who had consistently turned a blind eye to the family next door and their behaviour toward Alicia. After all, it was none of their business how they brought up their child, but seeing her so battered and bruised coupled with the story her father told about how he'd been ripped off after selling her for a spare part, was an abuse too far. A call was made to child protection services, which resulted in Anaïs being taken into care and her mother and father receiving short prison sentences. She saw them both once more when she was eighteen. She wanted to find out why they had done the things they had done to her but, on seeing and talking to them, decided to simply kill them.

Her father was first. Sitting across the kitchen table from her, he offered no excuses nor showed any remorse for his crimes. When he laughed at her, she smashed the glass of water she was holding and jammed it into his eye. As he screamed and thrashed around the room, she went berserk with the broken glass, stabbing and slashing him for all she was worth. When she'd finished, he looked like the contents of a butcher's bin.

Her mother, smothered in her husband's blood spatters, was too frightened to scream. In complete shock, she could only stand and watch as her daughter strode toward her.

The neighbours minded their own business.

She changed her name to Alicia Warren, stealing the name from a girl she once met, and set herself up in business in the only trade she knew. Sex. In particular, selling girls for sex. From there, she involved herself in the odd bit of cocaine importation and eventually graduated to the supply of human organs. By the age of thirty she had a business that stretched across Europe. America would be next. By thirty-five she was one of the wealthiest women in France and lived the lifestyle that went with it.

Now in her mid-forties, she radiated a calmness, burying the rage that had followed her from childhood. She carried herself with the kind of self-confidence that came from running a global business built on abuse and death. Compassion was not a trait that she possessed or encouraged in her workforce.

She stood with her hands behind her back as she listened to the news of her courier's demise in London, nodding occasionally. The bringer of this news was a slightly built man called Leon who had served her in a low-level role for many years.

She turned slowly. 'And how long before we can restock?'

Leon shrugged his thin little shoulders. 'Two days. Perhaps three.'

'Has our client been informed?'

'No, Madame. Not as yet.'

'Good. Leave that to me. Our surgeon in London?'

'It was he who informed me.'

'How is this accident being treated?'

'According to our surgeon, the police are suspicious. Two detectives have taken an interest in the case and are said to be investigating the courier. I understand they have searched his premises.'

'Did they find anything of note?'

'I do not know, Madame.'

Alicia drew a deep breath. 'Do we need to be concerned about these detectives?'

Leon shrugged. 'I understand they are most formidable.'

'Then let us keep an eye on them and decide whether action must be taken.'

CHAPTER TEN

Paterson sat with his elbows on his desk and his face less than a foot from the circular fan that was doing its best to cool him down. He didn't usually mind a bit of warm weather, but the English summer heat made him perspire unbearably.

'Everyone's back now, Ray,' said Clocks. 'Give it five minutes and we'll 'ave a debrief. Mind you don't catch yer face in that fan. We both know it's a bit loose now since the Childmaker nearly cut it off. Last thing we want is that thing spinnin' around an' landin' in someone's tea.' He chuckled to himself.

Paterson nodded, disappointed that he would have to leave the cool breeze so soon. He let out a heavy sigh and got up from his desk. The heat enveloped him again, and he cursed under his breath as he walked out into the kitchen to grab a glass of water before he started the meeting.

'Alright, everyone!' Clocks shouted. 'Let's 'ave yer. Debrief time. Let's go!'

The team gathered up their notebooks and various bits of paperwork and headed toward the back of the room.

'I swear to God it's getting hotter in here,' Paterson said to DC Gunn, whose desk was closest to the dial for the air conditioner. 'Is that thing on full?'

'Yes, sir. It's been on full all day as far as I know.'

'Great. Must be broken. Alright, everyone. Here we go.' Paterson went through their meeting with Dr Coleman.

'So we're still none the wiser. Dusty, how'd you get on with the name checks?'

'Reasonably well, guv.' Dusty Doneghan flipped open his notebook. 'It seems that Tony Dare and Lee Burkhan are affiliated with a registered NGO.'

Paterson shrugged.

'NGO stands for non-governmental organisation.'

'What's that, then?' said Clocks. He took a swig of his tea.

'NGOs — and there are literally thousands, if not millions, of them — are usually humanitarian aid groups that respond to some form of crisis. Generally non-profit.'

'Charities?' said Paterson.

'In effect, yeah. The larger, more well-known ones are Oxfam and — how d'you say it? — Médicins Sans Frontières. Sounds French to me. They can usually respond and adapt quicker than government organisations that are always bogged down by red tape. They're generally well thought of because not only do they respond quickly, they're well organised and deliver vitally important services — medical care, human rights protection, education, that sort of stuff. Little ones tend to do more local work.

'However, there have been a few problems with some of them not being too transparent with their budgets and accounting practices. Plus, as the staff are nearly always American or European, they sometimes go into these developing countries with plans that don't always sit too well within the local context. From what I can make of it, they tend to make a habit of overlooking the use of local expertise and end up barrelling their plans through and cocking things up, and that upsets the local population.'

Paterson nodded. 'Interesting. So who do our guys work for? Which NGO?'

'They don't work for anyone,' said Dusty. 'They've registered their own.'

'What? How does that work?'

'Not difficult. This is straight off the government's website — I'm paraphrasing: first you decide you wanna do it, then get three people for the board, make sure the charity has "charitable purposes for the public benefit", choose a name, choose a structure for it, create a "governing document", then you register as a charity with the Charities Commission then — bosh! Off you go.'

'Fuckin' 'ell!' said Clocks. 'It can't be that easy, can it?'

'Yep,' said Dusty. 'It can and it is. And that's what our two herberts have gone and done.'

'How long have they been established?' DC Gunn asked.

Dusty looked at his notebook and flipped a page. 'Since . . . 2001.'

'Christ!' said Paterson. 'If these two have been involved in stealing organs for twenty-odd years we could be looking at hundreds, if not thousands, of victims.'

The room fell silent as the thought sunk in.

CHAPTER ELEVEN

DC Yorkshire stopped Paterson as he was about to return to his office. 'Sir, I've arranged for a Zoom meeting for you and Inspector Clocks at seven o'clock, if you don't mind waiting another hour or so?'

'With?' said Paterson.

'My contact in Interpol.'

'Interpol?' said Clocks. 'Why'd you drag them in?'

'Because that's where my contact is now, sir. I did say in the briefing. Perhaps you never heard me.'

Clocks frowned. 'Oh, yeah. I 'eard you, Tetley, me ol' son. But you're so borin' I instantly forgot what you'd said.'

DC Yorkshire glared at Clocks. 'My apologies for being so boring, sir. Anyway, Interpol deal with cases of human trafficking across the globe. Although we have various departments that deal with aspects of human trafficking, Interpol are the big boys when it comes to this kind of stuff. If anyone knows what's going on here, my money would be on them.'

Clocks shrugged. 'Fair enough, Tetley. Cheers. Who is it we're talkin' to?'

'Fellah called Bill Sturman. He's been with them forever and this is his speciality. He's a really good man who knows his stuff inside out and back again.'

'Thanks, Colin.' Paterson preferred not to use Yorkshire's nickname, particularly after he'd done him a favour.

'I'll log you in to the meeting at seven and introduce you. Do you want me in the meeting?'

Paterson nodded. 'Sure, that'd be good. Can you take some notes for us, please?'

DC Yorkshire smiled. 'Of course. Can I get either of you a drink?'

'Yeah, I'll 'ave a drop of voddy,' said Clocks. 'There's some in Mr P's desk. Bottom drawer.'

'I was thinking more along the lines of tea or coffee, sir.'

Clocks sniffed. 'I'm sure you were, but I wasn't. So, voddy it is my son. Thank you very much.'

Paterson gave Yorkshire a nod. 'Little drop won't hurt. Pour yourself one if you want.'

'Thank you, sir, but I'll stick with tea.' Yorkshire gave a slight bow of the head and left the two men alone.

'Told you 'e was a wrong'un,' said Clocks. 'An' this proves it.'

'What? Because he doesn't want a drink?'

'Yep. Why would you not wanna drink at six of the p.m.? Traditional drinkin' time, that is.'

Paterson shrugged. 'Maybe he just doesn't want one. Maybe he's teetotal. No big deal.'

Clocks squinted his eyes. 'No? I'm tellin' yer, mate. If 'e's a teetotaller you can't trust 'im. Should be against the law, not 'avin' a cheeky snifter at six. Everybody does it.'

Paterson sat down on a desk and scooched himself back far enough so that his legs dangled. 'Anyway, back to the real problems of the world for now, John. If our boys Dare and Burkhan run an NGO, that means they could literally travel the world and do their shit. We need to find out if Interpol have anything on file for them and if they know where they are right now. Sooner we can catch these bastards the better.'

'Agreed. I mean, I've 'eard of this organ traffickin' but I never thought it'd 'appen in sunny Bermondsey.'

'I know what you mean. Perhaps the biggest problem in the world, mate, and it's everywhere. Everywhere.'

Clocks gave Paterson a sideways glance. 'You takin' the piss out of that Dr Coleman again?'

'What. No. I didn't realise I'd repeated myself.'

'Well, I did. I did.'

The two men broke into laughter just at the moment DC Yorkshire arrived with two small tumblers of vodka.

Clocks wrinkled his nose as he took his glass. 'You seem to 'ave run out of vodka, Ray.' He held the glass up to the light. 'Mine's fuckin' empty. Yours?'

DC Yorkshire sighed. 'I'm sorry, sir. I didn't think you'd want a big glass.'

'Did you not, Tetley? That's the trouble with thinkin', innit? Gets you into all kinds of trouble. Right now you're in trouble with me for shortin' me on the vodka, my son. So, if you don't mind — and even if you do — nip back and pour us a proper drink, there's a good lad. Off you fuck.' Clocks waved him away.

CHAPTER TWELVE

'Chief Superintendent Paterson?'

'Just superintendent,' said Paterson. 'Not chief. Thanks for taking the time to talk to us today, Mr Sturman. I appreciate it.'

'Bill. Call me Bill.'

Paterson and Clocks stood facing a 37-inch computer monitor filled with Bill Sturman's face. Although he'd only said a few words it was obvious that Sturman was from Manchester.

Paterson nodded. 'Thanks. I'm Ray, and this is DI Clocks. Johnny Clocks.'

'Good to meet you all. Right . . . Colin's given me the nod that you wanted to talk to me. Something to do with a possible organ-harvesting operation. That correct?'

Clocks frowned and gave Paterson a sideways look.

Paterson nodded. He spent the next few minutes filling in Sturman with as much detail as they had and ended with the names in the book.

'Don't suppose you've got any dates of birth for these guys?'

'Sorry,' said Paterson. 'Names only. Can't even give you a rough age. We do know, or at least we strongly suspect, that Dare and Burkhan are running a registered NGO under the name of GreatBritAid. Been running for about twenty years, mostly in France and . . . hang on . . . oh yeah, they've been mentioned in India too.' Paterson could hear Sturman's keyboard clacking away.

'Both countries are heavily involved in trafficking,' Sturman said. 'France with the refugees, sex workers, et cetera. And India, big on the old organ harvesting. Let's see what else we've got on them.' Paterson smiled at Clocks while they waited. 'Okay,' said Sturman. 'GreatBritAid have been flagged as suspected people traffickers in the past . . .'

'In the past?' Paterson interrupted.

'Yeah, but there's nothing else on their notes. It seems they came to our attention eight years ago, but there was insufficient evidence to pursue the investigation any further. We put them on our watch list, but nothing else has come to light about them since then. Obviously, that's now changed.'

'Okay,' said Paterson. 'Can you give me an idea of how all this works? This is new to us.'

'Sure. With France, as you know, it's a pass-through for refugees from the Middle East, Syria, Afghanistan, that sort of thing. These people are trafficked for all sorts of reasons. Work and sex mainly. What happens is, they meet with a transporter—'

'A what? Transporter?'

'Yeah, a man who, for an agreed sum, can arrange transport for them out of their home country and into France and then on to England. They usually pay a sum of money up front — non-refundable of course — and typically a lot more than these poor bastards can afford. They're then told where to be and at what time. Quite often, when they arrive at their departure point, there's no transport waiting for them and the transporter has nicked their money. Straight scam. If they go and demand their money back they're usually given a good shoeing by the transporter's "protection detail". In short, they're fucked.'

DC Yorkshire shook his head.

'So, for the ones who do get transported they think they've cracked it. But, what happens to these poor bastards is, they're told if they want to get across to England — which was the whole point — they then have to pay a ferryman. Obviously, a ferryman is the person or company that actually brings them across the Channel.'

Paterson nodded. 'Thank you,' he said, having filled another gap in his knowledge.

'Now . . . they haven't got any money left, of course. So they make a deal. They agree to work off the ferryman's debt once they're in England. To make sure that debt is paid off, the ferryman takes their passports off of them, promising to return them once they've paid up.'

'Why do they nick their passports?' said Clocks.

'Makes them toe the line. They can't claim to be in England legally if stopped, so they have to be on their best behaviour or they get nicked. Can't find work. Can't get somewhere to live. Can't claim any form of assistance without it. They desperately need their passports if they want to survive. So, they agree to do whatever work is necessary to pay the ferryman. If it's a family, Dad and sons do some labouring usually, even if they're kids. Mum and any daughters are put straight on the game.'

'Jesus,' said Paterson. 'I had a rough idea this went on, but I didn't know any real detail. Go on, please.'

'Wait 'til we get to the organ harvesting,' said Sturman, 'the blood markets. That'll raise your eyebrows.'

'Blood markets?' said Paterson.

'Yeah. Also known as red markets or bone markets.'

'Anyone want a tea?' said DC Yorkshire. 'This will take a bit of time and I'm aware of a lot of this stuff already.'

Clocks's head swivelled in his direction. 'I'll 'ave two sugars in mine. Oh, an' when I say "sugar" I mean two shots of vodka. That's what I *meant* to say.'

Yorkshire rolled his eyes. 'Same for you, sir?' he said to Paterson.

'Just tea, please.'

Clocks settled down as soon as Yorkshire left the room. He swung his feet up on the desk and leaned back.

'Okay,' said Paterson. 'Blood markets, then.'

'Massive,' said Sturman. 'You have no idea. Grab a chair yourself, Ray, and get comfy while I get a couple of searches done on your two suspects. It might be a few minutes.'

'No rush,' said Paterson. He rolled the chair from underneath the desk and sat himself down.

'We'll talk about India because that's where your boys have been flagged up. But what I'm telling you now is prevalent all across the world, even in the so-called developed world — the UK, America . . . There's no country that hasn't been touched by the blood markets in some way or other.'

'Go on, then. We're ready.'

'Ray, did you go to university?'

'Yes.'

'Did you have a biology lab?'

'Hmm, hmm.'

'And you no doubt had a complete human skeleton on display?'

Paterson said nothing for a second and then nodded. 'Go on.'

'You do know that was most likely real, don't you? Wasn't synthetic.'

'Seriously?'

'Hundred per cent. India used to have a reputation for producing skeletons of the human body for all of the best medical schools in the world. It started in the early days of medicine when these schools needed to teach anatomy to their pupils. They were in such pristine condition and bleached to a perfect white that the medical world couldn't get enough of them for lecture and lesson purposes. The suppliers had a deal with the local undertakers to bury the bodies and then dig them up later when the mourners had gone home. These bodies would then be stripped of the flesh and internal organs, the skeleton polished up and sent off to the customer.

'As the medical profession grew in leaps and bounds, so did the need for skeletons. Problem was, demand outstripped supply for a while until the Indians got a bit creative and decided to move things along a bit by bumping people off to plug the gap in demand. So, if you ever go back into a college or a classroom, there's a good chance you're looking at the skeleton of a murder victim.

'Then, as the market grew, the suppliers realised there was money to be made from sick rich people desperate to be healed. If you needed a kidney, no problem. They would find a "donor". Now, donors were not, and are still not, in short supply. When you have an extremely poor populace, where people literally cannot feed their children, they'll do anything to help them. If that means selling a kidney, then selling a kidney is what they'll do.

'Imagine this . . . You live in a ramshackle little town with fuck all to your name. And I do mean fuck all. The average monthly wage for someone living in a Mumbai slum is about 650 rupees. Nine dollars per month. *Per month.* For that, you have to rise at dawn, scrabble about in the rubbish piles to find bits of junk to sell. Or you can go to work in one of the toxic paint factories that will slowly poison you, and you'll be dead in your mid-thirties. Or — and this is a sought-after job, poor bastards — you get to clean out the latrines. And if you've ever seen a Mumbai toilet system, you'll know what I mean when I say "fuck that". You probably put in a sixteen-hour day for about four or five dollars a day.

'So, you and your family are sleeping in the dirt, and raw sewage runs in the gutter outside your little tin shack. You have three or four kids and you can't afford to put a piece of bread in their mouth. They're dying of hunger. Now, you know of a clinic in town, and there are usually two or three, where they'll pay you money if you're willing to sell an organ. Let's say a kidney.

'Desperate, you go to the clinic and offer to sell them your kidney. The clinic offers you a huge sum of money, say five thousand rupees — more money than you could even dream about — but still only about seventy US dollars, by the way. You could buy yourself a better tin shack, start a new life, and your kids would be able to live. Hurrah, right? Nope. You agree to the five thousand, they take you in and whip your kidney out. When you wake up, they bung you a heavily reduced fee, say a thousand at the most. That's about fourteen dollars. And then they kick you out the back door. Now, you can protest, but who to? It's not like they're gonna open you up and put your kidney back, is it? No. So you go to the cops. Like they give a fuck. Probably taking a bung from the clinic. So, you're royally fucked, your dreams have come to nothing and you're down one kidney.

'So, the clinic has a kidney for which they've paid about a tenner in English money and then they have it shipped overseas to an American clinic, where they will pay between three and five thousand dollars. Tidy little profit for the Mumbai butcher. The American clinic then charges their client something like two hundred grand for the kidney and probably as much as that again for the operation and aftercare. Big, big profit for the dodgy American doctors. As a business model, what's not to like? Everyone's happy, apart from the poor bastard who sold their kidney to feed their family.'

'Good God almighty,' said Paterson. 'That's unbelievable.'

DC Yorkshire entered the room backwards with three drinks on a tray, only two of which were tea. 'Tea's up, gents.' He put the tray down. 'Alcoholic beverage for you, Inspector.' Paterson and Clocks ignored him, wrapped up in Sturman's story.

'It goes on all around the world,' said Sturman. 'Do you know one of the biggest places for black-market organs?'

'Enlighten us,' said Clocks, taking a tea.

'Seattle, Washington.'

'No!' Paterson said.

'I shit you not. Not just computers and porn over there. Huge market. We've broken up several rings with the FBI right across the US. It's everywhere.'

Paterson rubbed his eyes. 'And this happens in Britain?'

'Everywhere. You may have just stumbled over an operation that will lead you down a rabbit hole if you don't hand it over to someone.'

'Hand it over? Who to?'

'Us,' said Sturman. 'We have the expertise and the technical know-how to get on top of this and make good use of the intel you've just given us.'

Johnny Clocks swung his legs off the table and sat forward, looking closely at the screen. 'Or, you can work with us, mate. We're not just a coupla numpties who fell off the back of a lorry, y'know. We caught the case an' we're stickin' with it all the way. Your job is to find out where our two suspects are right now and 'elp us lay 'ands on them — an' their pals, assumin' they've got any. So, that said, 'ow's it goin' with the checks your end?'

Sturman smiled. 'I heard you were direct, Mr Clocks. I like that.'

'Just as well, mate. 'Cos that's all you're gonna get.'

'Okay, GreatBritAid are currently active in India, funnily enough, in Mumbai. And in France. Flight passenger lists state that they both flew out to France on the fifteenth of last month. No trace of them having returned as yet. In fact, looking at the list for the last two years, it seems they've flown out a total of nine, ten . . . eleven times in total, and not once are they shown coming back in. Eurostar shows them travelling twelve times. Came back the same way nine times.'

'And that didn't alert you guys?' said Clocks.

'Why would it? As I said, an initial investigation proved negative and, quite frankly, we've neither the time nor the resources to watch everyone.' Sturman sounded apologetic.

'Well, they're obviously coming back in somehow,' said Paterson. 'What's your best guess?'

'Private plane. I would guess they go to the camps in France, pick a target, maybe a family, and fly them over on the pretext of work.'

'Okay,' said Paterson. 'I've heard enough.'

'Do you want to hear about how these gangs smuggle in kids for sex work? Similar operating procedure, except they promise to take the child to England but can't take the parents, as there's no room on the boat for them. Parents, desperate for their child to have a better life, agree — and that's the last they see of their little one. Off they go to satisfy the needs of the fuckin' fat, rich paedophiles of the world.'

'No thanks,' said Paterson. 'Save that for another day. Have you got any photos of our boys?'

'Yeah. I'll send them over to you. They're a bit old, but I think they'll be good enough. I've got some associates for you too, complete with names.'

'So as far as you're concerned,' said DC Yorkshire, 'they could still be in France, yes?'

'Could be,' said Sturman. 'But I can't be sure at the moment. I can get enquiries made, see if we can get eyes on either of them, and I'll let you know. I'll also put a marker on their names to see if they move off anywhere and where they're going to.'

Paterson nodded. 'Bill, you've been a big help. Thank you so much. I'll be in touch again very soon.' He ended the Zoom call. 'What d'you think, John?'

'What about?'

'What he just said. Weren't you listening?'

'Yeah, I was listenin', but I couldn't understand 'alf of it. Where the fuck is 'e from, Tetley?'

'Manchester, sir. It's where the UK branch of Interpol is based.'

Clocks wrinkled his nose. 'Really? Manchester?'

'Yes, sir. Manchester.'

'Well, that explains that, Ray. Foreign.'

'Don't fuck about, John. This isn't the time for it.'

Clocks shrugged. 'So what's the plan?'

'Plan is for us to go see the commissioner, tell him what we've got, get back to Sturman, tell him we're going to liaise with him and his pals in Interpol and pop over the pond and annoy the French, no doubt.'

Johnny Clocks's eyes lit up.

CHAPTER THIRTEEN

'Ray! John! Good to see you again. Come in. Come in.' Sam Morne had been the assistant commissioner of police during Paterson and Clocks's previous case involving the self-styled 'Bermondsey Knights', a group of mentally disturbed individuals who had taken to resolving long-standing family issues by killing their parents using medieval punishment methods.

One of the victims had been Sir Scott Anderson, the commissioner. AC Morne had been promoted after Anderson's death. He was a good man who felt sympathy for Paterson and Clocks in the way the Met continued to treat them and vowed to undo the problems that Anderson had caused them.

Paterson and Clocks were wary, though. History had taught them that the higher the rank, the less of a police officer they were and the more inclined to stab you in the back if they felt it necessary.

'Sir,' they said, together.

'Please,' said Morne. 'Take a seat. Make yourselves comfortable. Tea?'

'Will mine taste anythin' like vodka?' said Clocks.

Morne grinned. 'Unlikely, John.'

'I'll give it a swerve then, guv. Thanks anyway.'

'How's married life treating you, John?'

Clocks frowned. 'Bit early to say yet. It's only been a few weeks an' you were there, weren't you?'

'Yes. Yes, I was. Thank you for that. My wife and I had a lovely time.'

'Good to know.' Clocks looked around the room. Not much had changed since Anderson was in office. Just a picture of him in a black frame.

'Is she still thinking of going to work for Wallace?'

'Who?' said Clocks.

'Wallace. Wallace Young.'

'Oh, you mean Wol. Yeah. She's thinkin' it over. Pay's good . . . option to travel . . . that sort of stuff. She's got some time off, so I think she's seein' 'im this week.'

Morne nodded. 'Wish her well for me.'

Clocks forced a tiny smile.

Paterson and Clocks had spoken at length about Lyndsey going to work for Wallace Young in his new business adventure. Young used to be commissioner before Anderson, and although he and Paterson got off to a rocky start, they ended up being friends. Once Young had retired, he accompanied Paterson and Clocks to America to help chase down Albert Tanner, a vicious psychopath who once arranged for Clocks to be burned alive. Young had almost lost his life during an arrest attempt on Tanner, and without Paterson's financial expertise in ensuring he got the very best medical care, he would most likely have died.

Young had recently set up his own private investigation company with a remit to travel the world and provide 'assistance' to law enforcement agencies, governments and, of course, private clients of the wealthier kind. Paterson knew, however, that money would never be a driver for Young. Only justice.

Young's first two hires were a wanted ex-military sniper known and feared as the 'White Ghost', so called because of his albinism and his ability to avoid detection. But Young had found him. The other was a transvestite known as Alice, a tech genius who had frightened the life out of Johnny Clocks when he went to interview him with Paterson. Among other things, Alice ran a crèche for men who liked to dress as babies.

The next people he wanted to join him were Paterson, Clocks and Lyndsey. Paterson and Clocks turned him down. They had things to prove to themselves and to the Met. Lyndsey, however, wanted something more.

'So how can I help you two gentlemen today?' said Morne. 'Is it to do with your latest case? I've been told you've picked up on a possible organ-harvesting gang, correct?'

'Yes, sir,' said Paterson.

'Please . . . call me Sam.'

'Sam. Okay. Yes, it's a possibility.'

'Tell me about it, then.' Morne settled back into his chair. 'Don't leave anything out.'

Paterson didn't. For the next five minutes he and Clocks ran him through the full story and where they were at in the investigation so far.

Commissioner Morne sighed deeply. 'Jesus.' The room fell silent for a moment or two. 'So, I'm guessing you two are wanting to go to France, correct?'

'Correct,' said Paterson.

Morne shrugged. 'Okay. Look . . . this really is a case for the French authorities, seeing as how your suspects are thought to be in their country. You can of course go over and escort them back, but . . .'

'But what?' said Clocks.

'But I know that if I say no, you'll just take annual leave and go to France on a little holiday, won't you?'

Paterson and Clocks said nothing.

'And when you're on holiday you'll do all sorts of things, get into all sorts of trouble and no doubt piss the French off while you're at it. Am I right?'

Again, neither man said anything.

'So, I'll get on to the French and inform them of your imminent arrival and ensure that you receive assistance.

Much better to have you aggravate them with authority than without.'

Both men smiled.

'Thank you, Sam,' said Paterson with a little nod.

'Cheers, Sammy boy,' said Clocks. 'You know it makes sense.'

'Hmm,' said Morne. 'I hope it does. I take it there will be no interplay between you and your French counterparts, John?'

'Interplay, guv? What d'you mean? You mean you don't want me to fuck any of 'em?'

'No, no. That's not what I meant. That's inter*course*, John. How can I put this delicately? You won't be an arsehole to them, will you?'

Clocks grinned. '*Moi*? Don't see any reason that I would be, guv. I'm a big fan of the French. Love 'em, I do.'

CHAPTER FOURTEEN

DAY 2

Paterson glanced at his watch — 7 a.m. As early starts went, this one was more civilised. The main office thrummed with the sound of voices, most of which were unknown to him. His visit with the commissioner the day before had been fruitful, and he and Clocks had been granted permission to structure an operation around the surveillance and capture of the suspects, Dare and Burkhan. 'Operation Bone Diggers' called for specialist surveillance officers as well as his own team.

Standing to his right was Johnny Clocks. To his left stood Inspector Jim Leslie, the commanding officer of six highly trained surveillance officers now gathered in Paterson's squad room for a briefing. Paterson and Clocks had met with Inspector Leslie an hour before the officers began to arrive and had briefed him fully, both on the previous day's events and what they were now expecting of them. Paterson nodded to Clocks.

Clocks clapped his hands. 'Right, let's 'ave yer! Pay attention, you lot!' The voices died down to a murmur before stopping completely under Clocks's baleful stare. 'For those of you who don't know me, I'm DI Clocks, and this is Superintendent

Paterson. For the benefit of our team, we're joined by Inspector Jim Leslie and 'is intrepid little band of creepers or, as they like to be called, surveillance officers. Ray, all yours.'

Paterson gave Clocks a sideways glance before looking out into his audience. One or two of Inspector Leslie's team looked a bit perplexed by Clocks's parting remark. 'Good morning, everybody. Thank you all for joining us.' He spent the next ten minutes outlining everything that he knew so far, right up to the point of their Zoom call with Sturman.

'It was initially believed that our suspects were in France working at the camps, but it turns out that was incorrect. Our latest intel from Interpol has confirmed that both suspects are in fact in London. We now have addresses for both of them and we have local CID plotted up around their respective properties. Both have been confirmed as being at home. Now, we could go straight round and nick them, but we believe we've stumbled onto a European organ-harvesting gang.

'Interpol have confirmed that they're both booked onto the Eurostar out of St Pancras at eleven this morning. DI Clocks and myself will also be on that train along with Inspector Leslie's team. *My* team, I want you on full standby and ready to go for when these guys come back into the UK. The problem at the moment is that we don't know when, how or where they will arrive back, but I need you to be ready to move when we do. We'll call it through as soon as we know, so you can hopefully meet us in time.

'Once our suspects arrive back, Inspector Leslie will have a second team on standby who will take the lead on surveillance. We need to find out where they go to, once they're back. My team . . . you'll stay back, out of the way, but be ready to make any arrests. I'll make that call. Make use of local CID to assist if necessary. Ladies and gents, this is a fluid situation and one we can't make proper plans for. Everything, up to a point, will be dictated to us by our suspects.

'So, if there are no more questions, we're off to St Pancras.'

CHAPTER FIFTEEN

Paterson and Clocks showed their warrant cards to the guard on the gate for the Eurostar and slipped onto the train. The tiny earpiece Paterson wore would let him know when Dare and Burkhan were heading for the train. They slid themselves into a group of empty table seats, one row back from the seats they knew had been allocated to their suspects. Paterson sat by the window, leaving Clocks in the aisle with a good view of the two men when they boarded and sat.

Clocks pulled back the tab on his beer and took a slug from the tin and then another. He let out a loud belch that clearly annoyed a smartly dressed woman walking down the aisle toward him.

'How lovely,' she said, in a clipped, well-mannered voice.

Clocks punched himself in the chest. 'Glad you liked it, babe. Don't go too far, will yer? I've got another one brewin' up. If you want, I'll come an' find yer when it's ready, but listen . . . I don't want you to think I'm comin' on to yer or nothin'. I'm a married man.'

The woman fixed Clocks with a determined stare. 'Your wife must be so proud of you.'

'Oh, yeah. As it 'appens, love, she is. She once asked me to belch out the alphabet for her. I got up to 'M' before I ran out of steam. Personal best that was.' Clocks grinned and gave her a thumbs up.

The woman shook her head at him, and the look on her face was one of despair mixed with disgust. 'It's people like you that are dragging this country into the gutter.'

Clocks shifted about in his seat and looked across at Paterson, who gave a slow almost imperceptible shake of his head. Clocks smiled at him and turned to the woman. 'What d'you mean, *people like me*?'

One or two passengers were now taking a bit of an interest in the developing altercation.

'Your lot. Causing all sorts of problems wherever you go.'

'Oh, I see,' said Clocks. 'I geddit. You mean because I'm black, don't cha?'

The woman looked confused for a second and then horrified. 'Black?'

'That's right, love. I'm black.'

'But . . . but, you're not . . .'

'What? What did you say? Oh, so you're oppressing me now, are yer? You sayin' I'm not black enough for you? That's outrageous. Someone call the police, please. I'm being persecuted by this . . . this . . . *Karen*, and I won't stand for it any longer. I refuse to be treated like this because I'm a big, beautiful black woman.' Clocks slapped one hand onto his forehead. 'The stress. The stress is killin' me. Ray, 'elp me.'

Paterson looked at the clearly bewildered woman. 'I'm so sorry, miss.' He had already clocked that she wasn't wearing a wedding ring. 'I apologise for my friend. He has a brain injury. His mother shut his head in a door when he was a child.'

Her face flushed. 'I . . . I'm so . . . I'm so sorry. I had no idea.'

Clocks was smiling to himself and began bouncing up and down in his chair exaggerating his shoulder movements. 'Can we go to the park now, Daddy? Please, Daddy.'

Paterson ignored him. 'Of course you didn't,' he said to the woman. 'How could you? Look, it's not your fault.

He looks fairly normal on the outside, but inside . . .' He shrugged. 'He has all different sorts of days. Yesterday he thought he was Chinese. Today? Well, today he thinks he's Oprah Winfrey. He'll be alright soon.'

The woman, her gaze cast downward, nodded and choked out a couple more apologies before she shuffled along the aisle to her seat.

Paterson, tight lipped, was clearly annoyed. 'What the fuck are you doing, John?' he whispered. 'This is a fucking surveillance and you're playing the fool. What is wrong with you?'

Clocks smiled. 'What I'm doing, mate, is hiding in plain sight. Who expects two plain-clothes coppers to go around shoutin' an' 'ollerin'? Hmm? I'll tell you. No one. So, rather than sit there and run the risk of looking like two buttoned-up plain-clothes coppers, I decided to think out-side the box. You should try it.' Clocks turned and winked at the man sitting across the aisle from him. 'Alright, cocker?' he said.

'I think those seats are booked,' said the man.

'Yeah?' said Clocks. 'Well, if they are, then whoever booked 'em best show up a bit lively 'cos we're about to leave. And, if they do show up, I'll tell 'em to toddle off an' go find somewhere else to sit 'cos I'm comfortable now.'

The man frowned and went back to reading his Kindle.

'When are you going to grow up, John?' said Paterson.

'Me?' Clocks turned to Paterson with a suitably offended look on his face. 'It was you who told her I was a nutter.'

'Because you were acting like one. Grow the fuck up.'

'Sorry, Daddy,' said Clocks.

Paterson gave a nod of his head and pushed at the earpiece.

'Daddy,' said Clocks.

'What now?'

'*Can* we go to the park, please?'

Paterson chortled loud enough for the man with the Kindle to look up again. He puffed himself up and said,

'Can you two gentlemen please behave in a more decorous manner?'

Clocks sat sideways on in his seat and leaned over to the man. 'Listen up, mate. I would behave in a more decorous manner if I knew what the fuck a more decorous manner meant. Now, if you're gonna start using ten-bob words on a five-bob man, my advice to you is to fuck off and get back to reading your little plastic book and mind yer own business. *Comprende, señorita?*'

Paterson looked over to the man. 'And now he thinks he's Ray Winstone. It all happens so fast these days. I don't know where I am anymore.'

Two of the Met's finest officers sat back in their seats.

'Why do you do that, John?'

'Do what?'

'Make out you're black.'

Clocks shrugged. 'It's a giggle. When you say that, people freak. They just don't know what to say or do, an' they get paralysed with fear in case I 'ave some sort of black heritage and they've now gone from bein' just an angry person to an angry racist. Gets 'em every time. You should try it one day. Seriously. It's such a laugh to see their confusion.'

A tinny voice sounded in Paterson's ear. *'Two birds have nested.'*

Paterson nodded. 'Playtime's over, John. Put your toys away.'

Clocks grinned over at Kindle man. 'Daddy says I can't play with you any more, mister. Lucky ol' you.'

CHAPTER SIXTEEN

On the platform, Inspector Leslie and his team of officers boarded the train a few seconds apart from each other and on different carriages. A male and female pairing, posing as a young couple in love, were right behind Dare and Burkhan as they boarded, and it was the man, DC Peter Flight, who had given the signal that they were now on the train.

Thirty seconds or so later, Dare and Burkhan entered Paterson and Clocks's carriage and bumbled their way along the aisle. Every couple of feet or so, the two men mumbled apologies to the seated passengers who were being hit on the heads or shoulders by the large bags each carried.

Finally, they took their seats and set about making themselves comfortable, pulling out bottles of drink, a couple of paperbacks and a pen and pad each. The male and female officers slipped into a pair of seats five rows back. She gave a slight nod to Clocks as she made herself comfy.

The journey to Paris would take around two hours, and Paterson and Clocks's only job was to keep an eye on their two suspects without making it obvious who they really were. Clocks had already covered that aspect.

Paterson handed Clocks a paperback book and hoped that he would play the game, sit quietly and read it. For all of his shenanigans, Clocks was a highly professional operative and knew exactly when to toe the line. It was just that he couldn't help winding Paterson up and keeping him on tenterhooks. With people like Johnny Clocks, it didn't pay to show any sign of weakness or it would be picked up on and fully weaponised.

'What's this?' said Clocks.

'A book. Don't look so surprised. You must have seen one before.'

'Funny enough, I 'ave. An' I brought me own.' He reached into his backpack and pulled out a French phrase book. 'This is Lyndsey's. Said I could borrow it.'

'Really? You're going to try and speak the language? You?'

'Yeah. A bit. I want to demand their surrender when we get there, an' this is me bein' thoughtful, Ray. I thought it might be better to tell 'em in their own lingo rather than 'ave to shout at 'em in English.'

Paterson rolled his eyes. 'Their surrender?'

'Yep. They need to know when we get there that we're in charge an' they better not go gettin' in our way with their little stripy blue jumpers and bikes. Fuckers.'

'Well, I'm glad you've not taken to stereotyping people, John. Just keep your voice down, and it's probably best if you remember that this isn't 1415 again.'

'When? 1415? Is that the time?' Clocks glanced at his watch.

'Nope. The year. 1415. Battle of Agincourt.'

Clocks shrugged. 'Never 'eard of it.'

'It was during the Hundred Years' War.'

'Hundred years? I though the longest one was the Second World War. What was that? About six years, wasn't it?'

'I don't have time to explain what your history teachers should have. It was a battle in which the French had superior numbers and we, the English, beat them quite unexpectedly. They got, what you would call, "a right good hiding".'

Clocks smiled.

'And, for the record, we can't demand anything from them, let alone their surrender. We need them.'

'Do we bollocks, mate. All we need from the froggies is to fuck off out of it and let the professionals do their jobs. 'Ere . . . you know when Prince Phillip died?'

Paterson sighed. 'Yes, I remember.'

'Well, when they 'ad his funeral they 'ad a forty-one gun salute for him, didn't they?'

'Something like that.'

'Well, I 'eard that Macron was straight on the blower to Boris to surrender just in case.'

Paterson chuckled.

So did Lee Burkhan. Clocks looked at him.

'Sorry about that,' said Burkhan, leaning over to look at Clocks. 'Couldn't help but overhear. That was bloody funny.'

Clocks grinned. 'Mate. I've got a million of 'em. Get yerself comfortable an' pin back yer lug'oles. I'm John. Johnny Pratt. An' this is me boss, Ray. Ray Zens. I know. Couldn't make it up, could yer?'

Tony Dare got out of his seat to come and say hello. All four men were handshakes and nods. Kindle man, stuck in the middle of this sudden meeting of new travelling companions cleared his throat a bit louder than was necessary. Paterson could tell he was the type that if he had been reading a newspaper, he would have rustled it in annoyance. That was the trouble with technology, he mused. Rustling an e-reader didn't have quite the same effect.

'Come an' 'ave a sit-down with us, mate,' said Clocks. 'You seem like you both like a laugh.'

Dare looked at Burkhan, who nodded. 'Yeah, why not, mate? Better than having to listen to him bang on about work for the next two hours.'

Kindle man stamped his feet as he stood up, snatched up the briefcase next to him, dropped his Kindle in it and walked off to find another seat as far away from this little lot as he could find. Paterson grinned.

Burkhan dropped into the seat opposite Paterson as Dare sat himself down opposite Clocks. Glancing out of the window, Paterson deftly slipped out his earpiece and pocketed it. Clocks would do the same at the first opportunity he got.

Five rows back, the male surveillance officer was busily whispering into his radio and informing Inspector Leslie that, somehow, things had gone from the covert surveillance of two potential murderers and organ traders to the investigating officers having a laugh and a drink with the suspects.

'So, what work you in then, fellah?' said Clocks. 'Must be interestin' if your mate wants to talk about it all the way to Paris.' He held up his tin of beer. 'Cheers everyone. To new friendships.' The four men clanked their tins together.

'We're in the aid business,' said Burkhan.

'Aid?' said Paterson. 'What d'you mean, *aid*?'

'We travel around the world giving aid to people who need it the most. Y'know . . . earthquake victims, flood victims, that sort of thing. We have our own company . . . GreatBritAid.'

'Nice,' said Paterson. 'I've heard of you guys, I think.' He took a swig of his beer. 'Something to do with refugees, yes?'

Dare nodded. 'Yep, sounds like us. We do pretty much anything where people need help.'

'Sounds like a worthwhile job. Good on you both.'

'What line of business you two in?' Burkhan asked.

'Us?' said Clocks. 'Nothing as near as worthwhile as you guys. No, we run a cleaning business. We employ about eight, nine hundred people who spend their days and nights cleaning up all the shit in the country. Fancy dustmen is probably a good term.'

Burkhan tilted his head. 'I'm sure you're more than dustmen, boys. With a workforce of that many, don't be putting yourselves down. That's amazing. What's the name of your company?'

'You won't have heard of us,' said Paterson. 'We tend to keep out of the limelight and subcontract all of our workers out to the bigger names. We supply councils and private companies with our cleaning services.'

Burkhan nodded. 'So, what takes you to Paris?'

'Shit's everywhere, mate,' said Clocks. 'An' where there's shit, there's us. I mean, you've seen Paris, right? Frogs need a couple of professionals to clean up the dump they call a city because they weren't up to the job, and *voilà*, 'ere we are. The best in the business.'

Dare chortled. 'Point taken.'

'Dunno why they call it the city of romance either,' said Clocks. 'I once fingered a bird behind the wheelie bins outside a café when I was a teenager. Nothing too romantic about that, you think, but I did buy 'er a baguette on the way 'ome. So . . . y'know?'

Dare spat out his mouthful of beer, spattering Clock's suit.

'Oh, fer fuck's sake!' Clocks jumped backwards further into his seat and rubbed frantically at his jacket. 'Always me bastard suits.'

'Sorry.' Dare wiped his chin. 'But you're a funny bastard.'

'Ain't I just,' said Clocks. 'You 'ave no fuckin' idea.'

Paterson chortled. 'Honestly, fellah. When he gets the chance, he'll literally have you in stitches.'

CHAPTER SEVENTEEN

Two hours later, Paterson and Clocks stepped off the train at Gare du Nord station in Paris and shook hands with Dare and Burkhan, promising to keep in touch once they were back in England. They let Dare and Burkhan set off ahead of them while they made a show of fumbling for their passports in their bags on the platform.

Paterson watched as the two men were swallowed up by the crowds. 'That was bloody risky, John. We were just supposed to observe them.'

Clocks sniffed. 'I know. But now we know exactly where they're goin' an' how long they're goin' for. That means we ain't gotta fanny about following 'em all day long and riskin' gettin' clocked. Game'd be up then, wouldn't it? Best way is to front the fuckers out, get 'em a bit pissed up an' let 'em talk.'

Paterson nodded as he allowed more people to flow around him and head for the barriers.

'D'you think they know we're police? Cottoned on to us?'

'Nah, mate. Unless they're the world's best liars. They were too loose, too casual. If they 'ad us down for bein' Old Bill, they wouldn't 'ave chatted away so easily. Certainly wouldn't tell us too much about themselves, would they? Nah. We're safe.'

'I'm going to give Inspector Laurent a call, tell her we're here.'

'Who?'

'Capitaine Laurent. She's the equivalent of an inspector.'

'Law-ron?'

'*Oui*,' said Paterson.

'That's a funny sort of name, innit? Law-ron?'

'Pretty common here.'

'Got a "T" in it though, ain't it?'

Paterson nodded.

'So why ain't it pronounced "Law-rent"?'

'Don't worry about it. It's no big deal, is it?'

'No. It's not a big deal. It's just stupid. I'm gonna call her Law-rent.'

'Why would you do that? That'll just annoy her.'

Clocks grinned. 'Will it? Oh, no.'

Paterson dialled Capitaine Laurent's number and listened to the phone ring for a second or two. A female voice answered.

'Superintendent Paterson, *oui*?'

'Er, *oui*, yes. Paterson here.'

'*Bonjour, Monsieur*. Do you speak French, by any chance?'

'A very small amount, I'm afraid. Not a language I got around to. Sorry.' As he talked, he could see the male and female surveillance officers approaching. Neither of them looked happy. He turned his back. Clocks could talk to them.

The female officer, DC Patricia Laine, went straight to Clocks. 'Sir . . .'

'Yes, love,' said Clocks.

'The fuck was that about?'

'Come again?'

'You two. Inviting them over for a cosy little chat and a drink up.'

'Who the fu—'

'You broke every protocol in the book by your actions and may well have compromised this job.'

Paterson, half hearing the woman's raised voice, turned and frowned.

Clocks held up his finger. 'Right . . . 'old up, 'old up, love. Steady the bus. First of all, do yerself a favour, gel, an' shut yer trap. The fuckin' 'ell d'yer think you're talkin' to? You don't get to fuckin' lecture me on policin', alright? I saw an opportunity to get close to the suspects an' extract information. I took it. If you don't like it, tough. Fuck off back to Blighty an' take yer fake boyfriend with yer.'

'Sir,' said DC Peter Flight, the male officer. 'She's right. What you did could've compromised this mission.'

'Mission? Mission? What the fuck are you two? A coupla spies or summin'? This was a simple follow job, nothing elaborate. Bread-an'-butter work, mate. An' just so you know — so you *both* know — you're workin' for us. Your job was to follow, not to go trappin' off to a senior officer in the middle of Frogland like you're somethin' special. Now, if you're gonna stay, shut up 'an follow us. An' try not to lose us. If you're not gonna stay, off you fuck.'

Paterson hung up his phone. 'Problem, John?'

Clocks shook his head. 'Ken an' Barbie 'ere are givin' it large because we 'ad a jolly-up on the train with our suspects. Gone all self-righteous, they 'ave. Sayin' we could've fucked up their "mission".'

Paterson looked at the two officers. Their faces told him everything he needed to know, and for a moment he debated with himself whether to damp down the bad feelings that were brewing. Today, he just wasn't in the mood to smooth things over.

'Mission? Pair of silly bastards. Mind your own business. What we do is nothing to do with you. Understand?'

'Oh, no.' The female officer wagged her finger at him. 'That's completely the wrong attitude to take with me, sir. You're both senior officers and should know better. I refuse to be spoken to like that, and on my return to England, I'm gonna report you. Both of you.'

'Well,' said Paterson, 'you do what you need to do, but in the meantime, do your job. If you feel your "mission" has been compromised, then fuck off out of it and leave the policemen to do their job. Okay? Good.'

Johnny Clocks grinned. It wasn't often he saw Paterson narked and he was enjoying it.

'That will be going in my report too.' She turned on her heel and stormed off, DC Flight following behind her. Still in character, they held hands and headed off toward the exit.

'Fuck me, Ray,' said Clocks. 'Who set fire to 'er Tampax then? What's that all about?'

'Who knows? Who cares? Fuck the pair of them.'

'Well, thanks fer the offer Ray, but I'll choose me own friends.'

Paterson chuckled.

'What'd the frogs 'ave to say?' said Clocks. 'Was it, "I surrender"?'

'Funnily enough, no. Enough with the casual xenophobia, now, Johnny boy. We're in their playpark now.'

'It's not xenowhatsit. Not with the frogs anyway. It's part of our cultural histories, innit? We 'ate each other, don't we? Always 'ave, always will. An' you know why? I'll tell you why. Thanks fer askin'. I reckon it's because our countries were joined together millions of years ago an' a fuck-off big flood separated us, an' they ended up on their own and they made up some dodgy language, like a code of some sort.'

'You mean French?'

'That's it. Yeah. French. An' they ended up 'avin' to eat snails because that's the only thing the lazy bastards could catch.'

Paterson looked at his friend. 'What the hell are you banging on about? None of that makes any sense at all. None of it. Apart from the bit about them being lazy. That made sense.'

'Right? I knew you'd understand.'

'Look, just curb it, John. We need their help, and the last thing we need is for you to go giving them some of your made-up history lessons. And no cracks about surrendering all the time. Got it?'

Clocks shrugged. 'I'll try, but I can't promise. Besides, you know they're thinkin' the same about us. Apart from the surrenderin' bit. Brits don't do that. They don't like Brits bein' in their country 'cos we're all brave an' shit.'

'More likely because wherever we Brits go, we tend to get raging drunk and cause all sorts of problems. Fighting, shagging, smashing things up. Tends to piss people off.'

'No different from when they rocked up in the UK in 1066 is it? They did just that an' slung up a few castles while they were about it to let us know they were top Johnnies. So, bad luck. 'Ave a bit back.'

'Come on. Let's go. Capitaine Laurent is waiting for us. Her people saw Dare and Burkhan jump in a cab and they're following. We need to get outside and brief Laurent with what we've found out.'

Clocks nodded. 'That they're 'ere to nick a family an' chop 'em up for their giblets.'

'Yep. So, what we need to do now is stay in the shadows. Let the French put eyes on our two boys in the camp and then let us know when they make a move.'

Clocks nodded. 'Sounds like a plan.'

'Yeah. But it might change as we go along. Y'know . . . the usual.'

CHAPTER EIGHTEEN

Paterson held out his hand as Capitaine Vivienne Laurent approached him. Greetings out of the way, he decided it was better to bring up their social meeting with the suspects before the two whining undercover officers got to tell the world and his brother about it.

'Capitaine. Thank you for agreeing to help us. Although, I should tell you, things have changed a bit since we boarded the train.'

Laurent, beautifully dressed in designer jeans, blouse and lightweight jacket, nodded as Paterson spoke. She said nothing as he outlined their banter with Dare and Burkhan and the information they had gleaned from them, and she kept her silence as he brought her up to speed with the events in London that took him and Clocks to France.

'I see,' she said, once Paterson had stopped talking. 'That was a risky move to engage these two men. Very risky.' Her voice was smooth and self-assured and it was just accented enough to give Paterson a little thrill. That and her looks. 'I like your style. Takes . . . balls.' She smiled at him. 'And who is this?' She nodded toward Johnny Clocks, who was standing in the background flanked by two police officers. He was looking around the station, his rucksack slung over one shoulder.

'That's my number two, Inspector John Clocks. A good man.' He waved him over.

'Inspector Clocks,' Laurent said. 'It is a pleasure to meet you.'

Clocks looked the woman up and down. 'You an' all, love,' he said. 'You an' all. Sorry I didn't come an' say 'ello earlier, but I was lookin' for the nearest tea wagon.'

Laurent frowned. 'Tea wagon?'

'Yeah. Tea wagon — as in, where d'you get a cuppa tea round 'ere? I 'ear you lot are big on the ol' coffee.' He grinned at her.

'Us lot?'

Paterson rolled his eyes. *Not now, John. Please. Don't start.*

'Yeah. It's my understanding that the citizens of Paris are more likely to imbibe the beverage of coffee than they are tea. Somewhat akin to our American cousins. Myself, I prefer to drink tea.'

Paterson stared at him. It sounded polite, reasonably explanatory, but Paterson knew that Clocks was taking a sly dig at her.

'Of course,' said Laurent. 'Let us take you to your hotel, where I am sure the tea will taste much better than it does from one of the sellers on the platform. We can also talk better there.' She nodded to one of her officers, who opened the door of a Renault SUV. 'Mr Clocks, you can ride with my officers. Mr Paterson, you're with me.'

Clocks shook his head at Paterson's good fortune and clambered into the back of his vehicle.

'How far is the hotel?' said Paterson as he settled himself in the passenger seat.'

'About twenty minutes. Plenty of time,' said Laurent.

'For?'

'For us to get to know each other a bit better and to lay down some rules.' With barely a glance over her shoulder, Capitaine Laurent pulled out into the traffic to a chorus of honking car horns, squealing tyres and angry shouts.

'What rules would they be?' said Paterson, remembering a previous trip to Paris where he'd boarded a cab and felt that his life was in immediate danger from the driver's total lack of care for himself, his passenger and his fellow road users.

'You are guests in my country, so I expect you to respect her. You will at all times do exactly as I tell you. You will at all times be escorted by a French officer if you are on police business. Do you have weapons?'

'You mean, guns?'

'Yes. Guns.'

'No,' said Paterson.

'Good.' Laurent accelerated out of the train station and pulled across two lanes of traffic, once again showing an apparent lack of rudimentary driving protocols.

'Problem, Capitaine?' Paterson shifted uncomfortably in his seat.

'I hope not. But your reputation precedes you. It seems you and your Inspector Clocks have a problem with authority and violence, and during your stay in my country, I want you to understand that your little antics will not be tolerated. Do I make myself clear to you?'

Paterson looked out of the window as cars, seemingly hell-bent on colliding with them, swerved at the last second and threw themselves into the storm of traffic that surrounded them.

'Perfectly,' he said, without turning from the window. 'Well, now that we've established that you're the newly crowned first ever Queen of France, let me remind you that we're here for one reason only, and that's to track and follow the movements of our two suspects. There will be no *antics*, as you put it, nor will there be any violence instigated by us. Given the information we gleaned during our ride over here, we don't expect to be here too long at all but, that being said, we are being led by the movements of our suspects. So, thank you for the warm welcome. Please feel free to look me up the next time you're in England.'

Capitaine Laurent's face softened and she gave a small nod. 'I am sorry. I do not mean to be rude, but as I said, your reputation precedes you — and that reputation, as men of honour, does you no favours.'

'Well, reputations can be twisted out of all proportion by rumours. And we all know what happens when we listen to rumours, don't we?'

'I read your files.'

Paterson shrugged. '*Of course* you did. Ah well. What can you do?'

Capitaine Laurent jammed on the brakes, one hand firmly on the horn. She raged at the car in front of her that had suddenly stopped for no apparent reason before taking an angry swerve around it, cursing as she went. Paterson felt a little tingle in his stomach.

He glanced at his watch. 'Listen, now you've set out your stall, could I buy you dinner this evening if work doesn't interrupt us?'

'Have you not seen the ring on my finger?' she said without glancing at him.

'Yes. But I wasn't planning on marrying you. It was just an offer of dinner while I'm here in France. Two professionals bonding.'

She pursed her lips. 'Do you want to sleep with me, then? Is that what you want?'

'Well, I wasn't planning on it, but . . .'

She nodded. 'We'll have dinner at seven. But, so you know, you have no chance of sleeping with me.'

Paterson raised an eyebrow. 'Good to know. Dinner at seven it is.'

Laurent nodded again. 'Violence and abuse of authority is not the only part of your reputation that precedes you,' she said as she exited off the main road.

Paterson smiled. 'Can I ask? Your little speech. Would I be right in thinking that one of your officers would have given the same talk to Inspector Clocks?'

'*Oui*.' Laurent pulled up in front of the hotel.

'Oh, dear God,' he said under his breath, figuring that, by now, Clocks would have set Anglo–French relations back at least a thousand years.

Laurent switched on the window wipers in protest at the rain that was beginning to spatter the windshield. 'It seems you two have brought the rain with you.'

Paterson smiled. 'Only when we have to, *mon capitaine.*'

CHAPTER NINETEEN

The SUV carrying Johnny Clocks pulled up behind Capitaine Laurent's vehicle. Paterson doubted it would be a happy man who exited the car, and even before the wheels stopped rolling, he knew he was right. The back door exploded open and Clocks jumped out, bag already over his shoulder and his face like thunder. He strode toward Paterson with no attempt to speak to his hosts.

'You got the talk then?' said Paterson as he turned to enter the hotel. Clocks kept walking.

'What a fuckin' liberty! Talkin' to me like I'm some sort of snot-nosed schoolboy on a day trip to France.'

A doorman pulled open one of the big heavy doors and stood aside as the two men marched past him. He kept an eye on them as they presented themselves at the reception desk and watched as Clocks dropped his rucksack onto the floor and immediately started slapping the bell for attention. He turned lazily away from the small vignette in front of him.

'Go on then, John. Get it out of your system.'

Clocks wheeled around to face him. 'So, I'm mindin' me own business, never said a word to anyone. Nothing at all. I'm looking out the window at the scenery, or what there is of it in this shit'ole of a city, an' this big fucker sittin' next

86

to me suddenly starts givin' it large. Pointin' his finger at me an' tellin' me that 'e knows all about us . . . read our files . . . callin' us a pair of cowboys an' tellin' me that we're on French soil now an' that they ain't gonna put up with us struttin' about like we own the place.'

'And you said?'

'I said 'e could fuck off out of it and to get his fuckin' finger out of me face or I'd bite it off an' spit it out the window. Mouthy bastard.'

'Of course you did. And then what happened? Let me guess.'

'So, he puffed 'imself up like Johnny Big Bollocks an' started 'ollering something I couldn't understand, kept waving his finger at me, so I told 'im again. 'E ignored me, so I fuckin' bit it. Told 'im I would, didn't I? You know what I'm like. A man of me word, ain't I? I give 'im fair warnin', didn't I? Didn't I? Anyway, the geezer went fuckin' mental, didn't 'e? Lost 'is shit big time. Jumpin' up an' down in 'is seat, 'e was. You think he'd never been bit by an Englishman before.

'Anyway, I let it go before it got a bit too lively in there. Don't want a punch-up in the car, do yer? But 'e kept on an' on, waving 'is finger around an' showin' it to Pierre or whatever the fuck the driver's name was. I told 'im to stop being a fuckin' pansy an' to man up. Off 'e went again. Right up in the air. Whassa matter with these people?'

Paterson shook his head at the same time as a young woman stepped out of a back room and headed toward them.

'Good morning, gentlemen.' Her voice was melodic and heavily accented. 'How may I help you today?'

'Good question, babe,' said Clocks. 'We've come all the way from London to pick it up.'

The young receptionist looked confused. 'I am sorry, I do not understand. Pick up?'

'The rifle.'

'Rifle?'

'Yep. The one advertised on eBay. This is where we pick it up, the advert said.'

'John . . .' Paterson was getting weary. He knew this poor girl was going to be the butt of his ire for a moment or two.

Clocks ignored him. 'Yeah. We collect guns, an' I won an auction for a genuine Second World War French army rifle. It said it was in near perfect condition 'avin' never been fired an' only dropped once. Comes with a free white flag too. But that's well used.'

Paterson chortled. The receptionist looked even more confused.

'Excuse me, monsieur. I do not understand. Perhaps . . . perhaps the manager can help you?'

'It's okay miss,' said Paterson. 'He was just playing about. He's tired and hasn't been burped by his mum this morning. He's just a little cranky. He'll be fine. Ignore him.'

The girl looked relieved, even if she didn't know what exactly was going on. She handed them their respective key cards and they wandered off toward the elevators.

'So, what 'appened with you an' that Captain Low-Rent or whatever she's called?' said Clocks. 'She give you any mouth? An' by that I mean did she give you the same speech as I got?' said Clocks.

'Yeah. Sounds very much like it.'

'An' what 'appened?'

Paterson shrugged. 'Turns out we're having dinner this evening.'

Clocks stopped walking. Paterson carried on and pressed the elevator call button.

'What? Oh, turn it in, Ray. We're here, what, twenny bleedin' minutes an' you're on a promise? What the fuck do you say to 'em? I don't know 'ow you do it, I really don't.'

Paterson shrugged again. 'I don't know. Must be my charm.'

'Did she see it then? Your charm? I mean, I've 'eard it's a bit on the little side, but I didn't know it was charm-sized.'

'Very funny.' Paterson watched the lift numbers change. 'In any case, I doubt it'll happen now that you've opened up hostilities with the French again. The guy whose finger you threatened to eat is bound to go bleating to Mummy about you, and that should kill off my chances nicely.'

'Boo-fuckin'-hoo. Poor you.'

'Thanks for your sympathy.'

'You're welcome, mate.'

Paterson's phone rang. 'Capitaine Laurent,' he said, looking at the screen. 'Here we go.'

Clocks took over watching the lift numbers as Paterson paced up and down, trying to get a word in edgewise as Laurent tore into him about a vicious, unprovoked attack on one of her men by '*l'animal*' that was Johnny Clocks.

After a minute, Paterson, all smiles, said goodbye and hung up.

The elevator dinged and the doors slid open.

'What's she 'ave to say, then?' said Clocks, stepping in.

'Well, she doesn't like you and she's moved our date forward an hour. Seems she wants more time with yours truly.'

Clocks snorted. 'So, what do we do until you get yer leg over?'

'Look. In all seriousness, this is not a date and there's no leg-overs involved, okay? Two police officers trying to get along professionally and that's it.'

'Right you are, then,' said Clocks. 'Thanks for letting me know, you lying bastard. Anyway, what's the plan?'

'I thought we'd bypass waiting to get the nod from her troops. I'm going to give Dare and Burkhan a call and see if we can get the guided tour. You up for that?'

'About the only thing I am up for these days,' said Clocks as the doors slid shut.

CHAPTER TWENTY

At precisely 2 p.m., a taxi dropped Paterson and Clocks off at the top end of one of the flyovers in the Porte de la Chapelle area in Paris. Known locally as the City of Tents, the camp housed between 1,500 and 2,000 migrants, made up mostly of people from sub-Saharan Africa and Afghanistan. There was no way to tell the exact number of desperate people as the camp, like others before it, was illegal. New tents appeared on a daily basis and would only be constrained by the amount of available space, and that was shrinking rapidly.

Every so often, the French authorities would take a hard-line stance and evict the tenants from under the flyovers using the time-honoured tactics of force and a bit more force. This always led to hardcore fighting between the migrants and authorities which could go on for a few days before, in the end, the police gained control, but not before they took a few casualties for their troubles.

Waiting to greet them was Lee Burkhan, all smiles and handshakes as Clocks ducked his head into his shoulders as a small protest against the rain that had started as soon as they got into the cab.

'Ray! John! Good to see you both again. Didn't expect to see you guys so soon, if ever.'

Paterson contrived his best smile and it seemed to work. 'Well, our first meeting isn't until tomorrow, and never having seen one of these places before, I thought it would be a better use of our time than getting pissed up in the bar.'

Burkhan gave him a sideways look. 'Not sure I agree with your thinking there, mate. I'd rather be getting pissed in a pub any day than being here. Still, that's what we do.'

'Where's yer oppo?' said Clocks. 'Whassisname? Tony, weren't it? I'm shit at names. Never forget a face, mind. But shit at names.'

Burkhan chuckled. 'Yeah. Tony. Spot on. He's over at the first-aid post, helping out. We had some new faces show up here today. Not long ago, actually. Husband, wife and two kiddies. Poor bastards. Hopefully, we can get them over to the UK.'

'Give 'em a decent start?'

'Yeah. Wasn't sure they'd find their way here, to be honest. Seems they had a hell of a time. All sorts of grief, but make it they did.'

'Result,' said Clocks.

'Yeah,' said Paterson, 'result.'

'Duck under here, boys.' Burkhan gestured toward the flyover. 'You're getting soaked. Tea?'

'Now, you're talkin',' said Clocks. 'Don't s'pose you've got any Jammie Dodgers?'

'Dunno,' said Burkhan. 'Always got chocolate digestives, though. And I might be able to get someone to rustle up a plate of grub for you, if you fancy it?'

Clocks frowned. 'What is it?'

'Dunno that either. But it's usually a stew of some kind. Cheap 'n' cheerful.'

'Ooh. Stew. I love a stew. Got any dumplin's?'

'Oh yeah. Always got dumplings.'

'Lead on, my son. Lead on.'

They followed Burkhan as he took them under the flyover and guided them through the rows of tents, deep into the heart of the 'city'. Making their way through the narrow walkways, Paterson made the mistake of looking at some of the faces. They fixed him with a stare, as if they pinned their hopes on them — two men, well dressed and from the west, who might be their saviours, might give them a way out, might give them hope.

Families were huddled tightly together, sitting around small open fires — dangerous, given the abundance of nylon housing, but keeping the children warm was their priority. Although it was summer, neither sunlight nor warmth made it through the concrete canopy, and the wind, colder than it should be for want of sun, whipped through the makeshift walkways.

'Not far now,' said Burkhan. 'Tony'll be pleased to see you both. Had a right good laugh with you two fellahs, we did. Made the trip a bit more bearable.'

The smell of cannabis and alcohol mixed in with the smell from the makeshift toilets and general filth caused Paterson to heave slightly. He shook his head in silent protest at what he was witnessing.

A small boy of about ten ran out of nowhere and clamped his spindly arms around Burkhan's waist. 'Mr Lee! Mr Lee! Are we going, please?' The boy looked to be of Middle Eastern descent. Despite his ragged appearance, he looked well enough. Paterson knew from reading various news reports that the NGOs did the best they could to provide food, first aid and antibiotics and generally tried to make people's lives a bit more comfortable. Except for these two. These two were wicked bastards who didn't deserve to live.

'Hello, Baktash. No, I'm so sorry, son. Not today, not today. I'm sorry.' The boy's gaze fell and he gave a faint nod. Maybe tomorrow it would be his family's turn.

'Tomorrow, Mr Lee?' he said hopefully. 'Will it be tomorrow, please?'

Paterson hoped that this boy would never see Burkhan again in his life, and if things went his way, he never would. 'We'll see, Baktash. I'll do my best.' He started to prise the boys tightly clamped arms off of his waist when a harsh voice calling the boy's name made it unnecessary. The father. He berated the boy loudly despite Burkhan's protestations and made to hit him with his open hand. Paterson grabbed it on the downward swing and held it firm. The man's dark eyes flared at Paterson for his insolence and he tried to wrench his arm away. Paterson held him firmly and slowly shook his head. The father got the message pretty quickly. Paterson didn't give a fuck about him.

'Ray,' said Burkhan. 'You need to be careful here. Some of these people are armed. Knives . . . swords . . . the odd gun.'

'I'll be fine.' Paterson pulled his jacket straight. 'I can't stand people hitting kids. Gets my goat up.'

Burkhan nodded. 'You get used to it.'

Paterson swung his gaze toward Burkhan. 'Maybe you. Never me.'

'It's just over here,' said Burkhan, and he turned away from Paterson.

Paterson felt his stomach lurch as he caught the gaze of two small children looking at him. Filthy faces, filthy clothes. Snot dribbling from their noses and rheumy eyes — dead eyes, tired and hungry. He could feel his heart break. Children were his one weak point, and he hated the fact that they suffered. Guilt welled up inside him when it struck him that these people had nothing. He lived a life of luxury and was paid a good salary he didn't even need, money that these families could use to lift themselves out of this squalor and begin to build lives for themselves.

He resolved to do what he could to help as many as possible. The only question was, could he use Dare and Burkhan to put him in touch with the right people, legitimate people who could use the financial help, before he set about destroying the two of them.

CHAPTER TWENTY-ONE

Tony Dare's face lit up when he caught sight of his new friends, and he spent the next ten minutes ignoring the queue of people who needed his help while he caught up with what Paterson and Clocks had been up to since they went their separate ways at the station.

Paterson felt uncomfortable with Dare's indifference to the growing queue, and Burkhan was no better. He put it down to the fact that they were both inured to the suffering around them — that, and the fact that they were a pair of wicked bastards.

'Well, Ray 'ere is on a promise with some French sort 'e met at the hotel,' said Clocks. 'So, 'e's off to a flyin' start. Me, I just cracked open the minibar.'

Dare's eyebrows went up. 'Bloody hell, Ray. You're a boy. Good on you.'

Paterson shook his head. 'I doubt anything will come of it. John's already managed to piss off one of her kids. Bit his finger. So . . . y'know. Can't see it happening.'

'You bit his finger?' said Burkhan.

'Yep. Little French fucker was pointing it at me. Told him not to.' He shrugged. 'What can you do? Needed to be taught a lesson.'

Dare chuckled. 'Jesus. You really couldn't care less, could you?'

'Nope. Don't give a fuck, mate.'

'So, what's the score with this camp, then?' said Paterson. 'How'd it come into existence?'

'You remember the big camp at Calais?' said Burkhan. 'Got shut down a few years back?'

Paterson nodded.

'This is where most of them came to. It's not much, as you can see. But being under the flyovers gives some protection from the winter rain and snow.'

'And the authorities allow this?'

Burkhan drained his cup of tea and shook out the last remaining drops on the ground. 'They don't allow it, but they do turn a blind eye. They have to, really. There's just too many people, too many camps across this part of France, for them to do anything effective about it. Every so often, some politician gets a bee in his bonnet and orders a clear out. It's all punch-ups at dawn. Some get nicked, the place is cleared . . . a month later, they're all back. People have to go somewhere.'

Paterson sighed. 'I guess so. Do any of them get rehomed?'

'A few families, but not many. You have to understand that these people aren't particularly welcome here, so the authorities don't exactly go out of their way to help. Class them as a drain on resources. That's why they don't bother to stop them going to the UK. A problem moved is a problem solved.'

'But you sometimes help?' said Paterson. 'Help the odd family make it over?'

'Yeah. We do from time to time. It's a risky business but . . . you do what you can.'

'So, 'ow'd you decide it, then?' said Clocks. 'Why some families and not others?'

Burkhan shrugged. 'Medical grounds. Some people arrive with illnesses and injury. Some have severe medical conditions that require urgent care, and if we didn't get them into our country, they'd just die. Who the fuck wants to die under a shit-smelling flyover in the cold and rain.'

Paterson closed his eyes and rubbed his face for a few seconds. 'Jesus wept. Thank God for you two.' He locked eyes with Dare. 'You're a couple of saints.'

Dare kept his eyes locked on Paterson. He smirked. 'When we're not sinning.'

Paterson ignored the remark. 'Is there any way we can help?'

'No, not really,' said Burkhan. 'Not in a hands-on way. Donations always help, so you can support our work that way.'

'Of course. I'll have to run it all past the board when we get back, but I'm sure we can sort something out.'

'So, who's goin' back to civilisation, then?' said Clocks. 'Which one of these little families 'ave you picked out to be the lottery winners?' He looked around him at the sea of humanity at its lowest.

'Red tent over at the back. Just arrived. We're taking them back tonight before they're processed here as new arrivals.'

'Hasn't that already been done?' said Paterson.

'Yes and no,' said Dare. 'No checks are carried out to verify who these people are. The smugglers don't care. They just want payment. The driver doesn't care. He just brings them. It's all illegal, so he doesn't want to get involved over and above the risk he already takes. If he's stopped and his container is checked, he'll try and lie his way out of it by saying he was on an empty run and they must've all piled in while he was taking a piss at a diner. It's only when they arrive here that any sort of identity checks are made, and that's not a particularly thorough job.'

'Why not?' Paterson asked.

'Their passports get taken from them before they get here. We have no way of knowing who they really are, so we build up a rough profile to put on a form. Name, age, ethnicity, that sort of thing. We have interpreters here in the camps, but the migrants generally clam up like they've been told to. It's a basic description, but it might come in handy if any of them go missing.'

'Missin'?' said Clocks. 'What d'you mean, missin'?'

'Not everybody stays here, John, and none of them are prisoners. Some have other plans. Some have relatives here that they go to. Some make the decision to go into prostitution to make money. They move out and sleep rough in the cities. Gotta feed the kids somehow. Some, particularly young girls, are sold by the parents to the sex-trafficking gangs that operate here. Some are just snatched in the dead of night. Gone.'

'Fuckin' 'ell. They're sold by the parents?'

Burkhan nodded.

'Cunts! They need a fuckin' good 'iding, the dirty, no-good bastards.'

'It's not a nice world we live in, mate.'

'I know that, but sellin' your own flesh 'n' blood? You say there's gangs operatin' here as well?'

They stopped outside the red tent.

'Yeah. Nothing we can do. Authorities don't want to get involved and the gangs are powerful. Vicious bastards. It's all just money to them. You try and stop them and they'll kill you where you stand. No qualms about it.'

'This is unbelievable,' said Paterson.

Burkhan smiled. 'And this is just Paris. It goes on across the globe. The . . . whole . . . fucking . . . globe. Welcome to century twenty-one, boys.'

CHAPTER TWENTY-TWO

Paterson knelt down in front of the small child sitting out-side the red tent. 'Hello,' he said. The boy ignored him. His mother, father and sister were inside. Paterson heard a low groan come from inside the tent, and with permission from Burkhan, he poked his head through the flap, no longer interested in the child. The mother lay on her side, evidently in pain. Her pale and sweaty face was wracked in agony. She stared at him from beneath the grimy yellow puffer jacket that was draped over her body. 'What's the matter with her?'

Burkhan shook his head. 'To be honest, I'm not com-pletely sure. We think she has a problem with her appendix, according to her husband. Probably burst, judging by the state of her.'

'Why the fuck ain't she in the 'ospital, then?' said Clocks. He pushed past Paterson to see what was going on. 'Jesus, girl. You look a bit ropey.'

'No hospital will take her. She's an illegal. End of.'

'So, they're happy to let her die?' said Paterson.

'What can I tell you? It's just the way it works, Ray.'

'Is it? Well it's fucking disgusting. Can't we do some-thing for her?'

'We are. We're taking them back to the UK once it gets dark. We have a doctor with his own operating theatre.'

Paterson frowned. 'His own operating theatre? How's that work, then?'

'In this game, you have to be resourceful. You make friends, you get to know who you can trust. We'll weigh him off with a few quid and everybody's happy.'

'And they get to stay in the country? The UK?'

'Hm-hm.'

'Good. Poor sods.'

'So, 'ow they gettin' back to the UK, then?' said Clocks. 'Don't look like she'll make the train.'

'We have our ways, John. No offence, but this is a very risky move on our part, so we have to be a bit careful. You understand?'

'Yeah, mate. I don't care. Was just curious. You crack on.'

Paterson thought that it was bit late in the day to start getting secretive over how they transported their victims, given that he and Dare had pretty much told them their whole life stories. It flashed through his mind that perhaps they'd cottoned on that he and John were police, and if that was the case, it was game over. But, looking at Burkhan's face and taking in his whole demeanour, he wasn't convinced. He'd front it out a bit more, but he sensed they were getting to the limit of asking any more questions. Better to quit while they were ahead.

Clocks had other ideas. 'So, plane then?'

'What?' said Burkhan.

'Plane. If it's not the train, I can't see 'er surviving a boat trip, so that just leaves a plane.'

Burkhan stiffened. 'You ask a lot of questions, John. Why's that?'

'I'm a nosey fucker, mate. You boys 'ave got me intrigued. It's one of my loveable traits. If you don't tell me, I'll end up with a brain itch for the next coupla days. An' if I get one of those, I'll be a right bastard to be around. Biggin Hill for the landing?'

Burkhan turned away. But before he did, Paterson caught the flicker in his eyes. Biggin Hill it was.

'Well, sorry to give you brain itch, but it's best we keep it to ourselves. It's better that way. Safer.'

'Understood, Lee,' said Paterson. 'Thanks for doing this. I appreciate the tour. Certainly opened my eyes and, look, when we get back to England, I'll keep my promise and see what we can do about helping you boys out with some funds.'

'You going?' Burkhan looked surprised.

'Yeah. I've seen as much as I can take. I just wanna go back to my hotel room, get pissed and see if I can screw the arse out of that French bird who was coming on to me.'

'Good on you, mate. Give her one for me, will you?'

'That's a bit weird innit?' said Clocks.

Burkhan looked confused. It was a perfectly standard thing for an Englishman to say when a friend was about to get lucky. 'Weird?' he said.

'Fuckin' weird, mate. Think about it. He's doing the nasty dance . . .' Clocks thrust his hips backward and forward. 'And then he shouts out, "Here you go, gel. This one's from me mate, Lee. Enjoy!"'

Burkhan burst out laughing. 'You silly fucker. I love that sense of humour of yours. Brilliant.'

'Do we see ourselves out of the camp?' said Paterson.

'No. Make your way back to Tony. He'll see you out. I have to stay here and make arrangements with these folk.'

'Fair enough, mate.' Paterson shook hands with him, fighting back the urge to kill him there and then. An urge that told him he really did need to see the Met's psychiatrist when he got back.

As they walked away, leaving Burkhan to make whatever arrangements were necessary to get the family over to the UK, Paterson strained to keep himself under control. The psychological damage he'd suffered since he'd teamed up with Johnny Clocks was immense. Every day was a struggle with his mental health, but somehow he managed to convince his shrink that he was holding it all together. 'Just a part of the job,' he told her. 'I'm good. Stop worrying about me.' But, in his quiet times, alone, at home, the visions came: his ex-wife torn to pieces . . . dead girls, all victims of the same killer . . . colleagues . . . friends . . . all dead because of him . . . his face nearly peeled off by a crazed psychopath . . . a man sawn in half, head to groin . . . a woman with bamboo growing through her. It was enough to drive a man mad. He took in a deep breath as he walked back to Tony Dare.

'You alright, mate?' said Clocks.

'Fucking ace! You?' He knew that Clocks, for all his bluff and bravado, was feeling the strain too. Two ordinary men losing their minds was one thing, but these two particular men were dangerous and on the edge of losing their shit completely.

'Look, Ray. I know I can be a bit of a knob sometimes an' I take the piss pretty much all the time, but I really don't like these two fuckers one little bit. They've given me the ravin' 'ump — and you know what I'm like when that 'appens. So, first things first . . . what's the plan for savin' this little family?'

'They're leaving tonight, right?'

Clocks nodded.

'Then I'll call Vivienne—'

'Who's that then?'

'Capitaine Laurent. We tell—'

'Oh. First-name terms, are we?'

'You're not. I am.'

'Good point. I s'pose it 'elps to know who it is yer bangin'. Only polite, innit?'

'I've always found that to be the case. And as I've already said, there'll be no banging going on, so you'll have to switch off the movie in your head and go back to wanking off to *Love Island* or something.'

'Bit 'arsh, mate. No need for that. I'm married now.'

'And where is Lyndsey?'

'Dunno at the moment. Runnin' around with Wol's little band of investigators-cum-killers somewhere or other. Could be anywhere. She'll be back. We're good.'

'Anyway, I'll give her a call—'

'She'll be upset.'

'What? Who?'

'The French bird. Vivienne. You've made a date with 'er an' now yer blowin' 'er off without even sayin' sorry. Very ungentlemanly. You should be ashamed of yerself.'

'John, I just said I'm going to give her a call. I'll explain. She'll be fine. It was just a work thing anyway.'

'Hmm. Was it?'

'What d'you mean *was it*? You know it was.'

'Don't matter what I think, does it? Matters what she thinks. She thought she was goin' out for a slap-up meal at some expensive restaurant with a leg-over chucked in afterward an' now you're givin' the poor girl 'er P45 without even tellin' 'er why she's sacked. You can't keep goin' around leadin' women on like this. No good will come of it, mark my words.'

'What? I'm not leading anyone on. I was just trying to build a bridge between our two police forces.'

'Yeah, right. You were tryin' to build a bridge to 'er naughty bits, mate, that's what you were tryin' to do. So, 'ow you gonna explain it to 'er?'

'I'll tell her the truth. We got information that they're headed back to England with potential victims and we had to leave on the hurry-up. She'll understand.'

Clocks looked horrified. 'What? You're gonna tell 'er the truth? Are you mad? You never tell a bird the truth! Especially one you've just given the elbow to. You 'ave to say somethin' like, "It's not me, sweet'eart, it's you." That sort of thing. Make out you're all upset.'

'Right. Okay. Pretty sure that's not the right way of saying it, and I'm not giving anyone *the elbow*, for God's sake. Again, it was just a work thing!'

'Well, I dunno. Saw the look on 'er face when you asked 'er out. Pretty sure she's already at 'ome writin' up *save the date* cards for yer weddin'.'

Paterson sighed then rubbed his face. 'John, look . . . Do me a favour and shut the fuck up. I know you're on one of your wind-ups, but I'm tired and I *really* don't need to listen to you keep gabbling on about imaginary breakups and weddings. So give it a rest, mate. Please.'

Clocks nodded. 'Alright. Fair enough. But when you make the call put 'er on speaker so I can 'ear what she says. Deal?'

'What? Why?'

'Love it when a bird goes off on one in a foreign language. All sexy, innit?'

Paterson gave a little shrug. 'Yeah. It is a bit. I'll give you that.'

'I remember when I was a kid I saw a film with Sophia Loren in it. She was runnin' around in 'er bra and doin' 'er nut at some bloke in Spanish. Dunno what this geezer 'ad done, probably blown 'er out with no good reason like you, but she gave 'im a right good coatin'. I loved it. Got me first ever twinge in me down-belows on the strength of that.'

'Italian.'

'What?'

'Italian. Sophia Loren is Italian.'

Clocks twisted his face as he brought back the memory. 'She is?'

'She is. Definitely.'

'Really?'

'Really.'

'That might explain why I once walked all around Lake Como with a boner one year when I was on me 'olidays an' 'ad no idea why. Still. Don't matter. Principle is sound.'

'Principle might be sound, but you're bloody not.' Paterson skipped over the feet of an old man lying flat out in the gutter. He wasn't sure if he was unconscious or sleeping. 'We call Vivienne, tell her what we found out, and she can get eyes on them for when they leave the camp tonight. But we're running out of time to get the job jacked up.' He glanced at his watch.

'Yeah,' said Clocks. 'The French ain't known as speed merchants, are they? Don't see many of them winnin' gold in the sprintin' section of the Olympics. Takes the lazy fuckers long enough to walk around the track at the openin' ceremony. Three hours behind everyone else.'

Paterson ignored him.

'So, we know they're gonna land in Biggin Hill, yes?' said Clocks.

'He looked a bit shifty when you mentioned it, but that's not a guarantee.'

'I accept that, but we're gonna 'ave to go with it an' 'ope we're right.'

'Agreed.'

'So, what about us then? 'Ow we gettin' home?'

'Same way, but a lot faster. We're going straight to the airport now. Hopefully, we can charter a Lear. When they land, me, you an' the rest of the troops can follow them off. See where they end up and then we take the fuckers out. That said, if they land in a field somewhere or go to City Airport, we're fucked.'

'Nah, we'll be alright. Every dodgy fucker lands in Biggin Hill, mate. Trust yer ol' pal.'

'Hmm. Let's hope so.'

'I've never been in a Learjet.'

'Ah, you're in for a treat, then. Very nice way to travel.'

Clocks nodded. They were about a hundred yards from Tony Dare's little table. He still had a queue, so it would save them having to spend too much time talking to him.

'Ray . . .' said Clocks.

'What?'

'When we get back, which one d'you want to kill?'

CHAPTER TWENTY-THREE

Just after midnight, a private ambulance pulled into Biggin Hill airport. At the same time, a light aircraft began its approach, having crossed the English Channel from France. The ambulance driver knew from experience that the plane's passengers would be on board with him within the next fifteen minutes or so. He pulled a small flask from the centre console and poured himself a cup of overly brewed coffee, grimacing at the bitter taste.

As he watched the aircraft begin its descent, he noticed how it seemed to wobble from side to side and was grateful it wasn't him inside. Planes were meant to be big. This little thing . . . well, it was just a bit too rickety-looking to go anywhere, let alone across the Channel. He flashed his lights to let the pilot know he was waiting.

* * *

As the wheels of the light aircraft touched down, Paterson, watching from his car tucked away in Barwell Crescent opposite the airport, told his occupants that they were game on. Johnny Clocks, Monkey Harris, Dusty Doneghan and Tommy Gunn nodded and mumbled their acknowledgements. Monkey checked the tracker device that Inspector Leslie had given them earlier. Full signal.

'You figured out how to work that thing, Monkey?' said Paterson. 'We don't wanna lose his team.'

'Got it, guv. Was just this second checking it. Easy enough to work.'

'Why don't we use our phones again, guv?' said Clocks.

'I dunno. Inspector Leslie wanted us to use trackers. He's worried that they might pick up our phone signals or something. If we lose the surveillance vehicle then at least we can pick them up. That said, John, make a quick call to Leslie and tell him to follow the vehicle to its final destination then turn your phone off.'

Clocks pulled out his mobile phone and dialled.

'It's Clocks. Yeah. They're down. Guv'nor says to follow them to their final destination. All I can tell you is it's a private ambulance — so not gonna be too difficult to follow.' A few seconds later, Clocks hung up and turned the phone off. 'Ray?'

'What?'

'If we gotta turn our phones off to avoid detection, 'ow come we can use the radios?'

Paterson sat quiet for a second or two. 'That's a good point. No idea, actually. What'd he say?'

'He said that when this is over he's going to kick our bollocks in for tellin' his little crew to fuck off when we all rocked up in Frogland.'

'What? *Did* he?'

Clocks chuckled. 'No. But he's got the grip. Can hear it in 'is voice.'

'Come on, then . . .' said Monkey. 'What have you two done now?'

'Nothin'. Somethin'. We ended up 'avin' a laugh with Dare and Burkhan and, according to the stroppy little tart of a surveillance officer, we're not supposed to do that. Bad form, apparently. Short story . . . she slung 'er toys out the pram an' started givin' me a right good fangin'. So I told 'er to take a flyin' fuck. Tellin' me 'ow to do me job . . . cheeky cow.'

'Yeah,' said Monkey. 'Fancy her telling you about professionalism.'

Clocks held up his middle finger and twisted it.

Monkey smiled and shook his head.

Paterson unconsciously touched his earpiece, waiting to hear from the undercover officer hiding in the trees near the Heritage Hangar opposite the main runway. PC Jimmy Dent, equipped with night vision binoculars, was in control of the operation for the time being.

Paterson felt the butterflies waking up in his stomach and began to tap his foot gently. This anticipation was what fuelled him onward. Suddenly, a burst of radio chatter caused him to freeze.

'All units from OP1 . . . I have eyes on our prize. Travellers just left the bird and are now heading straight for their wheels.'

Paterson wrinkled his forehead. He got the gist of it, but English would have been better. 'Stand by, boys,' he said to his passengers. 'They're gonna start loading up the ambulance.' The officers clicked on their seatbelts. 'OP1 from Silver. Can you confirm how many?'

'Difficult, Silver 1. Total of six, maybe seven.'

'Thank you, OP1. Let us know when they're on the move.'

'All received.'

'Seven?' said Clocks. 'The frogs said only two boarded with the family. Where'd the other one come from?'

Paterson shrugged. 'Dunno. Anyone?'

'Might be a medic,' said Tommy Gunn, a quiet man by nature; it was easy to forget he was there sometimes.

'Oh, yeah,' said Clocks. 'Good thinkin' there, Batman.'

'Silver one and all units,' announced PC Dent. *'Travellers on the move. Heading for gate now.'*

'All received,' said Paterson. 'Here we go, boys.'

'Received by Bronze 1,' said Inspector Leslie.

The ambulance pulled into view and Paterson dropped his car into drive mode, foot on the brake. The ambulance stopped at the exit with its indicator flashing a left-hand turn. Five seconds later, it pulled out onto the empty A233 and drove straight past Paterson. Five seconds after that, a motorbike carrying a surveillance officer sailed past them heading in the same direction.

Paterson dropped the handbrake, drove to the end of the road, turned right and hung back. He had a pretty good view of the bike and would watch his tail light until such time as the bike peeled off in another direction to be replaced by a car. This swap would be repeated with a total of four cars and five motorcycles for as long as it took for their targets to reach their destination. And all the time, Paterson, Clocks and the others would be lurking in the background waiting for their moment.

'Where's SCO19 then, guv?' said Monkey Harris, referring to the Met's elite firearms unit.

'They should be a mile or so behind us. Leslie gave them a tracking unit too.'

Clocks seemed satisfied. 'How many shots on board? D'you know?'

'Two gunships, so ten officers. Plus us five all armed. Fifteen in total.'

'Fuckin' 'ell, guv,' said Clocks. 'I didn't know we were off to war. We goin' off to some pikey camp you didn't tell us about?'

'What?' said Paterson.

'Pikeys. The bloke 'iding in the trees called 'em travellers. That's the posh word for pikeys, innit?'

Paterson sighed.

'I thought this was quick take-down job. Lots of 'ootin' an' 'ollerin' an' wavin' our guns around like we know what we're doin', an' then off 'ome for tea an' biscuits. Hurrah! Didn't know we were going for a shoot-up with the pikeys. They're a right 'andful, that lot.'

'Clocksy, stop calling them pikeys. It's racist and, no, we're not going for a shoot-up with them — the travellers, I mean. You know exactly what's going on.'

Dusty chuckled. 'Best we just stay out of the way an' let Nineteen do their thing. They're a bit better at it than we are.'

'What?' said Clocks. 'Better than us? I don't think so, matey boy. Did I tell you about the time me 'n' Ray took out a bunch of nutters by 'ollerin' an' 'ootin' an' wavin' two plastic guns around at them?'

'You did, guv. Several times.'

Clocks had been dining out on the story for some time now. Unarmed and on their way for a showdown with a group of killers calling themselves the Bermondsey Knights, Clocks had the bright idea of stopping at an all-night convenience store that sold children's toys. It was a crazy idea and Paterson told him so, but it did work in getting the Knights to drop their weapons. 'That's because it deserves bein' retold over an' over again. Proper policin', that was.'

'What?' said Monkey. 'You bought a couple of toy guns and threatened a bunch of nutters with them. You only got away with it because it was dark. Otherwise they'd have killed the pair of you.'

'Would they, though?'

'Yes, they fucking would have. You got lucky and you know it.'

'Wasn't luck, Monkey boy. Confidence. It's all in the confidence, boys. Act like you know what the fuck you're doing and do it with conviction. That's my motto.'

'I thought your motto was, *You can't beat a big pair of tits*,' said Monkey.

Clocks grinned. 'It is. And I stand by that. But it's not my only motto, is it? I've got a ton of 'em. One for every occasion, me.'

'That defeats the object, doesn't it?' said Paterson. He drove carefully across a junction that showed a red traffic light against him.

'A little bit, I s'pose. But I like to be prepared. You never know when you'll need a new motto. That's my motto.'

Paterson rolled his eyes as the others burst into laughter. 'Keep it down a tad, boys,' he said. 'I need to hear the radio.'

He swung the car right, again taking care, as the lights were against him again.

The surveillance convoy made its way through the near-deserted streets for the next twenty minutes. Paterson watched the surveillance team swap over vehicles several times: drop back, move closer, drop back and occasionally disappear. He got nervous when they dropped out of sight but he trusted they knew exactly what they were doing. And they did.

CHAPTER TWENTY-FOUR

Ahead of him, Paterson could see what looked to be some sort of office block set back a few hundred yards behind a chain-link fence. He had parked up in a shaded area of the main road that ran past the front of the building and killed the lights on the car.

'What the fuck is this place?' said Monkey Harris.

'If I had to guess,' said Paterson. 'I'd say it's some sort of private hospital or a lab of some sort. Whichever it is, I'm pretty sure it's going to be the last stop for our little family of refugees.'

'What now?' said Clocks, leaning forward. 'We goin' straight in?'

Paterson shook his head. 'We wait until Jim Leslie gives us the nod. He's got eyes on now. He makes that decision.'

Clocks pushed himself deeper into his seat. 'Not 'appy about that, guv. The longer we delay, the more chance they've got to get on with the giblettin'.'

'Gibletting?' said Dusty. 'Is that even a word?'

'D'you understand what I meant?' said Clocks.

'Yeah, but—'

'Then it's a word. Leave it at that.'

Dusty sighed. 'Pretty sure that's not how language works.'

'Pretty sure I don't give a tiny sparrow's arse flap.'

Paterson pressed the earpiece with one hand and held up the other. The car fell silent.

'It's Leslie. They're in,' said Paterson.

Clocks livened up. 'Come on, then. Start 'er up and let's 'ave it!'

'Leslie says to hold. Place has some sort of security surrounding the building. Wants to get the lay of the land first.'

'Fuck that! While he's fannyin' about drawing maps an' shit, our little family could end up in the giblettin' machine. Let's go! Go. C'mon. Go.'

Dusty mumbled something from the back.

'What'd you say?' said Clocks.

'I said, "Fuck me, now there's a gibletting *machine*."'

'You're gettin' right on my tits, Dusty. Stop 'avin' a pop at me or I'll chuck you in the bastard giblettin' machine when we get in there.'

Dusty chuckled quietly. 'Sorry, boss. My bad.'

'Leslie says SCO19 are calling up electronic plans of the property,' said Paterson. 'Straight to their consoles. It's a fair-size building so they want to know what's what before they move in and storm the place.'

Clocks shook his head. 'If anyone of our little family dies in there, someone's gonna get their fuckin' bollocks kicked from arse'ole to breakfast time. This is madness.'

'Take it easy, John. We have to know what we're going into. How many hospitals have security outside of them?'

'Er, literally all of 'em.'

'What? Armed?'

'You never said they were armed.'

'You never let me get a word in. Leslie has just confirmed. Weapons seen. Guns.'

'We can deal with it.'

'I'm sure we can, but it's better to be safe than sorry. It won't be long.'

Clocks looked out of the window and sulked.

Again, the car fell silent, punctuated only by the sounds of rhythmic breathing as each man tried to quell his nerves. Waiting was always the worst part.

The minutes ticked by. Clocks rubbed his face and sighed loudly. Monkey Harris rubbed his temples and Paterson stared at the building. From where he was, he could just make out the odd silhouetted figure moving across what he assumed were the front doors of the building.

He jerked forward and started the engine. 'It's a go!' He spun the car around, tyres squealing on the dry tarmac. 'Nineteen are going straight through the gate!'

The team suddenly came alive. A pack of dogs about to be let out to play.

Ahead of him, Paterson saw the lead SCO19 vehicle heading straight toward him. It suddenly veered off and smashed through the chain-link gates, sending them flying open. Vehicle two was less than five yards behind, Paterson and his crew another twenty yards. Both vehicles screeched to a halt at the entrance to the building and the officers inside piled out.

For a second, the guards were taken by surprise but quickly rallied themselves. The two at the entrance raised their weapons.

'Armed police! Drop your weapons!' someone shouted. Clocks, Dusty and Monkey Harris already had their doors open for a running start. Paterson skidded to a halt.

'Back!' shouted Paterson. 'Stay put! Leave it to Nineteen.'

Shots were fired.

Clocks was out and running toward the fight.

'Oh, fuck!' shouted Paterson.

'Guv?' said Monkey.

'You lot! Stay put until I tell you it's safe.' Then Paterson was out and running.

The three officers in the back of the car looked at each other and decided to disobey Paterson. Sitting in the back of a car while their colleagues were in danger was not an option.

Paterson could see that the two guards at the entrance were down. Evidently, they'd chosen not to surrender. Two SCO19 officers were stood over them. A machine gun clattered across the floor, kicked away by one of the officers.

In his peripheral vision, he became aware that more was going on around him. SCO19 were shouting loudly and moving quickly. He looked to his right and saw another two men. These two were lying face down, arms and legs stretched wide with SCO19 officers pointing guns at them. They were no longer a problem.

Looking left, Paterson saw Clocks running full tilt toward a man who was raising his gun. The man had planted his feet and held the pistol in a two-handed grip. He knew what he was doing. In that instant, Paterson felt his stomach lurch.

Clocks would never make it in time.

CHAPTER TWENTY-FIVE

Clocks ran on. The guard's gun was now levelled at him. Paterson lurched forward. 'John!'

Two shots rang out. Clocks jerked to an awkward halt. The guard's face exploded. Behind Clocks and in front of the main doors, an SCO19 officer lowered his weapon. Two shots had finished off the guard: one in the head and one in the back, probably blowing his heart to smithereens. He'd certainly have been dead before he hit the ground.

Paterson breathed a sigh of relief. 'Christ almighty, John. You okay?'

Clocks looked stunned. 'What? Yeah. Yeah. All good. I'm fine.' He stared down at the dead man.

Paterson nodded. 'Thought you were fucked there.'

Clocks nodded. 'Me an' all. What just happened?' His voice was shaky.

'I think you owe someone a drink.'

The SCO19 officer strolled over toward them. 'Bit of a close shave there, mate. You okay?'

Clocks turned to look at him. He threw his arms around the gunman and hugged him like his life depended on it. 'Oh, mate! Mate. Thank you. Thank you so much. If I'da got shot, the wife woulda killed me!' He kissed the gunman on his cheek, which promptly got him pushed away.

'Yeah, alright,' said the shooter. 'No need for all that. You're welcome.'

Paterson grinned. He and Clocks had been through some shit together, had faced death more times than either wanted to, but this was the first time he had ever seen Johnny Clocks react like this. The scare factor on this one had gone through the roof. The pressure on Clocks was showing.

'Sorry, fellah.' Clocks let the man go. 'It's just that . . . y'know . . . really thought I was a goner there. Thought I'd 'ad me chips. I've got a wife and son.'

The SCO19 officer put his hand on Clock's shoulder. 'Well, glad you're okay. How old's your boy?'

'I think he's about twenty-four now. Only met him when I got married a few weeks ago.'

The gunman tilted his head to one side.

'It's a long story, mate. But thank you. Thank you.'

'No bother.' The shooter turned to Paterson. 'You wanna stay here while my team clears the building out? I have to stand down and surrender my weapon now. Protocol prior to investigation.'

Paterson shook his head. This man had just saved Clocks's life — and maybe his, if Clocks had fallen. Now he'd be subjected to the baying calls of the armchair critics who had all the time in the world to decide his fate. Paterson wasn't going to let him be thrown to the wolves on his watch. A fight for another day, but one he would relish.

Clocks snapped out of his daze. 'What? No fuckin' chance. Let's 'ave it!' He drew his sidearm and headed for the main doors. He hurried through them, Paterson behind him, taking in the scene. Two SCO19 officers were already inside, weapons raised. In front of them on their knees, hands behind their heads, were two surly security guards. They were under control and going nowhere.

Clocks raised his weapon in their direction.

'John . . .' said Paterson.

Clocks ignored him.

The SCO19 men were rooted to the spot, unsure.

'John!'

The SCO19 men suddenly jerked into life, their training kicking in.

Clocks holstered his weapon. 'It's all good, boys. Don't panic. Ease up.'

For the second time that night, Paterson breathed a deep sigh of relief.

Clocks walked up to the two security guards. 'Alright, lads. 'Ow's it all goin', then? Not too good?' The guards eyed him, warily. 'Just thought I'd let you know, one of your mates 'as got a dirty great 'ole in his face and one in his strawberry. Motherfucker tried to kill me.'

The guard nearest to Clocks scowled.

'What's your problem, mate?'

The guard fixed his eyes on Clocks.

Clocks kneed him in the jaw, tipping him backward. 'Is it that the bloke who turned 'is toes up was your mate or that 'e tried to kill me? Which upsets you the most, hmm?'

The guard groaned.

One of the SCO19 officers stepped forward. 'Stand back!' he shouted to Clocks.

'It's alright, boys,' said Paterson. 'Stand down. Leave him be. He's my responsibility.'

The officer looked at Paterson.

'I said *stand down*. Just do it.'

The officer lowered his weapon.

Clocks stood over the prone guard and grabbed him by the lapels of his Gore-Tex jacket, pulling him up slightly. 'Where's Dare an' Burkhan? Tell me now!'

The guard groaned again.

'D'you not 'ear me, fellah? No? Oh, well. I'll ask yer mate, then.' Clocks smacked him straight on the jaw. Blood gushed as the man's nose broke and his head bounced off the floor.

Clocks turned away. He kicked the second guard in the back, pitching him forward. 'Dare . . . Burkhan . . . Where are they?'

'Fuck off, hard man!' the guard said as he pushed himself back up.

Clocks grabbed him by the scruff of his neck, whipped out his gun and dug it into the back of the man's cheek. 'What'd you say t'me?'

The two SCO19 officers went straight back into high alert.

Paterson held his hand up to them. 'Lower your weapons now! Do it! That's a fucking order.'

There was a second's hesitation where the officers fought their instincts and training before they stood down.

'I said fuck off! And take that fucking little gun out of my face before I kill you.' For the first time, Paterson detected a heavy Russian accent.

Clocks looked taken aback. '*What?*' He lowered the gun. 'You serious?'

'You will not shoot me. You are police. I am not a threat to you. You cannot justify it.' He chortled. 'This is not Russia.'

Clocks shrugged, raised the gun and fired it next to the man's ear. The Russian screamed as he pitched forward again, this time with blood streaming from his ear.

'Can't kill you, mate, but I can make it difficult for you to listen to yer fuckin' Sony Walkman or whatever it is you backward pricks listen to these days back 'ome in Spetsnaz or wherever the fuck it is you come from.'

Paterson put himself between Clocks and the increasingly agitated SCO19 officers.

Clocks left the man lying on the floor. 'Stay with 'im, fellahs. My arrest. I'll deal, but I need you to watch 'im.'

'He needs medical attention, you fucking maniac,' said one of the officers.

Clocks looked around the foyer. 'He's 'ad a tickle, then. This looks just like an 'ospital, dunnit? Just 'ang about, then, an' I'll go find a doctor for 'im. Won't be long. Ciao!'

He headed through the double doors that led into a long corridor.

Paterson trotted behind. 'That was a bit uncalled for, Clocksy.'

'Cocky fucker, 'e was. I can't stand arrogance, know what I mean? Not so cocky now 'e's gone mutton in one ear though, is 'e?'

'He won't be happy.'

'Won't 'e? Oh dear, oh dear. That makes Uncle Johnny very sad. Maybe you can go back an' kiss it all better for 'im.'

'I'm just saying.'

'Well, say it to someone who gives a tiny rat's arse. Got lairy with the wrong one tonight. I'm not in the mood.'

'I can tell,' said Paterson. 'Did you see the tattoo on his wrist?'

'Nope.'

'I think he's ex-military or something.'

'Your point?' said Clocks.

'Point is, they don't normally look on the bright side of things as a matter of course. Chances are he'll come after you.'

Clocks stopped. 'Shit. I never thought of that.'

'I know. You don't often think things through.'

'You make a good point. You're sayin' 'e could be a problem in the future, am I right?'

'Could be.'

'Right. When we leave, remind me to shoot 'im in the nut on the way out. There you go. Problem solved. Now stop being a fuckin' worryin' little girly an' let's find our two bastards an' that family. I've got sixteen shots left in this Glock an' I wanna get good use out of 'em.'

They noticed a sign on the wall: *Theatres 1–4, Level 5*.

'Looks like they put on shows 'an all,' said Clocks. 'Maybe it's *Annie Get Your Glock*. I love a good musical.'

CHAPTER TWENTY-SIX

'I take it we're going straight to Level 5, yes?' Clocks closed the lift door behind them.

Paterson detected a strong smell of antiseptic wafting around. Too strong. His mind ran away with him: new patient . . . near to death . . . prepped for immediate surgery on the way to theatre . . . site of surgery swabbed with antiseptic. The woman was on her way to be cut open. 'Yep,' he said.

He looked at the floor numbers above the doors . . .

1.

'D'you reckon they know we're here yet?' said Clocks.

'Be surprised if they didn't.'

'So we can expect trouble?'

2.

'Yep.'

'Brilliant. It's been way too quiet so far.'

Paterson grinned. 'Stand away from the doors, Clocksy.'

3.

Clocks stepped to the side and leaned against the button panel. Paterson moved into the corner and dropped to one knee with his back to the wall.

4.

'Ready?' said Paterson.

'Born ready, mate.'

5.

The doors slid open.

Nothing.

Paterson and Clocks looked at each other. Clocks bobbed his head into the space where the doors had been. Paterson swivelled around, still low, arms locked, gun pointing into the corridor ahead of him.

Nothing.

'Trap?' said Clocks.

Paterson said nothing, his ears straining for any sound that would give an assailant away.

Quiet.

'Want to go first?' said Paterson.

'Do I, fuck. You go. You're the guv'nor.'

Paterson smiled. 'What if I ordered you?'

'I'd shoot you in the bollocks. And still not go.'

'Guessed as much.' Paterson stood and stepped out into no-man's land. He made his way carefully along the corridor, following the signs to the operating theatres, painfully aware that someone could be waiting in any of the corridors off to the side.

Clocks was behind him, walking backwards, covering the rear. Save for the sound of their footsteps, the silence in the empty corridor was almost palpable. At the end of the corridor was a sign: *Theatre 1*.

Paterson stopped. 'If they're coming for us, this'll be it,' he whispered.

'Why're you whispering?' said Clocks.

'In case they hear us coming.'

'And you don't think they'll 'ave 'eard heard our shoes clip-cloppin' along the corridor?'

'You make a good point. You go right.' Paterson moved fast and turned left. A metal baton swing at him, head height. He ducked and ducked again as the baton swung back, attached to the meaty fist of a large, bald-headed man.

* * *

Clocks ran right. A big man stood facing him, metal baton over his shoulder, ready to strike. Clocks kept running. The man swung his baton as Clocks barrelled into him and drove him into a wall. The man grunted and fell. Clocks holstered his weapon and raised his fists. 'Up you come, sunshine.'

The man threw his baton away and got to his feet.

* * *

As the baton swung away from him, Paterson punched his man hard on the nose. It didn't break. It didn't bleed. The man staggered backward but recovered quickly. He shook his head as if he was irritated rather than hurt. Paterson knew this one would be a handful.

* * *

Clocks's man was on his feet now. He ran at Clocks, head down, arms outstretched to encircle him. Clocks danced lightly to one side and shoved the man hard into the wall, dropping him again. This time, he was on him. He piled into the man, kneeing him in the face and body as the man tried to cover himself against the blows Clocks inflicted on him. After a few seconds, it stopped. The man looked up, straight onto Clocks's right-hander, which connected with his chin. He fell unconscious.

* * *

Paterson's man squared up to him. In a second, Paterson saw at least six weak spots he could hit which would render the man incapable of any further aggression. Instead, he raised his gun. 'Don't even think about it.'

The big man glared at him and moved forward slightly.

'I said *don't*. I *will* shoot.' Paterson's voice was calm, cool, but full of disdain. He waved his gun at the man. 'Turn yourself around.'

The man glared at him then spat on the floor. 'Fuck you, copper.'

Paterson shot him in the leg.

The man yelled in agony as the bullet punched through his leg, pushing out pieces of tissue and bone. He dropped back against the wall.

'I said turn around.'

'Fuck you, pig!'

Paterson shot him in the other leg, dropping him to the ground, screaming in pain. 'Do I look like I'm messing around with you?'

'You, fffffff . . . fuck!' The man was holding both of his legs, covering the bullet wounds and trying desperately to stop the flow of blood.

'Bloody 'ell, Ray. Was that necessary? Why not just shoot 'im in the bonce? Be done with it. That's two bullets you've wasted when one would 'ave done.'

'Just wanted to give him a chance.'

Clocks walked over to the groaning man and bent over, his hands on his knees. 'Can you 'ear me, cocker?'

Grimacing through the pain, the man glared at him. 'Fucking hell . . . Course I can hear you, prick. I'm not fucking deaf!' he said through gritted teeth.

Clocks nodded. 'Well, that can be arranged. As it 'appens, I know someone who's quite good at arranging deafness at a moment's notice.'

The man looked away from Clocks and groaned.

'Plan?' Clocks said to Paterson.

'We go in each theatre until we find our family.'

'And the other two clowns? Dare an' Burkhan?'

'We'll find 'em, John. Eventually.'

'And him?' Clocks nodded toward the stricken man.

'Leave him here. Not like he's gonna creep up on us, is it?'

Clocks walked away from the man and toward the theatre doors. 'Solid point there, Ray. Solid point.'

'You first?' said Paterson as they braced themselves against the wall.

'Again. No. You're the guv'n—'

Paterson stepped inside. He took it all in, quickly. The room was large, and dark except for the exceptionally bright lights that shone down on the naked body of a woman. Standing under the light, partly blocking his view, was the silhouette of a man with his back to them.

Clocks squinted into the gloom of the rest of the theatre. It could be that someone else was in the room and they'd missed them. Better to be safe than sorry.

'Armed police!' Paterson shouted. 'Put your hands up and step slowly backward away from the table. Do it now.'

The man, from behind, looked a bit slovenly, unkempt, but not so much as to give the impression he was incompetent at his profession. Paterson could see wires protruding from his ears. Headphones.

The man continued working. Paterson stepped forward and pushed the gun into the back of his neck. 'Armed police!' he shouted. 'Stop what you're doing and put your hands up.'

The man did exactly what he was told. Every step of the way.

'Put the scalpel down,' said Paterson. 'Now turn around. Take your time.'

Slowly, the man turned. The rubber gloves he wore were smothered in blood.

Paterson's jaw dropped first. Then his hands.

Clocks's eyes bulged. 'Oh, fuck me blind. No!'

CHAPTER TWENTY-SEVEN

Paterson and Clocks stood silent, in shock. This was the last thing they expected to see. The very last. The surgeon, a small man, looked as if the world had just collapsed and dragged him to hell.

'I'm fuckin' dreamin', ain't I?' Clocks said after a few seconds. 'Someone tell me I'm dreamin'. Please!' He inched forward. 'Are you seein' this too, Ray, or 'ave I 'ad one too many?'

Paterson couldn't speak. He shook his head. Denial.

Clocks circled around the small man and looked at the woman on the table. As far as he could tell, she was dead. The large opening in her body from her throat to her pubic bone area gave it away.

'Oh, fuck. You didn't?'

The little man said nothing. He too looked unable to speak and his eyes brimmed with tears. He was shaking.

Paterson stepped sideways and looked at the woman on the table. It was the mother of the family Dare and Burkhan had brought over. The mother they had sworn to protect. And failed. The ceramic floor tiles were awash with blood. On the metal table, Paterson could see all kinds of bloodied implements. There was a kidney in a small metal bowl and five blood-drenched plastic bags.

This little man had moved fast. Efficiently. He knew exactly what he was doing and he was comfortable with it. Paterson realised that this wasn't an operating theatre. It was a morgue. He should have known. The table the woman was on looked different. It had slightly raised edges and a drain.

Paterson could feel his eyes begin to water. He fought back the tears as he looked at the man, a man he knew and always thought could be trusted.

'Where . . . where are the others?' he said, softly.

The man shook his head. 'Next door,' was all he could manage. He began to sob. Softly at first and then great, chest-heaving sobs.

'Clocksy,' said Paterson. 'Nick him.'

Johnny Clocks moved forward, his weapon holstered now. This man was no threat to them. Not in the slightest. 'You're fuckin' nicked, you pissed-up piece of shit. The fuck could you do this? You're supposed to be on our side, fer Christ's sake.'

Alan 'Jock' Hudson, the Home Office's most senior pathologist, a man Paterson and Clocks had long considered a friend, fell sobbing onto the cold, grey tiles.

CHAPTER TWENTY-EIGHT

They left him crying on the floor.

Paterson went over to the table and looked down at the dead woman. 'I'm so sorry,' he mouthed silently. 'So sorry.' He looked her up and down.

Paterson turned away from the table. He grabbed Jock by the scruff of his neck and hauled him up, slamming his back into the cutting table.

Jock put his arms over his face. He knew what Paterson was capable of. Paterson grabbed him by the jaw and forced him backwards over the table.

'You . . . dirty, no good, fucking piece of . . .'

'I'm sorry. I'm sorry. I'm so, so, sorry . . . Please . . .' he snivelled.

Paterson let him go and jammed the balls of his hands into his own eyes. 'God!' he shouted. 'God all-fucking-mighty!'

Clocks watched Jock carefully. Like Paterson, he owed him his career after Jock wrote a favourable pathology report that skewed evidence proving Paterson had deliberately shot and killed the man who butchered his estranged wife. Clocks witnessed the whole event as it unfolded on top of Tower Bridge itself. Instead of arresting him for murder, he chose to support Paterson and cover it up.

As Paterson stood there, his mind racing, Jock must have seen what he thought was his only hope. He reached for the scalpel. Clocks was across the room before Jock could get a hold of it. He shoved him hard and sent him over the top of the cutting table, crashing onto the floor.

Paterson whirled around in time to see Johnny Clocks moving around the table toward Jock.

'You dirty, snivellin', murderin' little jock bastard! I'm gonna fuckin' kill you, you no-good prick!' He grabbed Jock's hair and wrenched him back up to his feet.'

'John . . .' said Paterson.

Clocks had Jock bent over the table, nose to nose, screaming more obscenities at him. Paterson could see flecks of spittle ejaculating onto Jock's face. For a moment, Paterson genuinely thought that he might bite the man's nose off.

'John!'

'What?'

'What're you doing?'

'This little prick was goin' for the scalpel. He was gonna cut your throat.'

'What?'

'Ain't that right, you snot-gobblin' little tosswipe?'

He pulled Jock's face tighter toward his own. If Jock Hudson was scared before, he was one step away from dying of sheer terror now Clocks had a hold of him.

'*Is* that right?' Paterson said.

Jock whimpered and shook.

'I asked you a question.'

Jock nodded his head furiously. 'I'm . . . sorry,' he whined. 'I'm so scared,' he whined.

'I know you're sorry, Jock. You've said that.' Paterson shook his head and walked around the table to join them.

'Drop him a minute, Clocksy.'

Clocks snarled and let him go. Paterson took over. He pulled Jock into his face.

'What you've done is bad enough, but then you try to kill me? I've done nothing to you, have I? Nothing. And you want to kill me so you can, what, run? How far do you think you'd have got before Clocksy caught you? You wouldn't have made the door, you dumb fucker.'

He snorted and pushed Jock away.

If he'd been a more compassionate man, Paterson may have felt just a bit sorry for the broken, snivelling mess before him. He was sorry that he was here, sorry that Jock was here, sorry the woman was dead, sorry the little family was now destroyed, but he wasn't sorry for Jock. In fact, he was deciding whether or not to just snap his neck and be done with it. He decided against it. There was information to be gleaned.

'You're going to tell me who's behind all this, Jock. Understood?'

Jocks eyes suddenly lit up with fear. Paterson saw it.

'Don't even think about protecting them, and don't even begin to think you can bargain with me. And don't try and give me all the bullshit about them killing you if you talk. I really don't give a fuck . . . Tell me something. You're married, aren't you?'

Jock said nothing, then nodded when Paterson's nostrils flared.

'Couple of grown-up kids, yes?'

Jock stared at him, searching his face to an unspoken question.

'Doesn't matter how I know. I just do. If you don't co-operate, then you need to know that your wife and family will find themselves victims of tragic road accidents a few months apart. You know we'll do it, too.'

Jock whimpered again.

'So, we're gonna take you back to the station and interview you. You will tell us everything — and I do mean everything. You'll waive your right to legal representation and you'll confess everything. You'll name names. You'll give written permission for us to search both of your homes and your office. If I think for one second you're trying it on . . . well, think about what I've just said. Be clear, there's no good outcome for you in this. Oh, and when we're done squeezing you for information, someone will leave a belt in your cell. You'll do the cowardly but right thing and be found dead the next morning.'

Jock slid back down to the floor, snot dribbling from his bright-red drinker's nose.

CHAPTER TWENTY-NINE

'Keep an eye on him, John. I'm gonna take a look next door.' Paterson headed off toward a door to the back of the room.

'Wait a sec. I'll come with you. You dunno what's behind there.'

Paterson carried on walking. 'Just stay with him.'

Clocks nodded.

Paterson raised his gun in a two-handed grip and booted the door inwards. He stepped into the room. Three bodies lay face up on a table. He could see they were already dead. He lowered his gun and rubbed his face with his free hand.

The lump in his throat felt like a small tangerine, and he swallowed hard as he looked at the child's face. All three had been harvested for organs. Not just the woman. He wiped away tears with the back of his gun hand and turned his back on the tragic little scene before him to rejoin Clocks.

'What's the score?' said Clocks.

Anger rose through Paterson. Blood rushed through his temples and a blackness lodged itself behind his eyes. 'Dead,' he said, his voice flat. 'All of them.'

Clocks's shoulders dropped. 'Ah, fuck . . .'

Paterson headed toward Jock. The little man whimpered as Paterson closed in on him.

'You did that?' said Paterson, pointing back toward the door with his gun.

Jock whimpered again. Paterson grabbed him by the jaw and started walking, pushing Jock backward until the man's back slammed against the wall. He pushed his nose against Jock's and jammed the gun under his chin. 'I said, *did you do that?* Did you? Did you fucking kill them? Answer me, you bastard!'

Jock Hudson crumpled like a wet paper bag beneath a waterfall, his eyes full of tears. Unable to avoid Paterson's gaze, he nodded furiously. 'I'm so . . . so . . .'

Paterson dropped his gun, grabbed Jock by the hair, swung him away from the wall and threw him across the floor, sending him sprawling. 'Don't keep telling me you're fucking sorry! Don't do it!'

'Ray . . .' said Clocks. 'Steady. You said we need him for answers. You're bang on. We do need answers. Now ain't the time to do this.'

His shoulders heaving, his fists bunched and breathing heavily, Paterson carried on toward Jock.

'Mate. If you do this, I wouldn't blame you. Fuck, I wanna do 'im meself. You know I do. But it won't get us closer to whoever's behind this. Right now, that's what we want. That's what we *need*.'

Paterson struggled with the rage inside of him, at odds with the part of him that was desperate to know more. The rage was winning.

'We'll lose, Ray. Me an' you. Everyone else loses too. More kids, more families killed if you do 'im in. Right now, he's our best 'ope.'

Paterson stopped. He turned his head but not his body. 'Soon,' he growled to Jock. 'Soon.'

CHAPTER THIRTY

Seated alone inside the interview room at Tower Bridge Police Station, Jock Hudson cut a pathetic figure. Hunched over and hugging himself, his red hair was tousled, his eyes red raw from crying.

Paterson looked in through the window and shook his head. Of all the people, he would never have had Jock down for crime. Certainly not murder. It reminded him of something that his father once told him: that you could never really know anybody.

'It's confirmed,' said Clocks. 'The ambulance driver was nicked, but no trace of Dare or Burkhan. Place was searched from top to bottom — twice. Nothin'. Fuckers 'ad it away on their toes.'

Paterson rolled his eyes. 'I thought the bloody place was surrounded. Jesus! Okay, then I guess Jock's *is* gonna have to tell us where they're likely to be.'

'I've given out an all-ports warning and gave the frogs a bell an' told 'em to keep an eye out for them slippin' back into the country. We've got someone keepin' an eye on Biggin Hill, but it's unlikely they'll go back there for a while. Certainly not tonight. You phoned that French bird you were knobbin'?'

'What? I never touched her.'

'But you were gonna.'

'If I got the chance. But it never worked out, did it?'

'Nope. But I've got a fiver that says you'll be straight back on the Eurostar when this is over to give 'er one.'

'Really? You think I'd go all the way over to France for a shag?'

'I would.'

Paterson grinned. 'Yeah. You probably would.'

'I definitely would.'

'Your Lyndsey'll be dead pleased about that.'

'She won't know, will she?'

'I suppose not. How d'you think it's gonna work out between you two?'

Clocks shrugged. 'Dunno. I tell you what, though . . . it's on track to be one of the shortest marriages on record. What's it been, a fortnight, three weeks?'

'Look. She's upset about you having a bastard son coming back into your life, of course she is. Your wedding day probably wasn't the best time for him to show up either, to be honest. Could have been a bit more sensitive.'

'What? Like 'is old dad, you mean?'

Paterson smiled. 'Exactly.'

'Ha!'

'What?' said Paterson.

'Just thought of something funny.'

'Go on, then.'

'He's a chip off the ol' Clock. Geddit? Block. Clock. Clocks. My name.'

'Hmmm,' said Paterson. 'Anyway, Lyndsey'll be back soon. She's not quit the job just yet, has she? You guys can work it out when she's back.'

'I guess,' said Clocks.

Paterson opened the door to the interview room. Jock Hudson jumped, startled by the sudden entrance.

'Ready, Jock?'

Paterson dragged out a chair and sat himself down. Clocks checked the recording equipment, video and audio, was working correctly and they began. Paterson reminded Jock he was still under caution and didn't have to say anything.

'I am Detective Superintendent Ray Paterson. My colleague is . . .'

'Detective Inspector Johnny Clocks,' said Clocks.

'Please state your name,' Paterson said to Jock.

'Alan Hudson.'

'Speak up,' said Paterson.

'Alan Hudson.'

Paterson nodded.

'I'm the investigating officer in this case and I'll be asking you questions about your arrest in the early hours of this morning. I note that you are here on your own and I understand you have waived the right to any form of legal representation. Is that correct?'

Jock raised his eyes slightly and nodded.

'I need a verbal answer. Please confirm you have waived your right to legal representation.'

'Yes, that's correct,' said Jock. 'I do not want legal representation.'

Jock's accent was thick Glaswegian and he'd been the butt of Johnny Clocks's humour for years, often making out he couldn't understand him, jokes about his drinking and his glow-in-the-dark nose. There was no humour today. Just cold fury.

'Thank you,' said Paterson. 'Now, you are known to both DI Clocks and myself. We have worked on a number of cases together and we know you as Jock. Do you mind if we call you that?'

'No.'

'Thank you, Jock. For the record, please state your profession.'

'I'm the senior Home Office pathologist.'

'Okay. Earlier today, DI Clocks and I arrested you inside a private hospital, the Betterment. When we found you it was in what appeared to be a morgue of some kind. On the table was a dead woman, a woman we now know to be Aisha Kalhad. We had followed her and her family from Biggin Hill airport, where she landed in the company of her family and two men by the names of Dare and Burkhan, and a third person as yet unidentified. In the ambulance that met them were two other men. One was the driver and he's been arrested. We don't yet know who the other man was.'

Jock's eyes flicked across to Clocks.

'Who was the other man, Jock?'

Jock cleared his throat. 'It wasnae a man.'

'S'cuse me?' said Clocks.

'It wasnae a man. Was a woman.'

'A woman? Who is she?'

'I cannae tell ye that.'

'Pity,' said Paterson. 'Could have saved us some time. We'll come back to that later. Going back to Aisha Kalhad . . . we know she was alive when she arrived at the Betterment. Fifteen minutes later, she wasn't. Her torso was opened from her throat to her pubis. In a box next to her was an organ transplant box. Inside, was what appeared to be a kidney. *Her* kidney. Your hands and apron were covered in blood. We know that she was ill, most likely due to her appendix — possibly her kidney — but she was alive and would most likely have recovered given proper care and attention.

'On a stand next to you, we also found five plastic bags covered in blood. They've been sent off for analysis, but to save us all some time, what was in those bags, Jock?'

Jock looked up at the camera, drew in a breath, shook his head and sighed. 'Carfentanil.'

'Carfentanil?' Paterson repeated. 'Jesus. I've heard of it. But for the record, Jock, clarify for me what carfentanil is.'

Jock cleared his throat. 'It's a synthetic drug, made from fentanyl itself.'

'And what does it do?' said Paterson.

'Makes money. Lots of it.'

'Tell me about it.'

Jock sighed again. He clearly knew he was done for and there was no point hiding anything from them. Paterson had said he had an idea of what it was, but in any case they would find out with a rudimentary Google search.

'It's extremely potent,' said Jock. 'Extremely. It's a hundred times more potent than fentanyl, five thousand times more potent than heroin and ten thousand times more potent than morphine. In America it's being laced with other drugs and in almost all cases causes an overdose leading to death.'

'Fuck me . . .' said Clocks.

'John!' Paterson nodded to the recorder. 'Recording.'

'What? Yeah. Sorry. Sorry. It's just that . . . Jesus. That's mad.'

'What was the plan, Jock?' said Paterson.

'Simple, laddie. To introduce it into Britain. Open another profit centre. Those five bags were the first to arrive.'

'So let me get this right . . . This poor woman was loaded up with these drugs and then smuggled into the country so that you could take them and her internal organs out. That right?'

'Aye. The drugs were a new thing she was trying. The organ thing was a long-standing racket.'

'She?' said Paterson. 'The woman you won't tell us about?'

'Aye.'

Paterson nodded. 'You were arrested on suspicion of the murder of Aisha Kalhad, her husband, son and daughter *and* on suspicion of being involved in a global organisation that deals in the sale and supply of human organs, and now it seems you're also involved in the importation of class-A drugs. So, one last time . . . you do understand the seriousness of the allegations against you, don't you?'

'Yes.'

'And you're still happy to proceed without a solicitor?'

'Yes.'

'Tell me how you came to be involved in all of this.'

'I . . . was approached.'

'By whom?'

Jock looked pained. 'I cannae . . . I cannae tell ye that.'

'You will,' said Clocks.

'This approach. Was it from a man or this woman?'

'The woman.'

'Is this the same woman you mentioned a moment ago?'

'Aye.'

'And what was it she wanted?'

'She wanted my skills.'

'And what skills are they?'

'I'm the senior Home Office pathologist. I'm a surgeon. Have been since I was twenty-six years old.'

'What did she want you to do?'

Jock squirmed in his seat and shook his head.

'What did she want you to do?' Paterson repeated.

Jock looked up at the blinking red eye of the CCTV that sat silently in the corner of the room. It wasn't capable of judgement, but the Home Office advisors watching the interview on monitors were.

'She wanted me to remove organs from deceased people and ready them for transportation for transplant into sick people.'

'These people were already dead, yes?'

'Aye. That's correct.'

'Except Aisha Kalhad was very much alive, wasn't she?' said Paterson.

Jock shook his head and replied weakly. 'Yes'.

'One question . . . How did Aisha Kalhad die?'

Jock Hudson swallowed hard. His eyes watered and he choked back the words. 'I killed her.'

Paterson took a deep breath. 'You killed her?'

'Aye, laddie. I'm so sorry. So sorry.'

'How did you kill her?'

Jock rubbed his face and closed his eyes. 'I injected her with a large quantity of air. Painless . . . and quick.'

'Did you do this on the operating table?' said Paterson.
'Aye.'
Were you in the ambulance at Biggin Hill?'
'Aye.'
'Why were you in the ambulance?'
'I'd received information from Mr Burkhan that the woman was seriously ill and would likely die. He wanted me to meet them and do all that I could to keep her alive.'

'What? Why?' said Clocks. 'I don't understand the logic 'ere. You were gonna kill 'er anyway, weren't you?'

Jock nodded. 'Time, John. It's important that the organ is removed surgically and placed into either the cold transport box or the patient as soon as possible. If it's not, then the tissue will die and make it useless. I couldnae operate on her in the ambulance, so I did what I could to keep her going until we got to the hospital.'

'And *then* you killed her. When it suited *you*?'

Jock looked down at his shoes. 'Yes. I'm so very, very sorry.'

'So am I, Jock. So am I.'

Paterson's phone vibrated quietly. He looked at the text message and showed it to Clocks.

'Seems you do have a solicitor. There's a woman downstairs demanding we stop the interview until she is present. I thought you said you were happy to proceed without one?'

'I was. I am. I don't know anything about it. Truly. I agreed to speak to you.'

'So, how does she know you've been nicked?' said Clocks.

'I dinnae ken. Honestly.'

'Your honesty ain't too high on my radar, Jock.'

Paterson looked across at him wearily and then clicked off the recording equipment to terminate the interview. When the room went quiet, he said, 'Who do you think it is, Jock?'

'I truly dinnae ken.'

'I bet one of our missing boys called 'er in,' said Clocks. Don't want 'im talkin', do they?'

'We don't have to let her in if Jock's waived his right,' said Paterson.

'I know. But we're intrigued, ain't we?'

'We are indeed. Hey, Jock. Perhaps she's come to kill you?' Paterson fixed his gaze on the pathologist and watched as the colour drained out of his face, nose included.

CHAPTER THIRTY-ONE

The two detectives stepped out of the interview room and into the main office. 'Monkey!' shouted Paterson. 'Get me two armed officers up here and keep an eye on Jock. Something's cropped up at the front desk.'

'Sure, boss. You go ahead. We'll watch him until someone gets here.'

Paterson and Clocks made their way downstairs to the main reception. Along the way, they picked up a couple of uniformed female officers to go with them. Paterson was going to have this woman searched for weapons or anything that could cause harm. He knew that there would be an almighty row. Solicitors almost never got searched, and if they did, there would have to be a solid reason for it. He wasn't sure that he could justify it, but at that point he couldn't have cared less.

He spoke to the station officer briefly, who pointed out the solicitor. A smartly dressed woman in her early fifties, she was certainly dressed for the role, right down to a fairly large sling bag hanging off one shoulder.

'Hi,' he said to the woman. 'I'm Detective Superintendent Paterson.'

The woman stood to shake his outstretched hand, but her eyes narrowed when she saw Clocks and the two uniformed officers standing in the doorway. 'I'm Susan Clarke from Erlanger and Partners. I'm here to see Alan Hudson.' Her voice carried that air of determination that most solicitors had, as if they were totally in charge and everybody else had better fall in line.

'Sure. Can I just ask, though . . . how did you know he was under arrest? I ask because he's being held incommunicado for the time being and nobody should have been aware of his detention.'

'I don't know anything about that,' she said. 'I got the call and was asked to represent him.'

'Who made the call?'

'It was from Mr Erlanger himself. Is there a problem?'

'Could be. As I said, I don't know how your Mr Erlanger knew we had Hudson in custody. It concerns me.'

'Well, that's something you'll have to take up with him, I'm afraid. Until then, I'd like to see my client, please.'

'I don't have a problem with it, but you'll have to be searched first, if that's okay?'

She met his gaze. 'Actually, it's not okay. I'm not going to be searched. I have a legitimate reason to be here and I demand to see my client.'

'You can demand all you like, babe,' said Clocks. 'But if you don't let us search you, you can turn around and toddle off out the nick. S'up to you.'

'I'm sorry . . . you are?'

'DI Clocks. Sheriff of this 'ere town.' He winked at her.

'Clocks? I've heard of you. Bit of an arrogant arsehole, I understand.'

Clocks grinned. 'I dunno where you 'eard that, babe, but you've been badly misinformed. I'm a *lot* of an arrogant arse'ole, thank you.'

'I'm sorry,' said Paterson. 'But you'll have to be searched or I will deny you access to your client.'

'On what grounds?'

'On the grounds that you shouldn't know ol' Jocky boy is 'ere,' said Clocks. 'An' that makes us wonder. An' when I wonder, I get a bit edgy. An' when I get a bit edgy, I tend to get even more arse'oley than normal. Right now, my arse'oleyness is on an upward tilt.'

'You two are unbelievable.'

'I know, right?' said Clocks. 'We're the Unbelievable Brothers.'

Paterson smiled. 'I like that. Sounds good.'

'So, what's the plan then, babe? You gonna let these two nice lady officers 'ave a rummage around in yer knickers or what? I'd do it meself like in the old days, but all you woke women get narky about it now. No fun anymore, the lot of yer.'

She glared at Clocks. Pure anger shone from her eyes. 'If you don't stand aside and allow me to see my client, Paterson, I will have your job. And DI Dickhead, here.'

'Oi, oi!' said Clocks. 'That's a bit 'urtful, babe. I'm an arse'ole, not a dick'ead. Thought we'd established that.'

Paterson smiled. 'That's that, then. I'm having you searched, one way or the other.'

Susan Clarke took an aggressive stance. 'No, you're not. I've done nothing to warrant it.'

'I have trouble believing you're a solicitor by your manner and bearing, and it's my belief you've come here to do harm to Alan Hudson. So, you will be searched regardless of whether you've come to see him or not. If you struggle, you may get hurt. So I suggest you play nicely and don't kick up a fuss. Ladies . . . Take her somewhere private, please. Full search.'

'Sir,' said the older of the two officers. She moved forward to take hold of Clarke's arm. As she did so, Clarke grabbed her hand and folded it into a wrist lock. The officer yelped in pain.

Paterson moved sharply, intending to push Clarke up against the wall. She kicked him in the top of his thigh, causing him to lose his balance then pushed the female officer into the other officer. They both fell to the ground.

Clocks jumped over them and grabbed her by the throat. She broke his grip easily and hit him with a solid uppercut, stunning him. She pushed him in the chest, shoving him off his feet.

And then she was out through the doors and running.

Paterson stood up and lost his balance. The kick to his thigh had deadened his muscle. He couldn't run. Clocks had had the wind knocked out of him and was struggling to get his breath. The two officers were in shock and stayed on the ground.

'Clocksy, you alright?' said Paterson.

Clocks held up a hand and fought for his breath. 'Yeah . . . yeah. Fuck me. That came out . . . that came out of nowhere, didn't it? Jesus.'

Paterson limped out into the street. She was gone. No point calling for a car to search for her. She knew what she was doing. Clocks staggered down the stairs to join him.

'What d'you think, John?'

'About her?'

'Yep.'

'I get the impression she didn't want anyone ferretin' about in her knickers. Miserable cow.'

'I would say a professional killer. Made quick work of us.'

'So, they do want Jock dead, then?'

'Looks like it.' Paterson limped back up the stairs.

'I don't see a problem with it, meself. Shoulda let 'er do 'im in. No loss.'

'He would've been a loss if we don't get more information out of him, and you're the one who stopped me from hurting him precisely for that reason. C'mon, let's properly rattle his cage. I'm tired of fucking around.'

CHAPTER THIRTY-TWO

Twenty minutes later, Paterson and Clocks, teas in hand, were back in the interview room with a visibly shaken Jock Hudson. Paterson had no intention of officially resuming the interview.

'Well,' he said. 'That all went swimmingly.'

Jock searched Paterson's face.

'Don't know who she was, but she got the drop on us and legged it out of the station. At a guess, I would say she wasn't a brief. I'd say she'd come to kill you. Presumably to stop you telling us what you know.'

Paterson sat himself down. 'But it's not going to, is it?'

Jock sat quietly.

'Look, Jock. I'm not gonna record this. You will be formally interviewed again at some point, but not right now. Right now, you're gonna tell me exactly what we want to know, and no fucking around. You understand me?'

Jock nodded.

'Good. Okay, so you were approached and they wanted you to help them with surgery. Did that seem reasonable to you?'

Jock sat himself up and wiggled around in his seat. 'I've had requests before. A lot of surgeons do. It's good money.'

'So, this is about money?'

'Yes. And I'm dying.'

'Do what?' said Clocks. 'Dyin'?'

'A.L.F.'

Clocks wrinkled his forehead. 'What? That cute little alien that used to eat cats? I didn't know it was a disease. How'd you get that, then?'

'Acute liver failure, John. The drink has done for me.'

Clocks shrugged. 'Told you it would. So, 'ow long you got, then? Not that I give a fuck.'

'I dinnae ken, laddie. Not long. Not long now.'

'So, what's that got to do with you killing people?' said Paterson.

'I needed money for the wife and bairns.'

'You can't be short of a few quid, Jock,' said Paterson. 'You're paid well and you've got two houses. Why would you need more money?'

'Gambling and drinking. I owe about two hundred thousand to various bookies, on- and offline. And when I'm drunk, I buy shit I dinnae really want. Certainly never needed. Bastard internet.'

'Two 'undred grand? Fuck me, that's 'eavy. You bein' chased for it?'

Jock nodded. 'I was until I threw in with this lot. They offered to clear my debts in full if I did some work for them from time to time.'

'An' that work was killin' people for their giblets?' said Clocks.

'Not at first. In the beginning it was all straight and above board—'

'Above board? Yer 'avin' a laugh, ain'tcha? Since when has it been legal to chop the bits out of people an' flog 'em on? Am I missin' somethin'?'

'It used to be until about 2009. But, like most things that involve the rich, it still went on. Money talks. What I meant about it being straight is that all the people I operated on had agreed to sell their organs on. Some did it for money,

146

some did it for family, some did it because they just genuinely wanted to help people.'

'So what changed?' said Paterson.

'Someone came to see me one day. Told me that things were going to be different. If they couldnae find live donors, then I had to use dead ones. Aye, I know what you're going to say . . . The dead cannae give permission to donate.'

'What about card carriers?'

'There's not enough of them to go around, Ray. People dinnae like the idea of giving up their organs when they're dead, despite all the campaigns.'

'Probably worried about people like you doin' 'em in if they're near to death. *No point in savin' this one. Put yer foot on 'is throat then tear 'im up. Might as well use 'is bits.* Is that 'ow it goes?'

'No, John. It doesn't.'

'Tell me about the person who came to see you. What was going to be different?' said Paterson.

'They told me they'd found a bigger pool of fresh organs. People that were generally in pretty good health and they would be brought in for me to . . . euthanise.'

'That's a fancy name for murder, innit?' said Clocks.

Jock carried on. 'I protested — of course I did. But I was in too deep. My debt was now owed to them, and they made it known that they'd destroy my life and my family's if I didnae go along with them. I didnae have a choice. You must see that.'

'You had a choice. There's always a choice. Why didn't you tell us? We'd have done something about it. You know we would.' Paterson rubbed his jaw.

'This started long before your time, boys. I've been doing this for nigh on ten years.'

'Ten years? So 'ow many people you killed?'

Jock looked down at his shoes again. 'About two hundred.'

'Two hundred?' Paterson was shocked. 'Two hundred! God all-fucking-mighty. Two hundred?'

'I'm sorry. Very, very sorry.'

'Oh, well. As long as yer sorry, that's fine,' said Clocks. 'I'd 'ate to think you weren't bothered about it, you no-good, murderin', pissed-up little jock motherfucker. Sooner your liver blows up the better.' Clocks's anger was visibly getting worse. He lost it. He grabbed Jock by the jaw and forced his head back. 'Right, piss'ead. Tell me who's behind this, tell me where I can find 'em an' tell me right now. If you don't, I'll sling you out the fuckin' window, pull you back in, sling you out again, drag you down to your morgue an' cut *your* fuckin' giblets out without killin' you first. I should think that'll be a bit painful. An' Jock, you *know* I'll fuckin do it.'

Jock's eyes filled with tears. He nodded furiously. 'Alright. *Alright.*'

'Jock,' said Paterson. 'As I said earlier, there's no way this ends well for you. You're dying anyway. Don't put yourself through the ignominy of a trial and a slow and painful death. Just do the right thing and tell us everything we want to know and help us to catch the fuckers behind this. If you do, then I promise not to let John hurt you.'

Jock nodded. 'Her name's Alicia Warren. She goes by different names, but I know her as Warren. She has a number of clinics in France and Mumbai. A couple in America and a few in Eastern Europe. That's all I ken. That's the truth of it.'

Paterson pulled a pen out a pocket and slid a piece of paper across the desk. 'Write down everything. Names she's known by and the addresses or as near as dammit for the clinics.'

Jock nodded.

'Do you know where she was headed next?'

He nodded again. 'Mumbai. She has a couple of older clinics there but I hear tell she's investing in several new ones. Sunk a lot of money into them.' He picked up the pen and began to write.

CHAPTER THIRTY-THREE

Paterson sat himself on the edge of a table and prepared to brief his team. Clocks was on the phone to someone and just about to end the call. Paterson waited until Clocks had hung up.

'Everybody . . . thanks for coming back in. I appreciate you're busy but we've had a significant breakthrough in this case. I'm sure you all know by now, and are as shocked as we were, that we nicked the borough's resident pathologist, Jock Hudson. We've had a chat with him and he's rolled over. We have a name for the suspect we're looking for.' He clicked a button on the tiny remote control he held, and the face of a woman, taken during a surveillance operation somewhere in India, flashed up on the screen.

'This is Alicia Warren. At least, that's one of the names we have for her. From what Jock tells us, she's the mastermind behind this whole operation, the Boss of Bosses, so to speak. According to the paperwork we have on her, she's long been suspected of being involved in the people trade in all its myriad forms and is the controlling force for a large number of gangs across the world. She is immensely rich and completely ruthless. She sees people as nothing more than a profit centre and has no form of empathy in the slightest, as attested to by the drug carfentanil we found inside our victim.'

Paterson pressed the remote and a grainy video flickered on the screen. It showed four men bound and on their knees surrounded by armed men. A woman walked toward them. Paterson hit pause.

'This was taken three years ago in Syria by a military drone that was flying reconnaissance for a completely unrelated job. It was on the lookout for a wanted terrorist believed to be holed up in a compound. Turns out the terrorist chappie wasn't at home, but they picked up this footage.'

Paterson pressed play. The woman crossed the courtyard and stood in front of the men. One of the armed men handed her a pistol. She calmly shot and killed all four with a single shot to the head before turning and walking away. There was no hesitation in any of her actions, no fuss.

'The CIA have confirmed this woman to be our Alicia Warren, although they also have aliases for her — Rachel Belkin, Lorraine Card, Janice Frost and Charlotte Mia. Earlier, a female solicitor arrived claiming to represent Jock. He claimed no knowledge of her, so we decided to have a chat with her in the foyer. I suspected she may have been sent to do harm to Jock. Turns out she did harm to us. Caught us all on the hop and put us down before we knew what was happening. She escaped.

'She can handle herself very well. She put two uniformed officers down plus me and Clocks. Hard on the ego chaps, I can tell you.'

'Any chance it was Warren herself?' said Monkey Harris.

Paterson shrugged. 'Maybe, but I doubt it. Too big a risk. And when you have that much money and her sorts of connections, why do it yourself?'

Monkey pointed to the screen. 'I get the impression she's a hands-on kind of girl.'

Clocks butted in. 'We've been onto Interpol an' they're keepin' an eye out for any movements on this bird. When they get a hit, they'll be in touch, but that ain't good enough. She's probably out of the country on false documents by now so the plan is to go and find her ourselves. Jock tells us she's building new clinics in Mumbai and she's been there a lot in the last few months, overseeing her investment. Bloody Mumbai! I ask yer, what self-respecting world-class villain fucks off to Mumbai?'

'Not a bad place to get lost in,' said Tommy Gunn. 'Packed to the rafters with people.'

'Who's asking you?' said Clocks.

'You said, "I ask yer." I thought you meant it.'

'Well, I didn't, so belt up. We've 'ad a word with the commissioner and we're off out there later this evenin' on a long — *very* long — shot. The commish wasn't 'appy at all when we told 'im what we wanted to do, an' it took all our powers of persuasion to convince 'im we're not on a jolly-up. We promised to bring 'im back a top-class curry. That did it for 'im.

'We're both completely knackered and we're gonna grab a coupla hours kip before we leave. Mr P. 'ere is payin' for an upgrade to Business, although he don't know it yet. I ain't doin' a fourteen-hour flight in cattle class an' I seriously intend to catch up on a shitload more sleep in comfort.'

'Thank you, John,' said Paterson. 'What he says is true. This is a long shot, but it's based on an educated guess backed up by information from Interpol and the CIA — who, as you well know, have eyes everywhere. They say she's been there a lot lately, which thinly corroborates Jock's story. Good enough to get us the go-ahead. Whether she's there or not remains to be seen, but at least we're going to the heart of this business.

'We're leaving later this evening, but that doesn't mean the fun stops here. Everyone who was arrested in that clinic needs to be interviewed. All of the security guards that were arrested . . . them too. And be careful. These are not your ordinary run-of-the-mill security guards. We suspect at least one or two of them are ex-Russian military, so watch your backs. Make sure there's armed support standing outside your interview rooms.

'Obviously, we're still on the lookout for Dare and Burkhan. They had it away on their toes when we stormed the building. The arrest of these two men is vital. I know it's a lot to get on with and we won't be here to help, but I know you can all cope. That said, I've spoken to the borough commander and he's agreed to giving you extra resources if you need them. Any questions?'

There was a collective shaking of heads.

'Okay. Back to work. We'll be in touch.'

CHAPTER THIRTY-FOUR

DAY 3

Less than seventeen hours after their direct flight from London landed in Mumbai, Paterson was trying to hail a cab to take him and Clocks to the main police headquarters.

'So, 'ow far is this 'eadquarters, then?' said Clocks.

'No idea. Hopefully not too long.'

'It's bleedin' 'otter here than it is back 'ome, innit?'

'D'you think?'

'Yeah, I do. I'm sweatin' me nuts off already.'

'Well, to be fair, you are in India, mate. It's generally known for being warmer here.'

Clocks pulled at his trousers. 'Think I'm gettin' swamp crotch.'

Paterson grimaced. 'Thought you always had that?'

'Nope. That's sticky crotch. This is swamp.'

'There's a difference?'

'Yeah. Sticky crotch is sticky and swamp crotch is, y'know . . .'

'Swampy?'

'Nah. Fuckin' disgustin'. All slippery an' smelly. Gross it is.'

'Oh, lovely. Thanks for that.'

'You're welcome.'

A cab pulled up and a fat, jovial little man jumped out of the car, grabbed their cases and threw them in the boot before either of them had a chance to tell him where they wanted to go.

'Please,' he said. 'Welcome to my cab. It is Grand Hotel you are wishing to go to, sirs?'

His accent was that of a man who had spent his entire life in this part of India and, looking at him, Paterson doubted he had ever left, even for a holiday.

'No, thank you,' said Paterson.

The driver looked nonplussed. All tourists went to the Grand to begin with. They usually moved off after a few nights when visiting other parts, but they nearly always started there.

'We need to go to Mumbai Police Headquarters, opposite Crawford Market. You know it?'

'Of course.'

''Ow long's it gonna take us, then, geezah?' said Clocks, as he dived in the back of the cab and scootched up against Paterson.

'One hour, sir.'

'An hour? Put the air con on, then. Good man.'

'There is an extra charge, sir. Fifteen percent.'

'Come again? Extra? Why is it extra? Just press the button.'

'I am sorry. It is company policy. They say we are to open the windows if passengers are too hot. Fifteen percent.'

'Fuck off, mate. Press the little button. Yer guv'nors ain't gonna know, are they?'

'Please, sir. There is no need to use this language.'

'There fuckin' is, mate. If you don't switch on the air con, me bollocks are gonna end up drownin' in a puddle of sweat all over your back seat. Press the button. Go on. Press it.'

'I am sorry. Company policy.'

'Okay, mate,' said Paterson. 'We'll pay the fifteen percent. Put the air con on, please.'

'What? Why are you payin' 'im to put the air con on? The little fat robber.'

'To be honest, John, I'm not paying him to put the air con on. I'm paying him because I'm hoping it'll stop you moaning all the way to Police HQ.'

'I'm not moanin', Ray. I'm sweatin'. An' I thought the little fat robber ought to know what'll 'appen if he don't put it on.'

'Well, he's put it on now, so just sit back and let your nads cool off.'

'I will. Thank you very much. Much appreciated.'

'You're welcome.'

The next hour was spent with Clocks tugging at his crotch every few minutes and moaning about the state of the country. He knew that parts of India were poor and very crowded, he just never knew how poor or how crowded. Street after street was lined with rundown, broken buildings, litter piled high and traffic like he'd never seen. When he wasn't pulling at his trousers, he was tutting and shaking his head.

One hour and ten minutes later, the driver pulled up outside the police station, hopped out of his cab and grabbed the bags out of his boot, dumping them unceremoniously on the ground.

'Oi! Careful, mate!' said Clocks. 'There's some expensive gear in those bags. If you've broke 'em, you'll pay for them. *Capiche?* He picked up his bag and shook it.

'Sorry, sirs.' The driver smirked. 'I did not mean to drop your bags.'

'How much do I owe you?' said Paterson.

'5,000 rupees, please.'

'What? Five grand? Five fuckin' grand? I know your country's got itself a rep for bein' a bit on the corrupt side of things but fuck me. Taking the piss, ain'tcha?'

'Rupees, John. It's about fifty pounds.'

'What? Fifty quid? He's takin' the piss, Ray.'

'I know. Don't worry about it. I'm not arguing over it.'

'Please tap your card on my phone, sir.' The driver scowled at Johnny Clocks.

'Do you wish to leave a tip, sir? I give you good service, yes?'

'You did,' said Paterson. 'Take fifteen hundred for yourself.'

The driver's eyes lit up. 'Thank you, sir. Do you need a driver, sir, while you stay in my beautiful country? I am most reliable.'

Paterson nodded. 'Tell you what. Leave me your number and I'll call you if we need you. But you'll have to put up with him moaning all the time. You okay with that?'

'Oh, yes, sir. I have heard many Australians before, sir. None of them complain like him, sir, but it will be okay.'

'What'd he say? Did 'e call me Australian? Oi! Did you call me Australian, porky?'

Paterson whirled around. 'John! Out of order, mate.'

'What now?'

'Don't call him "porky".'

'Why?'

'Supposing he'd been a Muslim?'

'He's not though, is 'e?'

'No. But he could have been. You have to think about what you're saying sometimes.'

'Alright, so even if 'e was a Muslim, what's that gotta do with anything?'

'You just called him "porky". Muslims don't eat pork.'

Clocks looked confused. 'I know that. I wasn't asking 'im if he wanted a sausage sandwich, Ray. I was pointin' out he's a fat bastard. There's a difference.'

Paterson shook his head. 'I'm sorry,' he said to the driver.

'It is okay, sir. My wife, she too says I am fat. And I'm not a Muslim.'

'I know you're not,' said Paterson. 'I was trying to teach him about being careful what he says to people. He can sometimes cause offence.'

'What are you then, fellah?' said Clocks.

'I'm a Sikh.'

'A what now? A sick?'

'No, sir. A Sikh. Sikh.'

'Oh. Like 'ide and seek?'

'Sir?'

'That's enough, John,' said Paterson.

'What? I didn't understand what he said.'

'You know exactly what he said and you know exactly what a Sikh is.'

'Do I? You're makin' assumptions there, Ray.'

'The turban didn't give you a clue?'

'Turban? Oh, course it is. Sorry about that. I thought he'd just washed 'is hair before 'e started work.'

Paterson sighed. 'You can be a right arsehole sometimes. D'you know that?'

Clocks grinned. 'Oh, yeah.'

'When we get back to London, I'm sending you on another race awareness course.'

Clocks shrugged. 'Can do if you like. It's a nice little day off for me. I'll be straight with you though. I think they're fed up trying to "wake" me up. One of the instructors said I was so unwoke 'e thought I was in a coma. All they do now is sit me in the corner an' give me tea an' dirty looks all day, so no 'ardship for me, is it? Still, I'm all up for a bit of lefty tree-'uggin' if you think it'll 'elp.'

Paterson shook his head.

'An' so you know, Mr 'ide an' seek, I'm not a bloody Aussie. They sound a bit like us because the last thing they nicked was our language when we chucked 'em all out of the country for bein' robbers. Like you, mate.'

'I'll give you a call if we need you. Thanks for your help,' said Paterson as he closed his door. 'You seem angrier than usual today, John. Did you miss one of your snacks?'

'Funny fucker you are.' Clocks pulled his shirt away from his back. 'I can't stand this 'eat. You know I can't.'

They headed toward the doors of Police HQ. 'Why did you come, then? Should have stayed at home.'

'Oh yeah? An' let you 'ave all the fun? Wouldn't miss this for the world.'

'What fun?'

'Early days, yet. I'm sure we'll 'ave some fun. C'mon, let's go an' wind up this mob. We can point out to them how they wish they were working for the Met police, the finest police force in the world.'

'*Service*, John. It hasn't been a *force* for years.'

'An' that's when it all went to rat shit, mate. When we stopped being a law enforcement institution and police inspectors all became "middle management". All downhill from there, I'm tellin' yer.'

'I know, mate. You're always telling me. Over and over and over.'

'Shut up an' listen. I'm tellin' you the truth. That 'appened shortly after we all changed over to being PC. Used to be a time when political incorrectness was all about 'avin' a laugh, but then all the buttoned-up lefties decided no one was allowed to take the piss out of people any more. You daren't get caught looking at a bird's chesticle area these days, let alone say naughty things. Sucked all the fun out of life, they 'ave.'

'You're just winding me up again.'

'No word of a lie, mate. Can't even *tell* 'em they've got nice bangers.'

'Pretty sure that was never okay.'

'I'm telling you. World's gone mental, mate. D'you know my little niece 'ad to read a book about masturbation in school the other day? *Forced* to read it. Was part of the study plan, fer fuck's sake. What's that all about?'

'Really? Which niece was that, then?'

'Skylar.'

'Oh, for God's sake. She's not little, John. She's twen-ty-two and at university. Probably been doing it for a good few years anyway. What's the big deal?'

'The big deal is . . . 'ang on. You've met her, ain'tcha?'

'Skylar? Yes. You know I have. Very attractive young lady, considering she's from your bloodline of wolves.'

Clocks frowned. 'You better not be imaginin' 'er?'

'What?'

'You. You better not be imaginin' 'er . . . y'know . . .'

'Imagining her what?'

'Y'know. *Polishing 'er sixpence.*'

'Polishing her sixpence? What does that even mean? What are you talking about now?'

Paterson pulled open the door and stood aside to let Clocks go through.

'You know exactly what I'm talking about. Don't be thinkin' anythin' dirty about my niece. There'll be trouble.'

Paterson grinned. 'Oh, John. Don't worry, mate. I wasn't imagining anything.'

'Good job an' all.'

'I was remembering.'

Paterson walked up to the front counter leaving a dumbfounded Johnny Clocks standing in the doorway.

CHAPTER THIRTY-FIVE

The station had been refurbished back in 2017 and was decorated in a Gothic Revival style. Money had been spent on flashing it out, but it somehow gave the feeling that the money could have been better spent. The place looked tired.

Paterson walked up to the reception desk and rang the little bell that sat next to a couple of pens and a pad of paper. Nothing official, just ordinary lined A4 paper.

A man wandered out of a back office to greet Paterson and Clocks. He looked about sixty and had a dour expression but was amiable enough to them. His English was quite broken but everybody managed to communicate, and within ten minutes Paterson and Clocks were sitting outside the commissioner's office.

'Wonder who that is?' said Clocks, pointing to a huge oil painting.

The subject of the painting was a nice-looking man, full head of dark hair and a neatly trimmed beard. His eyes, a dark, piercing brown, stared down at them like some sort of avenging headmaster. Paterson wandered over and looked at the little metal plate attached to the ornate gilt frame:

Police Commissioner Ram Devi, 2018. 'The very man we've come to see,' said Paterson.

'Blimey! Likes 'is old self, don't 'e?'

Paterson smiled up at the painting. 'I think it looks good.'

'I'm sure you do. Don't be gettin' any ideas above yerself an' start thinkin' you're 'avin' yer picture painted an' 'ung up in the office when we get back. That ain't 'appenin'.'

'Really? I think it's a great—'

'Mr Devi will see you now,' said an amiable woman seated behind a large oak desk. Prisha Singh was Commissioner Devi's personal assistant and the last gatekeeper for anybody who arrived to see him.

'Cheers, love,' said Clocks. He stepped aside to let Paterson in first.

The office was large, maybe eight times the size of Paterson's and four times that of the Metropolitan Police commissioner back at New Scotland Yard. The carpet was patterned, thick and opulent. A number of oil portraits lined the office walls. All were men, and Paterson guessed that all were past commissioners.

In the middle of the room, centred in front of two large window doors that led out onto a lavish garden area, was an enormous mahogany desk. Rising from behind it was Police Commissioner Ram Devi. Paterson could see straight away that the painting outside had been 'enhanced' to bring out some features that Mr Devi clearly did not possess. At least, not anymore.

This Commissioner Devi had thinning hair, a wispy moustache rather than a full beard and had put on a consid-erable amount of weight. Being generous, Paterson took the view that maybe things had been a bit tough at the top for Mr Devi and he was feeling the strain of high office. Devi rose, straightened himself up to his full five feet eight inches and walked around his desk to greet them. He had a heavy limp.

Clocks's left eyebrow rose up.

'Gentlemen, gentlemen. Please. Please. Come in.' The three men shook hands and made their introductions, and eventually Paterson and Clocks sat themselves down as Devi wriggled himself into his chair.

They went through the rigmarole of explaining why they were in Mumbai and the events that led them to their meeting with him. Every so often, Commissioner Devi would nod, touch his face and occasionally jot something down in what looked to be a handbound leather notebook.

'We were given some extremely good information that leads us to believe that the person behind these organ thefts has their main clinic here in Mumbai,' said Paterson. 'It is our intention to find out as much as we can about her whereabouts and her operation and then arrest her and bring her back to the UK to stand trial.'

Commissioner Devi nodded and sat himself back in his high-backed leather chair. 'I see. A woman, you say?'

'Yessir,' said Paterson. 'Alicia Warren. White, five-six. She has a number of aliases but we know her as Warren. So, the question to you is, can I count on your full support while we operate in your country?'

Devi took a deep breath. 'Of course, Mr Paterson. We want this filthy trade stopped just as much as you do, but there are difficulties ahead.'

Paterson shifted in his seat. 'And what would they be?'

Johnny Clocks was sitting in silence, watching the man. Clocks trusted few people in this life, probably only Paterson, and this man was unlikely to make his way onto the list any time soon.

'Well, these clinics are very hard to find. They operate . . . how do you say . . . underground. Yes. Underground.'

'Not this one. By all accounts she's been building some new clinics here to supplement her old ones.'

Devi flashed a look at Paterson. 'And then there is the matter of extradition.'

Paterson sat back. 'Is that a problem?'

'Do you have the relevant paperwork?'

Paterson eyed him up. Gone was the affable manner. 'It's coming,' Paterson said. 'Won't be long. I thought it professionally polite to come and speak with you first, before we started upsetting people.'

'Upsetting people? What do you mean?' Devi's body language was now defensive to the point of hubris.

'I mean that we intend to find this clinic and shut it down.'

'Shut it down?' Devi nodded slowly. 'How noble of you. Thank you for your concerns, but I do not think — no, I know — you do not have the authority to close down anything in this country.'

'What's yer problem, geezah?' said Clocks. The situation was beginning to nose-dive and this was as good a time as any for Clocks to bring it down a notch or two.

'My problem, Inspector Clocks, is that you are like our American friends. You think you can come into someone else's country and do whatever you like, whenever you like. That is not the way this works. If you want our help, I am happy to give it to you, but you will not close down any clinics or carry out any form of extradition without the correct authority. Is that clear?' Commissioner Devi looked back and forth at them both.

'Thought you'd be 'appy to shut down an illegal clinic.'

'*If* the clinic is illegal then, yes, I am happy to have it shut down. But not by you. *I* will close down any such clinics. Do you have definitive evidence that it is operating illegally?'

'Do you *allow* these sort of places to operate?' said Paterson. 'Legally or otherwise?'

'Otherwise?' said Devi.

'Yeah,' said Clocks. 'What my guv'nor is sayin' is, do you let them operate *illegally*? Straight question. Are you takin' the ol' brown envelopes in exchange for a quick look the other way? Y'know . . . you scratch my back an' I'll scratch yours. Nod, nod, wink, wink, say no more.' Clocks tapped the side of his nose.

Devi narrowed his eyes and took a deep, deep breath. 'You insult me? The commissioner of police for the whole of Mumbai?'

Clocks shrugged. 'Sounds like it, don't it? But don't think you're on yer own. We insult our own commissioner too. He gets a bit arse'oley too, but what can you do?'

'I think what DI Clocks is trying to say, sir,' said Paterson, 'is that we find it odd that you wouldn't want to be more proactive in closing down such a place and helping to alleviate the suffering and exploitation of poor and desperate people.'

'Was I?' said Clocks. 'I thought I was askin' if 'e was on the take. Perhaps you got a different subtext?'

Paterson rolled his eyes and murmured 'Jesus' under his breath. 'John. Shut up. Just shut up.'

Clocks looked genuinely hurt for a second but did as he was told.

'Will you help us, Mr Devi?' said Paterson. 'Can we rely on you and your officers for support?'

Devi tore his eyes away from Clocks and locked them onto Paterson. 'Of course. But understand that you are in my country. You have no jurisdiction here and what we say goes. If you do not agree, then you will have to wait for Interpol to tell you this woman has left the country. Then you can play cowboys somewhere else.'

Paterson thanked the commissioner, gave him the name of the hotel they would be staying at and left. They nodded politely to Devi's assistant and made their way out into the street.

''Ere, Ray! 'Ave a look, mate. One of 'is trotters was right on the wonky-donk, weren't it?' said Clocks.

'Yes. One's definitely a bit shorter that the other. Poor sod.'

'A bit? I reckon there's a good foot an' an 'alf difference. Reckon 'e needs a stepladder to do 'is laces up.'

'Don't be stupid. A foot and a half.'

'I knew a fellah like that once. Years ago.'

'Yeah?'

'Yeah. Nickname was "The Sniper's Nightmare" 'cos 'e kept bobbin' up an' down!'

Paterson burst out laughing. 'You bastard.'

'Seriously though. We 'ad a kid like that in school. We entered 'im in the egg 'n' spoon race on sports day. Mate . .

. shoulda seen it. The teacher 'ollered *go!* He took off, did a sharp left an' drilled 'imself 'alfway to Australia! To this day, it's still the funniest thing I ever saw.'

'That's cruel, John, and you know it.'

'Shut up, you ol' tart! It's just a joke.'

From across the street, a man was waving frantically at them. Paterson was quietly pleased to see their cab driver waiting. They dodged in and out of the teeming traffic and he gave the driver the hotel's name. The two men slipped into the back of the cab.

'Oh, I know what I meant to say . . . Well done, John. Nearly fucked it up again.'

'Fucked what up?' Clocks looked offended.

'Our meeting. Why'd you come out and accuse the commissioner of police of taking backhanders?'

Clocks shrugged again. ''Cos 'e is?'

'You can't say that. How do you know that?'

'Well, we're in India an' it's a well-known fact that all government officials, coppers an' the world an' 'is oyster are all as bent as a nine-bob note, mate. Trust yer Uncle Johnny.'

'That's you stereotyping again. I thought you were moving past all of this.'

'Well, you thought wrong. I'll bet you a pound to a pinch of shit that our commissioner 'ere is a wrong'un. I'll betcha.'

Paterson sighed and turned away, looking out of the car window.

'Sir,' said the cab driver. 'May I speak?'

'Yes, of course,' said Paterson. 'What is it?'

'Your friend . . . he is absolutely right. Everyone knows that Ram Devi is a bad man. He is involved in lots of criminal activity. Organ stealing is his main business, not police work.'

Clocks gave Paterson his biggest grin. 'Ray!'

'What?'

'Told yer.'

'I can help you,' said the driver.

'Help us? How?' said Paterson.

'What is it you are looking for?'

Paterson shot Clocks a sideways glance. 'A clinic. Some clinics. New builds.'

The cabbie nodded. 'Yes, yes. I know of them. I can take you to this clinic you are looking for.'

'For a price, I presume?' said Paterson.

'For a price. Of course. A good price.'

'See,' said Clocks. 'It takes a little fat robber to know a little fat robber. You're welcome.'

CHAPTER THIRTY-SIX

'Okay,' Paterson said to the cabbie. 'If you're going to be driving us around, what's your name?'

'Thank you, sir. It is Mohindra Singh.'

'I'm Ray and this is . . . Clocksy. Call him Clocksy.'

'Cocksy? I don't understand.'

'Clocksy! Cl . . . Cl . . . Cl-ocksy, you little numpty,' said Clocks.

Paterson chuckled. 'Look, I'll put you on twenty thousand rupees a day. For that, I'll need you to drive us around and introduce us to people who you think may be of use to us. If you find this clinic and it proves to be what we're looking for, I'll give you fifty thousand. How does that sound?'

Mohindra nearly crashed the car into a collection of rubbish piled up in the street. 'That is very generous of you, sir. I thank you from the bottom of my heart.'

'Well, you can thank me when we find this place.'

'Oi! Mo, me ol' cocker,' said Clocks. 'What's with Devi, then? You say he's involved in the organ racket. How do you know?'

'I have a cousin who works in the police force. He is a good man. A very good man.'

'And?'

'I am just saying, sir. He is a very good man.'

Clocks shook his head. 'Alright. Lovely. He's a good man, your cousin, but I'm not looking to fuck him, so I don't care 'ow nice 'e is. What *good* is he to *us*, then? Tell me that.'

'Oh, sorry. I thought—'

'We ain't payin' yer to think, son. We're payin' you to find this bird, find the clinic thingies and that's it.'

'What bird, sir?'

'What? Bird. Girl. It's English for *woman*. It means *woman*.'

Mohindra looked ever more confused the longer he spoke to Johnny Clocks.

'Bloody 'ell, Ray. We get the only little fat robber who don't understand English.'

'He understands it, John. Just not the way you speak it. To be honest, not many of us English understand it, if you want the truth.'

'Charmin', that is.'

'Right . . .' said Paterson. 'Your cousin in the police, Mohindra. How do you think he can help us?'

'Please, call me Mo. He is second in charge.'

'Of what?'

'Second in charge of whole of Mumbai police force, sir.'

'Oh, yeah? Why would 'e 'elp us?' said Clocks. 'Him and the commissioner ain't friends, then?'

'Yes, sir. Very good friends.'

Clocks squinted. 'So, why would he 'elp us if it 'urts his friend?'

'Money. If you pay him, he will tell you everything you want to know.'

'Money? That's it? He'd give up 'is mate for a few quid?'

Making no attempt to slow down, Mohindra swerved around a small child kicking a ball in the road. Paterson and Clocks slid across the back seat.

'Yes. Definitely. For money.'

'How much is it going to cost?' said Paterson.

'I'm not sure, sir, but I will ask him. He normally charges half a million rupees.'

'What? 'Alf a million quid? You can fuck right off, son.'

'Christ! Don't fucking start again, John. Rupees. About five grand in our money.'

'Alright, Ray. Keep yer girly bra on. Jeez.'

'Can you set up a meet for us, Mo?' said Paterson.

'Yes, of course. Tonight?'

'That would be good,' said Paterson.

'Stop the car! Stop the car!' Clocks shouted and began opening his door.

'What? What the fuck . . . ?' Paterson looked alarmed.

Mohindra slammed on the brakes.

Clocks jumped out and began running toward a small group of men. 'Oi!' he shouted. The men looked around as Clocks ran toward them. One of them held a stick over his shoulder, about to strike something. 'Fuckin' leave it alone!'

Through a gap in the group, Paterson saw a small brown dog tied to a post and cowering in fear. Clocks was at them now. He grabbed hold of the stick and got himself into a tugging match with the man. Clocks grabbed him by the throat with the other hand and pushed him away from the dog.

'Fuck you think you're doin'?' Clocks screamed. 'Fuckin' 'ittin' a dog, you prick.'

The man cursed and pushed back. His friends rallied behind him and started hollering.

Clocks wrested the stick from the man. 'Want me to fuckin' wallop you with it? Do yer?'

Paterson shouted. 'John! No!'

Clocks ignored him. 'Beatin' a little dog. You're an 'ard bastard, ain'tcha?'

'John. Let him go, mate. You'll start a riot.'

'Good. Don't bother me. Let's 'ave it, then.'

'John!'

The two men continued staring at each other long and hard.

Mohindra drew his cab closer. 'Mr Paterson, sir. We must go. It is not good to interfere in others' business.'

Clocks let the man go with a push and turned away. The other men in the group backed up slightly as he strode toward them, stick in hand. They parted as he walked straight past them and knelt down in front of the dog.

''Ello sweetie. 'Ow you doin'? Was the nasty man bein' a cunt, was 'e? It's alright. Uncle Johnny's got you now. You're safe.'

The little dog cowered away as Clocks reached out to him. After a minute of coaxing, the dog licked his hand and gingerly made its way toward him. Clocks picked him up.

'Fuck me, Ray. Poor little thing's shakin'.' He held the dog close to him and gently stroked the back of his head while muttering to him quietly.

'This is my dog! Give him to me!' said the man.

Clocks held the dog out to him. 'Come an' get 'im then, geezah.'

The man reached out to take the dog and received a kick in the testicles. He collapsed in a heap on the floor. The crowd started shouting and waving their arms.

Clocks looked at the crowd of men. 'He belongs to me now, an' if any of you fuckers wanna 'ave a row about it, bring it on.' He walked back toward Paterson and Mo.

One of the men started forward after Clocks. Paterson moved in front of him and held his hand up. 'Back you go, fellah. It's better that way.' The man stopped and continued shouting, this time directly at Paterson. Paterson smiled and walked away.

'And what are you going to do with it now, John?' said Paterson as he clambered back into the cab.

'Dunno.' Clocks sniffed. 'Didn't really think about it.'

'Go on. You didn't think about it? That's not like you. You're normally such a careful thinker.'

'I know, right? But what can yer do? Wasn't leavin' the poor little thing to get beaten to death by that no-good fucker. Not 'appenin', mate.' Still holding the dog close to him, Clocks climbed into the back seat and pulled the door closed. 'S'pose I can take 'im 'ome with me. Lyndsey likes dogs,' he said as Mohindra drove them away.

'How can you take it home, John? How are we going to get it on a plane? It has to be checked over, given papers and quarantined when we get home. It's gonna cost a small fortune.'

'Is it?'

'Yeah, it is.'

'You wanna dog, Mo?'

'No, thank you, sir. I have cats.'

'There you go, then. Perfect. Somethin' for 'im to play with.'

'No, sir.'

'Right. UPS it is, then. I'll parcel 'im up an' post 'im 'ome.' The little dog licked his face. 'Like that idea, don'tcha, boy? Yes, you do. You do.'

The little dog got more excited as Clocks played with him. 'Oi! 'Old up. Fuck me, 'e's only got his lipstick out!'

'His what?' said Paterson.

''Is lipstick.'

Paterson turned around to look at the dog. He chuckled at the dog's little erection. 'Seems he really has taken a shine to you.'

'Dirty little sod,' said Clocks. 'I like him. Mo, find out 'ow I get 'im back to the UK. There's fifty quid in it for you.'

Twenty minutes later, Mohindra screeched to a halt outside the hotel. 'Leave him in the back, Mr John. I will see to it. I will call you. Have a good evening, my friends.'

Paterson and Clocks watched the taxi pull away, leaving a cloud of dust in its wake.

'You trust 'im, Ray?'

'Not in the slightest.'

'Think he could be settin' us up?'

Paterson nodded. 'Maybe.'

'If 'e is, then bagsy I get to kick 'im up 'n' down the street first. Deal?'

'Deal.' Paterson as he headed toward the hotel entrance. 'I need to make a call.'

'Who to?'

'Tell you soon. I need to find out if he's busy first.'

Clocks nodded as Paterson stepped into the hotel lobby.

'Dunno about you,' said Clocks. 'But I don't 'alf fancy an Indian.'

'A what?'

'An Indian. A curry. Is *that* right? 'Ave I offended anyone by sayin' that?'

'You're alright but, just for the record, it's not called an Indian out here.'

'Innit? What's it called, then?'

'Food, Clocksy. Just food.'

CHAPTER THIRTY-SEVEN

'Take a seat.' Alicia Warren gestured for him to sit. Here, in this office, Commissioner Devi held no power. He was nothing but a useful pawn in her game. She owned him.

'What is so urgent that you could not speak to me over the phone? You coming to my office in daylight is . . . inconvenient. It does not do for people to speculate even further.'

'Miss Warren . . . please forgive me. I felt that this should only be discussed in private.'

'Do we have a problem?'

Devi nodded quickly. 'Yes. I was visited by the two police detectives I told you were coming. They know who you are and what you look like. They also know about your clinics here in Mumbai.'

Warren took a deep breath as she processed the information. When she spoke, she kept her voice in monotone, cold. 'And what do they want with me?'

'I fear they are here to arrest you and take you to England. They know that your courier in England was not legitimate and they have somehow traced this back to you. These men are not like any others. They have no fear. There is one . . . a loud man, brash . . . rude. He is . . . how is it said? *Itching?* Yes, itching for a fight. The other man — younger, his superior officer — is quiet and well-mannered but, of the two, he is the one I feel is most dangerous. There is something in his eyes, Miss.'

'Do they know we are connected? Of your involvement?'

'They suspect, Miss. I do not think they have evidence or I would not be sitting here in front of you today.'

Warren narrowed her eyes. 'Are you saying that they have threatened you, the commissioner of police for Mumbai?'

'Yes, miss. They have no respect and, as I said, no fear.'

Warren stood up. 'Thank you for coming to me. You were right to do so. Please close the door on your way out.'

Devi, confused, stood. 'Yes, yes, miss. Of course. But . . . what are you going to do?'

'Do not worry yourself any further. I will give them something to fear, Devi.'

CHAPTER THIRTY-EIGHT

Paterson lay in his bed watching the ceiling fan go around and around. Outside, the rain had been falling for the best part of two hours straight. Wherever they went in this world, the rain seemed to follow them. A few minutes' reflection on this morbid idea faded as other random thoughts drifted in and drifted out of his troubled mind.

The sessions he'd had with the Met's psychiatrist were not bringing him any real comfort or closure on the things he'd seen, and he certainly couldn't tell her in any real detail about some of the things he'd done. Even worse, he couldn't tell her about the things he was still prepared to do if he felt the situation called for it.

His mind drifted back a few years to before he and Clocks had become friends, to when his life remained on track for great things. Tipped to be the Metropolitan Police Service's youngest ever commissioner, his career was shaping up to be covered in glory and greatness. After retirement, high public office would call. He would sit on the boards of various blue-chip companies and be called upon as a consultant and business guru.

Then some crazy bastard tore up his estranged wife in a frenzied attack, and everything he'd achieved and dreamed of died with her. After that, it was a downward spiral of cocaine, drink and thoughts of nothing but revenge. When it came, it was swift, brutal and without hesitation. A single shot between the eyes of the killer, one of his own goddamn team, and it was done. Life was different from then on.

Johnny Clocks, a sergeant at the time, had witnessed the shooting. The two of them had started out hating each other with a passion. Paterson was rich, handsome, used to getting whatever he wanted, played by the rules and was a high-flyer headed for the top spot at New Scotland Yard. Clocks couldn't have been any more different. Brash and arrogant, he was the kind of man who thought rules were for 'nancies', and the only places he was likely to go was one rank up to inspector — just to get him moved — or prison. Two different worlds had fused together the second Clocks made the decision to back up Paterson and stand by him.

Since then, they'd become inseparable. The more they worked together, the more each man pushed the boundaries of what they could get away with. Neither cared what anybody else thought of them. They had each other and they shared the same vision: justice. And an awareness that sometimes you had to do wrong to do right.

He thought of Lyndsey, Clocks's new wife. An SCO19 officer, she was a crack shot with a rifle and the toughest woman he'd ever known. He still couldn't understand why she'd married him.

Like most people, she started out with a grudge against Clocks for his insensitivity and cockiness. Clocks had overstepped one boundary too many, and she let him know with a right-hander he never saw coming. The heart wanted what it wanted, Paterson supposed. And now it looked like she would join up with Wallace Young's little crew.

Wol, as they called him, was an ex-commissioner of police who, after a shaky start, had become the only real ally the boys had. He was an unconventional man in the sense that he was one of only a tiny percentage of high-ranking police officers who was still that: a police officer, someone with a sense of purpose beyond himself. He'd gone into bat for them on more than a few occasions, but retirement called for him and he left the police with a big payout, a fat pension and a sense that he was now free to inflict punishment on the criminal filth that still angered him.

He'd set up his own company, a private security firm, and invited Paterson and Clocks to join him. It was tempting, but Paterson refused. There was still more to do in the police. Clocks stayed loyal to his friend.

A peal of thunder rolled across the night sky and brought Paterson out of his thoughts. He lifted the half bottle of rum he'd bought in the hotel bar and finished the last few drops. He closed his eyes, felt the room sway precariously and wiped away the small tear that rolled down his cheek. He'd confirm his plan with Wallace Young in the morning.

CHAPTER THIRTY-NINE

Johnny Clocks lay on his bed, looking up at the ceiling fan. The bastard thing was broken and he was sweating like the proverbial pig. He thought about Lyndsey and uncharacteristically, found himself reflecting on his life. Up until Lyndsey had found out about his son, it had been pretty much okay.

He got to put away bad people, annoy senior management, prick the pomposity of anyone who thought they were something special and generally have a good laugh all the way through life. Things went tits up from time to time, but, hey, that was just normal. *Don't dwell on it. Don't mope about it. Just get on with it.* The key to a happy life was acceptance. There were things you could control and things you couldn't. The trick was to worry about what you could control. Fuck what you couldn't.

He finished off his half bottle of cheap whisky and rolled over onto his side. In his mind's eye he saw Lyndsey's face. He closed his eye and sniffed as a small tear wound its way down his cheek. He wiped it away with a finger.

'Fuck it!' He shot up out of bed and staggered toward the toilet. 'Bastard fuckin' curry!' He sat himself down and followed through on an enormous fart.

CHAPTER FORTY

DAY 4

Paterson strolled into the lobby of the Leela Mumbai Hotel and looked around. Behind him, Clocks did the same, but he was looking for someone different.

'You see anyone, John?' said Paterson.

'Nope. Not yet.' A hand tapped Clocks on the shoulder. He spun around, fist cocked. Always alert. His face lit up. ''Ello, sweetheart,' he said, as Lyndsey pulled him in close. She kissed him as if they'd been apart for years.

Paterson raised an eyebrow and smiled. Behind her, he saw the little troupe they'd come to meet. He left Lyndsey and Clocks to it and made his way over to a table tucked away at the back of the lobby.

Wallace Young stood to greet him, a smile all over his face, hand extended.

Paterson smiled back. It was always good to see this man. 'Hello, Wol. How are you? Thank you so much for coming. Appreciated.'

'You kidding me, Ray? This sounds like it's gonna be a riot. Wouldn't have missed this for the world.' Young shook Paterson's hand, pulled him in for a man hug and then nodded toward Lyndsey and Clocks. 'Those two should get a room.'

Behind Young, sitting at the table with his head slightly bowed and a cap pulled down over his eyes, was a man Paterson had never expected to see again in his life. He broke away from Young and sat himself next to the man. Powerfully built, he exuded a quiet, calm confidence that neatly hid his callous nature.

'Liam . . .' he said. 'How are you?'

Corporal Liam Bailey, ex-British Army and one of the world's most wanted men, lifted his head slowly. His face, flecked with little brown marks, was as white as a sheet, his eyebrows somehow whiter. Paterson knew it didn't stop there. An albino, Liam Bailey's nickname was whispered throughout Africa: the White Ghost. Paterson and Clocks got to meet this particular killer when a number of African church leaders in Bermondsey were shot dead.

Bailey had tracked a warlord and dictator by the name of General Abrafo and his wife to the UK to stop them from killing children in the name of sacrificial witchcraft. Hampered by Abrafo's diplomatic status, Paterson had found his hands tied at the highest level. In desperation, he'd agreed to work with Bailey to track and kill Abrafo and his wife.

His mission over, Bailey had vanished. Paterson had thought that was the end of it, until Young mentioned to him that he was thinking of starting up a group of investigators that would travel worldwide to sort out 'problems', and that he was looking to contact Bailey for his particular skill set.

An army-trained sniper of the highest calibre, Bailey also possessed a multitude of additional skills, all of which would stand the little squad in good stead. Those skills and Bailey's complete lack of conscience made him a deadly and highly effective operative and one that Paterson wasn't yet sure could be trusted.

'How are you, Ray? You look . . . well.'

Paterson knew he didn't. He'd crawled through too much shit in his life for it not to show on his face.

'Yeah. I'm alright. Y'know. Another day in paradise and all that.'

'Where's Clocks?'

Paterson looked over his own shoulder. 'Making out with his wife by the look of it. Liable to be thrown out if they keep carrying on like that.'

'I heard he has a bastard son.'

Paterson screwed his eyes up slightly. 'Hmm, hmm. So the story goes.'

'Do you believe he knew nothing about his existence?'

Paterson felt himself get irked. 'Yeah. Absolutely. It happens.'

The White Ghost nodded slowly, like he was mulling it over. 'I suppose.'

'Anyway,' said Paterson. 'None of our business. Want a drink?'

'I'll get them, Ray,' said Young. 'I've opened a tab. I could do with a bloody good drink. Damn, this place is hot.'

After a few minutes of catching up, their drinks arrived. Lyndsey and Clocks were still playing kissy-kissy.

'John!' Paterson shouted. 'Put her down and come here! Wol's bought a round.'

Clocks let Lyndsey go and, taking her hand, pulled her toward the table. 'Fuck me. Wol's put 'is 'and in 'is pocket? What's 'appenin' in the world? I can't 'andle this.'

Paterson stood up. He and Lyndsey threw their arms around each other. 'Lynds! How are you?' He was genuinely pleased to see her.

'Ray! I'm good. I'm good. You look well.'

'Do I? It's the facelift I got from the Childmaker. Made me look years . . . older. You and John made up, I see.' He pulled a chair out for her. 'C'mon. Sit down. Watch the show.'

'Show?'

Paterson sat down beside her and watched Johnny Clocks and the White Ghost eye each other. He folded his arms and smiled. 'This could be good.'

'John . . .' said Bailey. An acknowledgement of Clocks at least.

'Who's that?' Clocks made a show of peering under the baseball cap. Bailey looked up at him. 'Fuck me. It's not. Is that . . . ? It is. It's Michael bloody Jackson! Big fan, mate. Big fan. You look like you've put on weight. Being dead must suit you.'

'Still a prick, I see,' said Bailey.

'Of course. That's why you love me, innit, Bumpy, me ol' son?'

'Rest assured I don't love you. Not at all. And don't call me Bumpy.'

'Why'd you call him Bumpy?' said Lyndsey.

''Cos of the amount of people 'e's bumped off!' Clocks raised his glass. 'Everyone. A toast. The White Ghost. The world's most miserable assassin.'

Everyone raised their glasses.

'Keep your voice down, John,' said Bailey. 'I'd appreciate you not announcing me to the whole fucking room.'

'Oh, leave off. You announced yerself when you walked in fer Chrissakes. You look like Casper the fucking Ghost. Not like you can 'ide in the shadows, is it?'

Lyndsey grimaced. 'John . . . don't start.'

'What? It's only banter. He knows I don't mean it, don't you, Bumpy? Ray, if 'e takes that cap off, can I borrow yer Ray-Bans? You know I've got sensitive eyes.'

'Well, now you ladies have caught up, shall we get on?' said Young. He turned his attention to Paterson. 'When you're ready, Ray, you can brief everyone. Quietly, of course.'

Paterson launched into the details of the case and where they were with it. Lyndsey and Young nearly fell over with shock when they found out that Jock Hudson was heavily involved and actively killing people for profit. Paterson told them that Hudson had given up the boss, Alicia Warren, and went on to explain who she was and what she did for a living.

'We've been to see the commissioner of police here in Mumbai. Goes by the name of Devi. I get the sense that he is, as John says, a wrong'un, and neither of us trust him.'

'So, what is it you want from us?' said Young.

'I need you to track her, find out where she is and find out as much as you can about her clinics here in the city. We have an informant who can give you the addresses.'

'You have an informant already? I'm impressed.'

'It ain't a proper informant,' said Clocks. 'It's a little fat cab driver with dodgy teeth who's probably robbin' us blind with makey-up information.'

Paterson glared at him. 'Yes. Thank you, John. Very helpful as always.'

Clocks shrugged. 'Just sayin', mate.'

'Can we trust the info?' said Bailey.

'Truthfully,' said Paterson, 'I don't know. What I do know is that, out here, money talks loudly, and I've greased his palm with the promise of more. We'll just have to see.'

'What's he come up with?' said Young.

'Nothin',' said Clocks.

Paterson nodded. 'Hmm. Yeah. So far, nothing. But he has promised us a sit-down with the commissioner's number two, who from what I can make out, is all about the rupees.'

'Yeah,' said Clocks. 'We'll 'ave to give 'im a fair ol' straightener to get 'im on board an' give up what we need to know.'

'So, again,' said Young, 'why us? If you're going to get the information straight from a high source, what's the point of getting us here?'

Paterson gave a little smile. 'Well. There's a chance Devi could be setting us up to get us killed, so I thought it prudent to have you guys in the background. With two snipers on the team, it should be a good insurance policy. The pay will be good, Wol.'

'Ray. Some things are not about the money. If you two are in the shit, we're happy to help.'

'What?' said Clocks. 'Even the Milky Bar kid there?' he nodded toward Bailey.

Bailey nodded. 'Why not?'

CHAPTER FORTY-ONE

Johnny Clocks glanced at his watch: 3.17 a.m.

Lyndsey had fallen asleep within minutes of their love-making, and although falling asleep straight after sex was normally his thing, he found that he woke frequently feeling hot, sticky and uncomfortable. A drink was needed. He left a note for Lyndsey saying he was going downstairs to the bar in case she woke up.

As he walked down the stairs to the lobby, his head throbbed. Whether from the heat or lack of sleep he didn't know nor much care. He'd wandered into the brightly lit lobby and asked the receptionist if there was any chance of a drink despite the ungodly hour. He knew it was a slim chance but was worth the ask.

'I'm sorry, sir. I cannot serve you after hours. There is a machine over there that will give you a drink.'

The receptionist pointed out a vending machine stacked with soft drinks. Clocks peered at it, nestled between two doors. 'Mate, do I look like I drink bleedin' Fanta? I wanna proper bevvy. I fancy a whisky.'

'No, sir. There is no alcohol in it. Only soft drinks. Coke, Pepsi and water.'

'I'm not a ten-year-old boy, mate. That's no bloody good to me, is it? I want a proper drink.'

'I am sorry sir. The bar is closed.'

'I know that. You've already said. But seeing as it's stupid o'clock in the mornin' an' there's no bugger about, you could slip out the back and pour me a nice little drinky that your bosses won't know anythin' about. I could take it off of you and go an' creep over to one of the little tables in the corner there an' everybody's 'appy. What d'you reckon? Sound like a plan to you?'

'I am sorry, sir. The bar is closed.' He pointed toward the bar area, shrouded in darkness.

'I know, mate. We've done that bit, but come on. Do us a favour, eh? I'm 'ot, sticky an' knackered, so be a pal for me. Good man.'

'I cannot, sir. It would be a disaster for me to serve you alcohol after the bar has closed.'

'A disaster? Why is it a disaster? An earthquake's a disaster. I only want a little drinky.'

'We could lose our licence, sir.'

Clocks threw his arms up in the air. 'Oh, leave it out, mate. Lose yer licence? Who's gonna know? No fucker's awake apart from me an' you, an' I'm on me last legs. Seriously?'

The receptionist eyed him warily.

'Sir, are you the English policeman?'

Clocks sniffed. 'Would it make a difference if I said yes?'

'It could do, sir. Are you Mr Paterson?'

'What? Paterson? Yes. I'm Paterson. Yes.'

'I see, sir. That is different, sir. English police are very welcome here. I love English police. What can I get you?'

'A large gold watch would come in 'andy?' Clocks said.

'Sir?'

'Sorry. Sorry. A whisky. Scotch. Whatever. Don't care. Thank you.'

'Certainly, sir. One moment please.' The receptionist smiled and walked away from the bar. A few minutes later he returned holding a large tumbler of whisky.

'Oooh! Look at that. You beauty. Cheers, geez. Saved me life, you 'ave.' Clocks took a slug of the drink and punched his chest a couple of times as the liquid burned its way down to his stomach.

'Sir, would you please take a seat in the back there? I do not want to get into trouble for serving you a drink.'

Clocks looked over his shoulder and noted an empty booth in a dimly lit part of the lobby where he could tuck himself away out of sight of any nosy manager who might be wandering about. It was unlikely given the time, but he didn't want to get the receptionist into bother.

'Yep. No worries, mate. Ooh. While you're at it, nip back an' get me the bottle, eh?'

'No sir. That I cannot do.'

'Don't see why not, cocker. You're in the shit for givin' me this, so yer might as well be shot for a sheep as for a lamb.' Clocks looked sideways. 'Wait. Is it "shot for a lamb as for a sheep" or what I said? I dunno. I think that's right. Anyway, off you go before I report you to yer boss in the mornin'.'

He slid himself into the semi-circular leather seat and took another swig. That one went down a bit better.

Alone with his thoughts and his drink, it wasn't long before his head started to droop. Several times he would snap awake then drift back into a light sleep.

He woke with a start. It took him a second or two to remember where he was and he automatically lifted his wrist: 4.13 a.m. As he rubbed his eyes, it dawned on him he wasn't sitting alone.

CHAPTER FORTY-TWO

Four heavy-set men with thick, dark beards had inserted themselves into the booth with Clocks, two each side of him, and they were all staring at him.

'Mornin' ladies,' he said with a nod. He sat himself upright. 'What can I do fer you all?'

'You are Paterson?' said the man nearest to him. He was powerfully built with thick curly hair. A pinkish looking scar cut through his brown skin from forehead to cheek creating an ugly frame for his missing eye. This guy had lost at least one fight. His three companions all bore different facial deformities, which suggested they were not strangers to violence and not too good at avoiding it either.

'I might be. Who wants to know?' Clocks realised he was in serious trouble. Stuck behind a table that was bolted down and flanked by two men either side of him was not the most conducive place to fight.

'Are you Paterson?'

'As I said, I might be.'

'You will come with us,' said Scarface.

Clocks looked at his glass. Only a little drop left.

'Nah. Don't get me wrong. I like an orgy as much as the next man but I like *my* pussies with a little bit less hair on 'em than *you* pussies sittin' 'ere. Last time I saw a growler like that on a bunch of cunts was in some seventies porno. I mean, fuck me . . . you an' the 'Air Bear Bunch 'ere could set up the Mumbai branch of Build-a-Bear. You'd make a bleedin' fortune stuffin' them.'

'You will come with us.'

Clocks gave this man the hard stare. 'Hmm. No sense of humour, 'ave yer? Nah. I don't think so, mate.'

'If you do not, it will be bad for you.'

Clocks picked his drink up and drained the glass. 'Bad for me? What? Worse than this piss driddle 'e calls whisky. You reckon it can get worse than that?'

Scarface said nothing.

'You're a chatty fucker, ain't yer? Right, look . . . It's been a hoot meetin' you lot, but you're borin' the life out of me now. So, be good boys an' slide yerselves out. I'm goin' back to me bed.' He gave them a dismissive wave with his glass as he started to slide himself sideways. Scarface reached inside his jacket pocket. Clocks threw the tumbler and hit him above his good eye.

Chaos broke out as Clocks struggled to stand upright, hampered by the fixed table, and bent double. He grabbed the man nearest him by the hair and slammed his face onto the table, stunning him as blood burst from his nose.

A man to his left reached across the table and pulled on Clocks's arm, dragging him down and across the table. Clocks lashed out wildly as the other three used their numerical advantage to get him under control. Scarface pushed a gun into Clocks's face and quietened him down.

'Get up, Paterson! You will come with us.' He wiped blood away from a deep cut over his eye, the result of Clocks's hurling the glass at him, and sniffed at the blood that dripped from his nose.

'Fuck you, Noddy!'

One of the men hit him on the forehead with the butt of a gun, hard enough to subdue him but not hard enough to put him out. They dragged him off the table and manhandled him roughly to a standing position.

'Where we goin' then, fucker? Anywhere good?' Clocks made an effort to shake himself free from the grip of the two men that held him. He quickly realised he couldn't.

'You will see, Paterson,' said Scarface. 'You should not interfere in things that do not concern you.'

'Oh, I see. That right, is it? Killin' people for their bits an' bobs. Not my concern? Should be everyone's concern.'

'But it is not. Now, come.' The two men dragged him away and marched him toward the entrance.

'Who sent you? Was it the bird, Warren? Or Devi? My money's on Devi.'

Ahead of him, with his head down, was the receptionist who'd brought him the drink.

'Wait a minute,' said Clocks.

His two captors ignored him. Clocks dug his heels into the carpet and leaned back.

'I said, wait a minute.' The two men stopped. Clocks turned to Scarface. 'I'll come with you, mate, just tell your two 'airy lovers 'ere to lemme go. I ain't gonna run. I wanna walk out on me own. *Comprende?*'

Scarface nodded to the two men and they released their grip on him. He shook himself as gesture of defiance.

'Oi!' He turned to the receptionist. 'This on you, is it? You grass me up to these wankers, did yer?'

The man ignored him and kept his head down.

'Oi! I'm fuckin' talkin' to you, you cowardly prick.' The man looked up, and the second he did, Clocks lashed out and landed a backhanded fist on the man's nose. The man yelped in pain and clutched his face.

The two men latched onto Clocks again.

'You cannot be trusted, Paterson,' said Scarface.

'I said I wouldn't run, mate. Didn't say I wouldn't whack this little arsewipe, did I?'

As they forced him toward the door and the black van waited outside, he glanced at a clock hanging on the wall: 4.22 a.m. He knew Paterson was coming for him at seven and Lyndsey would be up at about the same time. They'd find him if they followed his trail.

A trail starting with the receptionist.

CHAPTER FORTY-THREE

DAY 5

Paterson hopped out of the taxi and asked Mohindra to wait for him. He was five minutes late and wasn't happy about it. Being late wasn't his thing and he always worked on the basis that it was better to be an hour early than a minute late.

He scanned the lobby for Clocks. No sign of him. He checked his watch: 7.05 a.m. He pulled out his mobile phone and dialled Clocks's number. After a few rings, a sleepy sounding Lyndsey answered.

'John's phone,' she mumbled.

'Morning, Lynds. It's Ray. Sorry to wake you but is John there? Has he done it in? We're supposed to meet downstairs in the lobby at seven and it's five past.'

'John!' Lyndsey called.

Paterson strained to detect a response; there was nothing.

'I'll see if he's in the shower,' Lyndsey said. He heard her call his name again. 'He's not here, Ray.'

'Okay, hun. I'll give him a couple of minutes.' Paterson tried not to sound concerned as he hung up. But John never went anywhere without his phone, and Paterson knew that

Lyndsey would be having the same thought. Sure enough, the phone rang and he answered it.

'Ray!'

'I know,' he said. 'I'll wait for you.'

'Five minutes.' She hung up.

Paterson looked around the lobby. Two receptionists. One male, one female. They were engaged in a deep discussion, with the man touching his nose every few seconds. Paterson deduced that this was the night shift to early morning shift changeover. He took one last glance across the lobby in case he'd missed Clocks sitting somewhere then went over to the two receptionists.

'Excuse me,' he said.

The woman looked up at him with her best courteous smile. 'Yes, sir. How may I help you?'

'I was supposed to meet a friend here at seven but I can't see him anywhere. Can you tell me if you've seen him, please?'

'Of course, sir. What does he look like?'

'No one has been in the lobby as yet, sir,' chipped in the man who'd been rubbing his nose. 'I have been here all night.'

Paterson stared at him. 'No one? Seems odd. This is a hotel, isn't it? People come and people go all the time, surely?'

'Yes, sir, but not this morning. It has been very quiet.'

Paterson nodded. 'What happened to your nose, fellah? Your eyes are a bit swollen too.'

The man unconsciously touched his nose. 'It is nothing. I had an accident. I walked into a door.'

Paterson smirked. 'Was this door a middle-aged Englishman with an attitude, by any chance?'

The receptionist flinched just enough for Paterson. 'You've got five seconds to tell me what happened. One . . .'

The man startled and the woman backed away.

'No sir. It was an acc—'

'Two.'

'Please. It was—'

'Three, four, five!' Paterson vaulted the desk. He grabbed the man by the throat and rammed him up against the wall. The female picked up the desk phone.

'Where is he? What happened to him? Tell me!'

The man looked terrified. 'Sir . . . Please . . .' he gurgled.

'Hey, bitch! Put the phone down. Now!' The female receptionist looked startled as Lyndsey marched across the lobby at a clip. 'Put it down now!' The woman did as she was told. Lyndsey's tone told her that to ignore her would be a bad mistake.

'Who were you calling anyway?'

'Po . . . police. Police.'

'No, you're not. Not now.' She jumped the counter to join Paterson.

'What's he done, Ray?'

'He knows something. Look at his face.' Paterson held the man firm.

'What happened to you?' she said to the frightened man.

He gurgled as Paterson squeezed his throat tighter.

'I said, *what happened?*'

'I might be wrong,' said Paterson, 'but I'm betting those baby black eyes and swollen nose are a note from Clocksy . . . *come and find me*. This fucker knows what's going on.' He released his grip. Lyndsey took over.

'That right? You know where my old man is, do you?' She dragged him down to the floor and put him on his back. 'You will tell me or I'll hurt you so bad you'll wish you'd never been born. Tell me!'

Paterson heard sirens blaring in the distance. He glanced at the woman, saw where she was cowering and noticed that underneath the desk was a panic button. He shook his head. 'She's called the police. We've not got much time, Lynds.'

She put two fingers either side of the night porter's nose and twisted it hard. The man yelped in pain. 'Tell me!'

Paterson jumped the counter and headed to the main doors. 'I'll hold them back for as long as I can,' he said.

'*Tell me!*' Lyndsey twisted the man's nose again. 'Tell me or I'll pull this bastard thing right off your face!'

The man was in so much agony that the woman took action. She left her cowering position and hit Lyndsey over the head with the receiver from the telephone.

'Fuck!' Lyndsey yelped and let go of the man. She batted the woman across the face, sending her sprawling against the counter, then turned back to the man. She toed him in the ribs to keep him down and turned her attention back to the woman.

'Don't!' she yelled at the same time as she held up a finger. '*Don't!* Stay out of this. Nothing to do with you.'

The receptionist was in a state of shock as she held a hand to her stinging cheek.

'They're here, Lynds!' Paterson shouted. 'Squeeze him harder!'

From outside the lobby came the sound of cars skidding to a halt, followed by slamming car doors and heavy, urgent footfalls.

Paterson timed his exit perfectly. He flung the door open and it hit the first running man full in the face, dropping him like a brick.

'Oh, Jesus!' Paterson threw his hands up and looked down at the dazed policeman. 'I'm sorry. I'm so sorry. It was an accident.'

A second policeman rushed to his colleague's aid and knelt down to help. The others stood still, surprised by this unexpected turn of events.

'I'm sorry,' Paterson said again. 'Totally my fault.'

One of the policemen gathered his senses and decided that he still had a job to do and that job was inside. He pushed Paterson in the chest as he tried to get past him.

'Hey!' said Paterson. 'I said it was an accident. No need for—' He stepped forward quickly; his left leg went behind the advancing man and his left hand pushed at his throat, knocking him backward and tripping him up. As the policeman sprawled to the ground, Paterson spun sideways and punched another policeman with the back of his hand, knocking him backwards. The kneeling policeman was shoved sideways by Paterson's foot.

One of the two remaining pulled his gun. Paterson, close to him, reached out, grabbed his wrist, pushed the gun away and punched him in the forehead. As the man fell, Paterson took the gun from him. He whirled around to the last policeman and pointed it at him.

The policeman was in the process of drawing his gun. 'Ah, ah,' Paterson said. 'Don't do that, pal. Don't do that.'

The policeman put his hands up.

'Good boy,' said Paterson. 'Now, take their cuffs and cuff them all up.'

The policeman looked at him.

'Cuff 'em all up. Come on! Do it!'

The policeman looked confused.

'Great.' Paterson sighed. 'I get the only Indian in India that doesn't speak English. C'mere.' He beckoned the man forward with the gun. As the man approached him, Paterson smacked him between the eyes with the butt of the gun, sending him reeling backwards before dropping to the floor. With everybody down, he set about handcuffing them all himself. More sirens were approaching.

CHAPTER FORTY-FOUR

A crowd of armed police officers ran toward them, guns drawn and shouting. Paterson and Lyndsey had made a decision. Hands behind their heads, they waited calmly for them.

'Did he tell you anything?' Paterson said.

Lyndsey shook her head. 'Whoever he's protecting, he's terrified of them.'

Paterson nodded.

'You sure about this?' she said. 'Just giving up?'

'No point running, is there? We've got no info from the desk clerk and everyone and his brother will be looking for us. Best we give up now, get this over with and get in to see the commissioner. That's our only chance.'

'Chance? You kicked the shit out of six of his finest.'

Paterson grinned. 'If that's his finest then God help them all.'

'You!' shouted a police officer. 'Get down! Get down!'

Paterson looked him in the eye. 'Don't shoot! We are English police officers. Diplomatic immunity.'

Lyndsey glanced at him. 'We don't have diplomatic immunity, Ray,' she said out of the side of her mouth.

'I know. But they don't know that, and I'm betting no one wants to be the one to start a diplomatic incident.'

'Crafty bastard.'

'Thank you.' He looked over at the pile of officers he'd walloped and watched them stagger to their feet, helped by their colleagues. 'I demand to see Commissioner Devi. He knows us!'

Two officers approached Paterson and the braver of the two drew his cuffs. He looked wary as he got closer. Paterson nodded and held his hands out in front of him. Lyndsey did the same.

Cuffed up, they were bundled into the back of a police van.

'I hope you know what you're doing, Ray. John could be anywhere now.'

'I know. But if anyone can tell us where he is, it'll be Devi.'

CHAPTER FORTY-FIVE

Twenty minutes later, Paterson and Lyndsey were standing in Commissioner Ram Devi's office. He was not in a happy mood. Neither were Paterson and Lyndsey. Time was marching on and Clocks could have been anywhere by then.

'You have caused many problems, Paterson. And you, miss.'

'Yeah, well. Sorry about that. But someone has taken my husband and I want him back. Unharmed. Right now. Understand me?'

Devi bristled. 'You do not talk to me that way. I am the commissioner.'

'And I'm your worst fucking nightmare if you don't tell me where my John is.' Lyndsey was struggling to contain herself.

'You threaten me, woman?'

'Making you a promise, dickhead.'

'What is it that makes you think I know anything?'

'Because you know everything that goes on here,' said Paterson. 'I know you're on the take from criminal gangs and I know you're heavily involved in organ trafficking. Clocks didn't just disappear, and you know it. Now, either you tell me where he is or I swear I'll make your life a fucking misery.'

Devi snorted. 'How dare you! Who are you to accuse me of this? I cannot help you, Paterson. I *will* not help you.'

Paterson moved forward slightly.

Devi didn't flinch. 'You have assaulted six of my men and the hotel staff. Why should I not have you thrown into prison? Or deported?'

'You can,' said Paterson. 'But think of the shit storm that would cause. Bad idea. Your men are fine. I barely touched them.'

Devi glared at him. 'Leave my office. Go back to your hotel and stay there. My men will find your Inspector Clocks. Do you understand? *We* will find him. Not you. Do not leave your hotel and do not assault anyone else.'

'I'll see what I can do. And you've got thirty minutes to report to me, Devi. Understand? Half an hour. And it better be with John's exact location.' Paterson turned on his heels and left the almost apoplectic Commissioner Devi sitting at his desk.

CHAPTER FORTY-SIX

'Well, that went badly, didn't it?' said Lyndsey.

'Maybe.' Paterson hailed a cab. He wasn't surprised when he saw that the driver was Mohindra. Paterson opened the door for Lyndsey and she slid in, bumping up against a middle-aged Indian man in a sharp suit.

'Mo!' said Paterson. 'Thought it might be you. Who's he?' He indicated the man next to Lyndsey.

'This is my cousin, Kulminder Singh. Ram Devi's second.'

Paterson slammed the door shut and looked over his shoulder. 'Good to meet you,' he said.

'Yes, sir,' said Kulminder. 'You too.'

'You know what happened to my friend?'

'Yes, sir. They have taken him to the clinic.'

Lyndsey stiffened slightly, urgency in her voice. 'What clinic? Where is it? How far away?'

'It is close. No longer than fifteen minutes. Mohindra knows where it is.'

'Are you sure that's where he is?' said Paterson.

'No, sir. I cannot guarantee it, but I believe that is where he is.'

'Okay then,' said Paterson. 'It's all we've got. Let's go, Mo. Put your foot down.'

'Wait!' said Kulminder. Mohindra took the cab out of gear.

'What?' said Paterson. 'You're not coming with us?'

'No, sir,' said Kulminder. 'I'm here to arrest Devi. Behind us is a squad of my best men. They have not been corrupted and are loyal to me. Devi has gone too far. The capture of your friend is too much. He must be stopped now.'

'Why didn't you stop him before this?' said Lyndsey.

Kulminder shrugged slightly. 'Money.'

'Wait . . . money?' said Lyndsey. 'You on the take as well?'

'Yes, I have taken money. I am ashamed of my actions, but I will put things right before I must go to prison. This I promise.'

Paterson turned to Kulminder Singh. 'Listen to me . . . Do not arrest him now. If our friend isn't at this clinic then I'll need to come back here to lean on Devi. A lot harder this time. If you try to arrest him now, he might run.' Suddenly Paterson chuckled.

'What's so funny?' said Lyndsey.

'Nothing. Just realised what I said.'

'What?'

'Well, Devi's got one leg shorter than the other. John said something about him going around in circles. I just had a vision of him trying to get out of his office on the hurry-up.'

Lyndsey smiled. 'Sounds like my John.'

'If Devi does manage to get away, then we may lose our only lead to John for good. Understand?'

Kulminder was clearly mulling it over. 'What you say is true, sir. I will wait, then.'

'Good man,' said Paterson. 'Listen though . . . I need you to distract him somehow. Keep him busy while we do what needs to be done. I don't want him to get wind of this until necessary. Understood?'

'Of course.'

'Okay then. I need a favour.'

'What is it?' said Kulminder.

'Can we take your officers with us to this clinic? You said they were loyal to you, so I can trust them to play right with us? Yes?'

'Of course. I will tell them. Good luck in finding your friend.' Kulminder stepped out of the car and walked over to his officers.

Mohindra spun the car around and they headed off in the direction of the clinic. Paterson looked back in time to see an armoured police vehicle pull out behind them. Kulminder's loyal officers.

CHAPTER FORTY-SEVEN

Johnny Clocks drifted out of unconsciousness, woken by the sound of woolly voices. He vaguely heard his name mentioned above a metallic clatter. Above him was a series of blurring streaks of light, and he felt himself moving backwards at speed. It took him a few seconds to realise he was strapped down to a trolley.

He shook himself awake and took it all in. Walking briskly by the side of him was a woman. Alicia Warren. He tilted his head forward as far as he could and saw Lee Burkhan pushing the trolley.

'Hello, John,' said Burkhan. 'Good to have you back with us.'

''Allo Burkhan. Fancy seein' you 'ere.' He shook his head, desperate to remove the fuzziness. 'It's good to see me, is it?'

'It really is, John.'

'You won't think so when I get up off this table.'

'Really? It's a good job you won't be getting off it then, isn't it?'

'Whatcha got in that bag?' Clocks eyed the medical kit slung across Burkhan's shoulder.

'Something to help you sleep, John.'

'I've just woke up from a kip. Can't sleep me life away, can I?'

'Mr Clocks,' said Alicia Warren. 'At last we meet.'

Clocks chuckled. 'Ooh, 'ello. D'you know that woulda sounded a lot better if you'd twirled your moustache as you said it. Who the fuck are you, babe?'

'I'm the woman you've been looking for.'

'Really? No you're not. You're not Suranne Jones, are yer? If you are, you look a *lot* different in real life than you do on the telly. Didn't know you 'ad a moustache, Suranne. They do a good job with the ol' make up, don't they? Can't see it all on the telly.'

Warren touched her top lip absentmindedly. 'I am not this . . . Jones woman.'

'You're not? Fuck. That's a disappointment. I always dreamed of bein' tied down on a trolley by 'er. Ah, well. That's a wank for another day, then. Look . . . whoever you are, don't worry about the tash, love. Nothing a coupla litres of industrial-strength bleach won't sort out.'

'I have heard you are a funny man. What is it they call you . . . Timex?'

'Oi! Only my oldest friends call me that. So, before you do, we need to get to know each other better. Know what I mean, sweet'eart?' He winked at her. 'I know you're not Suranne, but I'll give yer a go anyway. You've got an 'alf-de-cent pair of tits on yer for an old bird. Bit saggy, but what the 'ell.'

'Oh, we're going to get to know each other well. Very well indeed.'

Clocks yelped as the trolley smashed into the corner of a wall that Burkhan had failed to negotiate properly. 'Fuckin' 'ell, son! Where'd you learn to drive? France?'

'Sorry!' said Burkhan, instinctively.

'S'alright. Be careful, though. You don't want to damage me before we get to where we're goin', do yer? I'm guessin' you're gonna damage me properly when we get wherever we're goin'. Am I right?'

'Spot on, mate.'

'What we after?'

'Kidneys.'

'Kidneys? Nice. She started making pies, then?' He nodded at Warren. 'Fat cow looks like she's a bit too fond of a pie.'

Warren stopped and pulled the trolley backwards. Burkhan stopped too. She looked down at Clocks.

'You would do well not to insult me anymore, Mr Clocks. I am not fat nor do I have a moustache.'

Clocks looked her up and down. 'Well, I think it's safe to say you're a bit sensitive about your weight an', to be fair, I swear I could hear your thighs rubbin' together as we came down the corridor. Sort of a swishin' noise. Y'know what I mean? And you forgot about your saggy tits. Or are you okay with them?'

Warren drew in a deep breath.

'S'alright, love. Don't you worry yerself. They must 'ave an Indian branch of Weight Watchers out 'ere, surely? You can pop down there an' tell 'em yer story. Y'know . . . you're depressed 'cos you can't get a boyfriend 'cos you're fat an' 'airy an' ugly. Probably got snail breath an' all. So you took up pie eatin' as an 'obby and before you knew it . . . wallop! Fat as a barrel, an' shares in Greggs shot up tenfold.'

Clocks knew he'd got to her now as he saw her clench her jaw. 'As for the tash . . . well, p'raps it's a caterpillar. Difficult to tell from 'ere.' He squinted at her. 'Let's 'ave a proper look.'

Without thinking, she bent closer. Clocks drove his head straight onto her nose. She staggered backwards and fell against the wall.

'Dunno what it was, love, but best to drown it, I think. Blood was all I could think of.'

Burkhan stood frozen then ran around to Warren. She pushed him aside as she regained her balance and glared at Clocks before she launched herself at him. Screaming obscenities in French, she punched him in the face several times, drawing blood from his nose and mouth. When she stopped, Clocks spat out a gob of blood onto the floor.

'Ouch.' He smiled at her. 'I've got a bit of a twinge in me down-belows now, love. Thanks for that.'

'You bastard, Clocks! You bastard! Burkhan! Take what we need and take everything else from him too. You understand me? Hollow him out and feed it to the dogs.'

'Oi, love! You've got somethin' red 'angin' under yer nose. I think yer caterpillar's dead. I got it for yer though, didn't I? No need to thank me. You're very welcome.'

Holding her nose, she stormed off as Lee Burkhan pushed the trolley into the service elevator.

'Not smart, John. I was just gonna take a kidney, patch you up and kick you out, but now . . .'

'Can I tell you somethin, Lee?'

'You will anyway, so go on.'

'You know you're a dead man walkin', don't cha? Ray will fuckin' destroy you for this, an' it won't be an easy death.'

Burkhan smiled as he pulled out a syringe from the bag around his shoulder. 'And you, Johnny Clocks. You're a dead man lying.'

CHAPTER FORTY-EIGHT

'You got a plan, Ray?' Lyndsey asked.

Paterson watched the streets slip by as Mohindra weaved frantically in and out of the slums and past wasteland. He nodded slowly. 'Yeah. Straight in through the doors. No fannying about. No tiptoe Secret Squirrel shit. We go in, we find Clocksy, we get out. Anyone else there of interest, in they come too. We are not fucking around today.'

'I like the sound of that,' she said.

Sixteen minutes later, Mohindra had the clinic in sight. From the outside, there was nothing to indicate what went on inside.

'There it is.' Mohindra pointed into the distance.

Paterson looked at the chain-link fence that seemed to be the only form of solid defence that he could see. There was a hut with a guard inside by the gates, but no one patrolled the grounds and there were no guards with guns. That was good enough for him.

'Pull up, Mo. I want to have a word with the guys behind. They're gonna have to go straight through that fence and up to the main entrance. We'll follow on.'

Paterson bailed out of the car and was back in under two minutes. 'Okay, we're good to go. And, for good measure,

Kulminder instructed them to give us a gun each plus three clips of ammo. I like this!'

He handed Lyndsey one of the guns. She quickly and expertly checked it over. It had a full clip. She pulled the slide back, putting a round in the chamber.

'Lynds. We only use these as a last resort. We need to be a bit shrewd.'

'Gotcha.'

The armoured van carrying Kulminder's squad drove around them and picked up speed.

'Go! Go! Go!' Paterson shouted. Mohindra slammed his foot on the accelerator and dropped in behind the van.

Paterson ducked instinctively as one of the gates came flying up and over the van, over the top of their car and bounced violently on the ground behind them before it stopped. He caught the flash of brake lights in his peripheral vision and heard the sudden shout of Kulminder's men as they jumped out, weapons drawn, and started screaming at anyone within earshot.

Paterson and Lyndsey got out of the car and ran toward the main entrance, where Kulminder's squad of officers were defending the building, backs to the door in a semi-circle, machine guns held high.

Paterson, running, fired at the glass door ahead of him. It shattered into a million little pieces that caught the light from inside, causing them to sparkle like diamonds. He ran straight through, his feet slipping on the broken glass. To his left was a reception desk. Behind it, a large man with a terrified look on his face. Paterson went straight for him. He ran around the desk, pointed the gun straight at the man's head.

'Someone was brought in earlier! White man. Dark hair. Where is he?'

The receptionist, shaking, was a bit too slow to answer.

Paterson kicked him in the chest, knocking him down. 'Where? Tell me!'

He fired a shot into the ground near to the man's head. 'Top Floor! Three! Please . . . please don't kill me!'

Paterson turned away. Lyndsey was already hitting the button for the elevator.

'Two of you stay here,' she said to Kulminder's officers. 'Two of you take the lift. The rest with us.'

She ran for the stairs. Paterson and the rest of the squad followed her.

Each set of stairs was taken like the professional she was: gun high and pointed ahead, careful at the junction where the stairs turned, back to the wall. At the fourth floor, she kicked the door open and waited. No shots. She crouched low and poked her head inside a corridor.

She stepped in. Paterson covered her. Empty.

'We're gonna have to check every ward as we go,' she said.

'No, it'll take too long,' said Paterson. 'I say we find the operating theatre and go there.'

'What? The operating theatre? If they've—'

'We'll worry about that if we have to,' said Paterson. 'You boys, split up and check these wards. We're fine. We know what we're doing.'

He watched Kulminder's officers make their way along the corridor and peel off, two to a ward. Paterson and Lyndsey made it to the end of the corridor and peeped around one of the corners. An overhead sign said *Operating*.

They headed toward it. Ahead was a room with the lights on.

'Here . . .' Paterson said. They crept up to the door and he took a careful look through the square window. 'Fuck!'

'What? What's the matter?' said Lyndsey.

He pushed the door open. 'They know we're here,' he said.

CHAPTER FORTY-NINE

Paterson and Lyndsey stepped into the room to see a bare-chested and unconscious Johnny Clocks lying on a trolley. Standing behind Clocks with a scalpel pressed against his throat was Lee Burkhan. Clocks was bleeding from a wound in his side.

Lyndsey let out a sharp breath. 'John!'

'Hello, Ray,' said Burkhan. 'I thought there was something not quite right about you two.'

'Did you now?'

'I did. Tony thought you were okay. Me? Nah. I had you pegged.'

'Yeah, course you did. You're a fucking genius. Tony's not that bright though, is he? Where is he? Counting his fingers somewhere?'

'Let him go!' Lyndsey raised her gun and pointed it directly at Burkhan.

Burkhan pulled the knife tighter. 'Ah, ah! Don't do that.'

Paterson held his hand up. 'Hold it, Lynds. Who cut him, Burkhan?'

'I did.'

'*You* did?'

'Yeah. Did I not mention I was a surgeon?'

'Nope. That bit never came up.'

'My bad. I trained straight out of university.'

'Why'd you give it up?'

'This is more lucrative. Much more.'

'Why'd you need Jock Hudson, then?'

'Volume, Ray. He took care of the merchandise in the UK while I did elsewhere, along with others. Besides, we cleared his debts. He owes us, so we might as well put him to work.'

'Merchandise? Is that what they are to you?'

'Pretty much. I find it helps if you don't think of them as people, you understand?'

Paterson stared at him.

Lyndsey slowly moved to the side. It didn't go unnoticed.

'Just stay there and he won't get hurt,' said Burkhan.

'Seems a bit late for that,' said Paterson. 'Have you taken anything from him?'

'No. Was about to when you and your friends turned up. He'll be fine, provided you don't try and stop me leaving here.'

'Not gonna happen.'

'A shame. For him, not for me.' Burkhan pressed the blade tighter against Clocks's throat. A small trickle of blood ran from the wound.

'That's enough,' said Paterson. 'Leave him here and go.'

Burkhan shook his head. 'Leave him. No chance. Not while you two have guns. He's coming with me until I'm out of here.'

Paterson raised his gun.

'Oh. That's not clever, Ray. You know you can't shoot me before I pull this blade across his throat. And even if you do, there's a very good chance I'll pull it as a reflex. Either way, he's fu—'

The bullet from Lyndsey's gun hit Burkhan in the shoulder, smashing into the bone and jerking Burkhan's arm and the scalpel away from Clocks's throat. That little gap in time and space was all she needed. A double-tap to his body and Burkhan died before he hit the ground.

She and Paterson ran to Clocks.

'Shit!' Paterson peered at the wound in Clocks's side. 'This is deep. He needs a hospital. Now!' He spun the trolley around and headed for the doors. 'Lynds! Get some compression bandages for him. Catch me up!'

He rammed Clocks through the doors and ran along the corridor, the trolley's wheels wobbling uncontrollably as it went. When he got to the lift, Lyndsey caught up with him. She tore open a pack of bandages and pressed them onto Clocks's wound.

Kulminder's squad followed them down into the lobby. One of them was on the radio demanding that an ambulance meet them.

The lift doors burst open and Paterson pushed his friend out into the lobby, past reception and out into the night air. He stopped by the armoured vehicle.

'How long before the ambulance gets here?' he demanded of an officer.

'Five minutes, sir.'

'Good. Stay with him. Lynds . . . keep the pressure on. I won't be long.'

'Where are you going, Ray?'

'To cause a problem!' he called back.

CHAPTER FIFTY

Paterson strode back into the reception area and made a bee-line for the fire alarm on the wall. He punched it, shattering the glass and setting it off. A piercing wail screamed through the corridors and offices of the clinic. He turned to the receptionist he'd put on the ground earlier. The man, being watched over by one of Kulminder's men, looked terrified as Paterson came straight toward him. He cowered as Paterson rounded the desk for a second time that day.

'Please, sir. Please. I know nothing.'

'How many people in this building?'

'Please . . .'

Paterson grabbed him by the jaw and forced him back into the wall. 'How fucking many?'

'Five patients and . . . about ten doctors. Maybe fifteen nurses. A few other staff. Not many.'

'Where is the owner? The woman. Tell me now or I swear I'll take your fucking head off its shoulders.' He jammed the gun into the man's cheek, digging it into his flesh.

'I . . . d . . . d . . . don't . . . know. I swear. I don't know.' His eyes filled with tears. Paterson believed him.

Over the wailing of the fire alarm, raised voices could be heard as staff in the hospital began a panicked evacuation, running for the exits. Some were pushing trolleys with patients on, some were pushing wheelchairs and some were just saving their own skins.

Paterson turned back to the receptionist. 'Now, I need two things from you . . . First, addresses of all of the clinics owned by the woman. Understand?'

'Yes. Yes. Of course.'

'Next . . . do you smoke?'

'W-what?'

'Do you smoke? Simple question.'

'Y-yes.'

'A lighter. You got one?'

'What?'

'A lighter. I want a fucking lighter.'

'Under the counter.' The man nodded toward the desk. 'In that brown box.'

Paterson pulled out the lighter. 'Get me that list by the time I get back. Understand?'

The receptionist nodded.

'Officer!' Paterson called back. 'Arrest him for me.'

He walked over to the lift and got in.

Getting out on the third floor, he made his way to the furthest ward. Entering, he walked to the back of the ward, turned and with a couple of clicks of the lighter, set fire to the bed nearest to him. He systematically set each bed on fire as he made his way out. He smashed bottles of any flammable-looking liquid he came across to help with the process. He set fire to chairs in offices and curtains at windows. He set fire to waste bins. Anything that would burn, he burned. Without turning to see what he'd done, he made his way to the next ward and did the same. Doctors and nurses were too busy fleeing to take any notice of him.

At the third ward he came to, he noticed that a couple of orderlies were frantically trying to move patients.

'Step it up, boys!' he shouted to them. 'This whole fucking building is going up.'

He made his way down, floor by floor, making sure each one was burning properly until he reached the ground floor. The receptionist looked terrified as Paterson strode toward him.

Paterson thrust out his hand. 'List.'

The man handed over a hastily scribbled note.

Paterson walked out into the hot midday air just as several windows blew out and equipment exploded. A busy day ahead.

'Jesus, Ray. Did you set fire to the place?' Lyndsey asked as glass rained down and thick black smoke poured out of the windows.

'Yep.' Paterson looked over her shoulder and watched Clocks being lifted into the back of an ambulance. 'How bad is he?'

'Nowhere near as bad as it looked, thank God. We got to him in time. A paramedic here said that the wound is reasonably deep but hasn't hit anything vital. Maybe a dozen stitches, painkillers and some heavy antibiotics and he'll be up and running. They'll keep him in overnight for some rest and make sure the effects of the anaesthetic wear off.'

'Good. Stay with him and keep me posted.'

'What are you going to do?'

He grinned. 'I've got a list of the other clinics she owns and I'm gonna fuck up each and every one of them.'

'Jesus, Ray . . . that's crazy.'

He cocked his head sideways slightly. 'Is it? Seems reasonable to me. Besides, you'll know I'll get bored sitting around in a hospital. Might as well use the time productively and piss this bitch off a treat.'

'Miss!' an ambulance man called. 'We have to go, please.'

Lyndsey waved to him. 'One second!' She turned back to Paterson. 'Be careful, Ray.'

'I always am. You know me.'

'She'll come after you now and she won't stop.'

Paterson kissed her lightly on the cheek.

'Fingers crossed.'

CHAPTER FIFTY-ONE

DAY 6

Paterson was taking breakfast in his hotel room while watching the BBC World News. An aerial shot of a burning building filled the screen and the ribbon at the bottom of the shot said that at least seven other similar buildings had been set on fire.

He grinned as he bit into his toast. The press never got anything right, he mused. It was three, not seven — plus the one where he'd saved Clocks, so four in total. Not a bad day's work by anyone's standard.

He glanced at his watch: 8 a.m. Clocks had called him at seven to tell him he was fine — in a bit of pain, but well enough to work. Paterson knew he would be. Clocks was not one to miss a fight if one was going, and things were shaping up to be a bit tasty.

He turned his attention back to the TV. He'd sent a clear message to Alicia Warren. A message that said they were coming for her and they were coming hard and fast. She would go one of two ways: stand her ground or run. His money was on running. People like Alicia Warren weren't stupid. She'd want to live to fight another day and she'd want the odds in her favour.

But he had a plan. He'd already spoken to Lyndsey and told her what he wanted her and Wol to do. There was a knock on the door. Paterson carefully checked the spyhole and opened the door.

'Morning, John. How are you?' He hugged his friend in the doorway.

'What? 'Ow am I? Oh, yeah. Mustn't grumble. Apart from the fuckin' pain, I'm as good as gold. Now fuck off with the cuddlin' malarkey, you big drip.'

Paterson stepped back.

'I've got an eight-inch gash in me side where the fucker wanted to whip some bit or other out and a dozen or so internal stitches 'olding me guts in.'

Paterson rolled his eyes. '*Holding your guts in.* You're fine.'

'Says you. Ooh. Is that toast? I love a bit of toast.'

'You on any medication?'

'Yep. Painkillers. Mumbai's answer to paracetamol. Shit stuff.'

'Can you eat or drink?'

'Yeah, course I can. I'm not fuckin' disabled.'

'I meant, are you allowed to.'

'I know what you meant. I'm fine. Besides, I'm only after a bit of toast. That won't kill me, will it?'

Paterson shrugged. 'It could. Could get stuck in your throat. Would be funny if it did. I can see the headlines now. Top 'tec killed by slice of toast.'

'Take more than a bit of hard bread an' butter to do me in, son.'

'Help yourself. It's a bit cold now.'

Clocks picked up two semi-warm bits of toast and buttered them thickly. 'Got any jam?'

'No. Marmite if you want it.'

'Fuck that. I'd rather eat me own scrotum than touch that shit. Probably taste better.'

'I dunno.' Paterson buttoned up a crisp, white short-sleeved shirt. 'The way you sweat, I should think it tastes just as salty.'

Clocks chuckled. 'So what's the plan? You found out where this Warren bitch is?'

'Not yet. Working on it, though.'

'So, 'ow's that comin' along, then?'

'We're going back to see Commissioner Devi. Rattle his cage something chronic.'

'Yeah?' Clocks bit into his second slice.

Paterson nodded. 'When you were taken at the hotel last night, was Lee Burkhan with them?'

'Yeah. The fucker was in the van, waiting. He 'ad the raging arseache when they bundled me into the van.'

'Why?'

'They were comin' fer you.'

'For me?'

'Yep. The blokes that took me asked me if I was you and I said yes. Well, I didn't say yes, but I didn't deny it.'

'You silly bastard. Why didn't you tell them you weren't me?'

'Figured they'd take me anyway and then go looking for you. Once I was in the van, Burkhan realised it was me and threw a wobbler. Too late by then, of course. So, it was me or nothing.'

'What was it he wanted me for?'

'From what I can make of it, a couple of things. First off, you're reasonably young and fit. Good giblets. Second, Alicia Warren wanted us off her back. Getting rid of you and then presumably me was her plan. She's got the 'ump with the pair of us for some reason.'

'She'll be more upset this morning.' Paterson nodded at the TV.

Clocks watched for a moment. 'That down to you?'

'Yep.'

'Fuckin' 'ell! You torched eight of 'er buildin's?'

'Four. You know how the press exaggerate. Apart from the one you were in, they were empty, still being built. They went up a treat.'

'Nice as you like. Good on yer, yer ravin' psychopath. I'm proud of yer.'

'I prefer the term "high-functioning sociopath", John. Much closer to the truth these days.'

CHAPTER FIFTY-TWO

As he climbed the steps to the police headquarters, Paterson wondered if he and Clocks would have to fight their way in to see Commissioner Devi this time. He ran over the layout of the station in his mind, trying to recall, as best he could, where Devi's office was in relation to the front desk.

The immediate plan was to speak to the desk officer and ask to be let through on the basis of some made-up, hush-hush meeting they had arranged together, and if that didn't work, leap over the front counter and force their way through.

'You sure about this, Ray?' said Clocks. 'Only I reckon half the Indian police force is looking for you now that you've set light to 'alf of Bangladesh.'

'We're in Mumbai, Clocksy.'

'Yeah, whatever. Same thing, innit?'

'Not really, no. Bangladesh is about—'

'Yeah. Don't care. All I care about is us not gettin' our collars felt once we stroll in large as life.'

'Don't worry about it. I've made provisions.'

'Provisions? You mean you've made us a packed lunch? I didn't think we'd be 'ere *that* long.'

'Plans, you idiot. Plans.'

'It was a joke. I know you've made plans. But it all 'inges on us gettin' past the bloke on the front desk, don't it?'

Paterson opened the door to the station. 'Stop worrying. We'll get in. Trust me.'

Clocks shook his head as he watched Paterson walk into the foyer.

Paterson put the man behind the desk in his mid-to-late thirties. He was a big lad who looked like he could handle himself if things went sideways, but by the time Paterson stood in front of him he'd already worked out at least four ways he could incapacitate him if the need arose. There were only two other policemen in the room as far as he could tell and he didn't anticipate them being much of a problem.

'Morning,' he said. 'We're here to see Commissioner Devi. He's expecting us.'

The big man eyed Paterson up for a couple of seconds. 'Who shall I say it is?'

'Oh, it's okay. He knows who we are. We're from London. If you can just let us in, we'll make our way to his office. We know where it is.' He showed him his warrant card.

'From London?'

'Yep. That's us. Where it always rains.' Paterson beamed him a big smile. It failed.

The man's eyes shifted from one of them to the other. Clocks threw him an awkward smile and gave a curt nod of the head.

'Please,' said the big man. 'Come through.' He jumped off the stool he was sitting on, raised the wooden flap on the desk and beckoned to them.

'Nice one, squire,' said Clocks as the big man dropped the flap back down.

'I will tell the commissioner that you are on your way.'

'No need, fellah,' said Paterson. 'As I said earlier, he is expecting us.'

They headed toward Devi's office, smiling politely at people they passed in the corridor.

'Evidently, that big fucker ain't watched the telly this mornin', 'as 'e?'

Paterson grinned. 'Even if he has, there's been no mention of any suspects as yet, and I'm guessing Devi hasn't put me up as a suspect for the fires. At least, not yet.'

As they rounded a corner, a police officer in front of them stopped in his tracks and reached for his sidearm. Paterson was already moving. With his right hand he punched the man in the shoulder, separating the joints. The man yelled in pain but Clocks headbutted him in the face, knocking him spark out.

'Fuck!' said Clocks as he rubbed his forehead. 'I shoulda just punched 'im out.'

'Why didn't you?' said Paterson without breaking his stride.

'Force of 'abit. Been doin' it since I was a kid. Seems natural. Fuckin' 'urts though. Geezer's nut was like a lump of concrete. Wonder why 'e went for 'is gun?'

'I dunno. Perhaps my picture is all over the telly by now. Who knows? Are you alright? The wound?'

'Wound? I've 'ad worse than that shavin', mate. Don't you be worryin' about me.'

The policeman's yell hadn't gone unnoticed. A door opened and a man poked his head out, straight onto Paterson's elbow. Expecting trouble from within the office, Paterson darted inside. It was empty.

'The gods seem to be with us, John. Drag the other one in here.'

Still rubbing his reddening forehead, Clocks did as he was asked. Once both men were inside, Paterson took the key out of the door and locked it from the outside. It wouldn't hold them for long, but both men were out like a light. He didn't expect them to wake up anytime soon.

Paterson pulled out his phone and pressed a button. 'Right. Texts sent.'

Clocks gave him a knowing nod. 'Okay then. 'Ere we jolly well go.'

Paterson tapped gently on Commissioner Devi's door.

'Come,' said the voice from inside.

'Good morning,' said Paterson as he strolled in. Commissioner Devi's eyes widened.

'Alright 'op-along, me ol' cocker?' said Clocks with a big wave. 'Bet you weren't expectin' to see us, were yer?'

'What . . . what are you doing here?'

'We've come to see you,' said Paterson. 'Thought we could have another chat. If you're not too busy, that is?' Paterson pulled up a chair and sat himself down. Clocks stood by the door, his hands held in front of him, doing his best to look like a bouncer.

'What do you want?' said Devi.

'All in good time,' said Paterson.

'These clinics. These fires. This is you, right?'

'Correct. Impressed?'

'You bastard! I am going to have you arrested for this. You will rot in prison here. You have no idea what you've done. You are a fool. She will kill you. She will have you both torn to pieces for this.'

'Do I look bothered? Clocksy, do I look bothered to you, mate?'

'I'm goin' with nah. What about me? Do I look bovvered?'

Paterson turned around. 'Nope. You never look bothered.' He turned back to face Devi. 'There you go, commissioner. Seems we're not bothered. Tell you what. Why don't you come and arrest us yourself? Not got the balls for it?'

'Fuckin' 'ell, Ray. We'll be 'ere all day while he drills 'imself into the carpet!'

Paterson laughed.

'Do us a favour, Devi, me ol'mate,' said Clocks. 'Go an' get us a cuppa tea?'

'*Tea?*' said Paterson. 'This isn't the time for tea.'

'Yeah, I know that. I just wanted to see if 'e could bring it in without spillin' any.' He mimicked Devi's limp.

'She will have us all killed, you fools.'

'Yeah, you said.'

'What do you want? What do you want?'

'For you to tell us where Alicia Warren is.' Paterson crossed his legs and picked at a bit of lint on his trousers.

'I do not know. Now, get out of my office. Get out!'

'Not happening until you tell me what I want to know. So, rather than waste too much of my time, best you get on with it.'

Commissioner Devi snorted. 'Who is it that you think you are? You cannot come into my country and set fire to our buildings. You cannot come into my police station and start bossing me around. You cannot talk to me like this. I run this district. I am your superior officer even if you are not in your bloody England.'

Clocks bristled. 'You ain't superior to anyone, mate. You might 'old a senior rank but that don't make you superior in any way shape or form. Besides, do we look like we give a fuck about rank?'

Devi's face flushed and he balled his fists.

'Oh. Look out, guv. 'Op-along 'ere's gone an' got the 'ump with us. Run away!'

'No more. No more. I will not have this. You will not disrespect me in this way, you bastards. I will have you arrested. Now!' He reached for the phone on his desk.

A small *pock* noise announced the arrival of a bullet as it punched a small hole in the window behind Devi. He recoiled in terror as the bullet bit into the desk an inch or so from his hand.

'Oh, dear, oh dear,' said Clocks. 'Who the bleedin' 'ell did that, I wonder? That's criminal damage where we come from. A crime.'

Devi spun around to look at the window. 'What . . . ?'

Paterson smirked. 'Oops.'

'You bastards!' Devi's nose flared and he flashed a set of yellowing teeth that showed years of neglect. 'I will have you killed for this!'

'Seems everyone's going to be killing us. Unlikely though.' Paterson raised the index finger of his right hand.

Another gentle *pock* sound. Another bullet dug into Devi's desk.

Clocks ambled over to the window. 'I wonder who keeps doing that? I think you've got a sniper out there somewhere. That's two 'oles in your window now. You got any good glaziers in this neck of the woods?'

'Before we came into your office, I sent two texts that set out your *very* limited options,' said Paterson. 'The first sees your head exploding across this office of yours. The second sees you getting arrested.'

'Lemme know if you're goin' for the first option Devi, me ol' son,' said Clocks. 'If you do, I need to get out of the way. I really don't need all your snot 'n' gore over me clothes. I can't tell yer 'ow many of me suits 'ave been fucked since I started workin' with 'im.' He aimed a thumb at his partner.

Paterson smiled. 'So, the first option is what happens if you decide to be big and brave and refuse to tell us where Warren is. The second option is what happens if you decide dying isn't for you. In the end, the only difference is in the outcome for you. Hole in the head or prison. Make your choice.'

Clocks looked at his watch. 'You've got ten seconds. I'm startin' Mr Clocks's naughty clock now, Devi. You ready. And . . . go!'

Devi's arrogance gave up on him. 'Alright! Alright! I will tell you. Please don't kill me. Please.'

'That's up to you. Where is Warren?'

Devi took a deep breath. 'France. She has gone back to France.'

'Whereabouts in France?' said Paterson. 'It's a fair old size,' said Paterson.

'Paris. She has an office there.'

'Give me the address.'

Devi shook his head. 'She will kill me if I do that.'

'Have you forgotten about the bullets in your desk already?'

'You are a bastard!'

'I know. But if you keep calling me that, I'm going to get upset and probably have you killed anyway.'

'Yeah,' said Clocks. 'Don't do that, 'op-along. He's a very sensitive man.'

'I am,' said Paterson, frowning.

Devi opened the drawer, pulled out a piece of paper and wrote down the address.

Paterson stood up, took out his mobile phone and pressed another button. Devi frowned at him.

'Well, it's been a pleasure talking to you, but we have to go now,' said Paterson.

Clocks opened the door and Kulminder Singh walked in, followed by three armed police officers. The two men glared at each other across the room.

'I will get my coat.' Devi limped over to the coat stand and took down his jacket. He pulled out a gun from inside it and swung it toward Kulminder a second before a bullet punched its way through his leg, dropping him to the floor in screams of agony.

'I'm guessin' the ol' White Ghost weren't 'avin' none of that ol' bobbin' up 'n' down malarkey,' said Clocks.

Paterson looked out of the window and waved. 'I guess not.' He headed for the door.

Kulminder stopped him. 'Thank you for this, Mr Paterson. Thank you. You will both be safe in my country now, and I will have you escorted to the airports. Where will you be going next? Home?'

'No. Paris. Me and him have a date with the same woman.'

Clocks stepped over a crying Commissioner Devi. 'I 'ope it's that bird you were gonna shag before we came 'ere. She was a *right* ol' sort.'

CHAPTER FIFTY-THREE

DAY 7

Capitaine Vivienne Laurent stood beneath an umbrella in an attempt to keep herself dry from the small monsoon that had suddenly broken out. She didn't look particularly happy as they stepped off the private plane Paterson had chartered. It may have been a result of the rain, but Paterson figured it could just as likely have been because he left without saying goodbye.

'*Bonjour*, Mr Paterson. How lovely of you to come back to France.' Her tone was just the right side of sarcastic with a touch of ice.

Paterson inched under her umbrella and beamed her a smile. '*Bonjour*, Capitaine. Thank you for meeting with us. Much appreciated.'

'Come. We will go back to the station and you can fill me in on the details as we ride.'

Clocks pulled up the collar of his jacket and watched as Paterson wheedled his way under the umbrella to some small measure of protection from the rain. He shook his head. 'Alright, love? Just thought I'd let you know that I'm back 'ere too, just in case you 'adn't noticed.'

'Ah, Johnny Clocks. Yes, I see you. You can ride with Pierre.'

'Why can't I ride with you this time?'

'I don't like you.'

'Oh, I see. You're still 'oping Ray 'ere is gonna give you a seein' to, aint'cha? An' you don't want me cramping yer style.'

Laurent stared at him. 'What did you say, you filthy pig?'

'Oi! 'old up a bit, love. That's a bit strong. No need fer that, was there?'

Paterson could see from the look on Clocks's face that he was genuinely insulted. He also knew he wouldn't let this go. 'John . . . don't, mate. It's not worth it.'

'Not worth it? I ain't lettin' some frog call me a pig. Out of order.'

'But you can call me a frog?' said Laurent.

'Yeah, why not? Everyone in the world calls you frogs. It's a term of endearment. The world loves you lot with yer crackin' sense of fashion and yer tiny food, yer piss-poor sense of humour an' yer fuckin' uppity attitude.'

'John, please . . .' said Paterson. 'Just get in with Pierre. For me.'

Clocks scowled at Laurent. 'Oh, alright. Because it's you,' he said, in a mocking tone. He looked across at Pierre, another big man, at least six foot six. He had arms like tree trunks and his soaking wet shirt showed off every toned muscle in his upper body.

'Alright, mate?' said Clocks. ''Ow's it 'angin', then?'

Pierre glared at him. 'It is good, my little friend. Does your one hang?'

Clocks looked down. 'I'm in me forties. Everythin' 'angs now, mate. Word of advice . . . Don't get too comfortable with looking like a Greek god, me ol' son. Gravity'll get yer one day. It starts with a beer belly then before you know it, bosh! You're a fat ol' fucker.'

Pierre snorted and opened the door for him. 'Like you?'

'Oi. Cheeky monkey. I'm not fat, mate. I've 'ad a rough coupla days, so I thought I'd give me stomach muscles a bit of time off for good behaviour.'

'How long have they been off now? It looks like a few years to me.'

Clocks gave him a little grin. Game on.

'Mate. That's a bit 'urtful. I'm tryin' to 'ave a conversation with yer and yer bein' rude. I know you can't 'elp bein' rude because you're French an' everythin' but that's exactly why nobody likes yer. None of yer. All up yerselves thinkin' yer summin' special when you're not. Oh . . . just in case yer didn't pick up on it back there, I was windin' yer guv'nor up about the world lovin' all of yer.'

As Clocks stepped into the car, Pierre closed the door, catching him on the shoulder. He yelped in pain as it struck bone. 'Mmmmotherfuuuucker!' He shot daggers at Pierre and leaped back out of the car.

'I am sorry. Did I hurt you?' Pierre's smirk sent Clocks through the roof.

'Fuckin' 'urt me? Nah. You couldn't 'urt me if you tried, son. You fucked me off though.'

Paterson saw that Clocks was getting ready to lay into the Frenchman. 'John!' he shouted.

Clocks ignored him as he squared up to the bigger man.

Pierre looked at him. 'I said that I was sorry. Get into the car, my little friend.'

'Don't fuckin' tell me what to do, yer big prick! Why'd you slam the door on me? What was the point of that?'

Pierre shrugged. There were a lot of things that aggravated Johnny Clocks. Chief among them were arrogance and indifference. Pierre was demonstrating both.

'John!' Paterson headed toward the two men. 'What's the matter?'

'Nothin'. Me an' Kermit 'ere are just 'avin' a little discussion on manners. Nothin' fer you to worry about.'

Pierre bristled. 'What did you call me?'

'You deaf as well as French? I called you Kermit. As in Kermit the Frog.'

Pierre grabbed Clocks by the lapels of his jacket and pushed him back against the car's door frame.

'Pierre!' Capitaine Laurent ran toward them. 'Stop it!'

Clocks landed a right-hander square on the Frenchman's jaw, causing the big man more anger than pain.

By the time Paterson got to them, Pierre had Clocks's lapels clenched in one fist and was drawing back the other.

Paterson grabbed hold of it. 'Enough! Pack it in!'

Laurent pushed her way between the two men. 'What the hell! You two are grown men. Police officers. You are acting like schoolboys.'

'Sorry, miss.' Clocks glared at Pierre.

She yanked them apart. 'That's enough! Both of you!'

'C'mon, John. You ride with us,' said Paterson.

'What?'

'With us. You can't behave yourself, can you? So, with us.'

'Fuckin' 'ell, Ray. I found the only Frenchman with the balls to fight an' you wanna split us up.'

'What did you say?' Capitaine Laurent rounded on him.

'Nothin'.'

Laurent was bristling. 'Yes, you did. You said that the French were cowards.'

'No, I didn't,' said Clocks. 'I *insinuated* the French were cowards. I refer you to Exhibit One, your honour: World War Two.'

'Fuck's sake, John. Give it a rest.' Paterson pulled him away from Pierre, who was still doing his best to intimidate Clocks by standing far too close to him.

'What? Truth's truth, mate.'

'Why do you English always go on about the war?' said Laurent.

'Because you lot weren't in it,' said Clocks.

Pierre pulled himself up to his full height. There was a mix of anger and hatred in his eyes for this annoying little man.

'Of course we were in it!' Laurent retorted.

'Yeah, but not for long, were yer? You all gave it a swerve as soon as Adolf and 'is firm came gallopin' over the 'orizon. *Ooh. Look at the time, lads. It's surrender o'clock.*'

Paterson pulled Clocks further away from the two French officers. Pierre was a danger all on his own, but right now his money was on Laurent belting Clocks in the mouth.

'I'm sorry, Capitaine,' he said. 'John can be both stupid and ignorant of the facts sometimes. He is what we call a "fuckwit". In his defence, his mother shut his head in the door when he was child.'

Clocks smiled. 'That she did. She was teachin' me the importance of takin' yer lumps like a man.'

Pierre lurched forward. Paterson dragged Clocks away and out of a situation that was rapidly descending into chaos. He pushed him toward Laurent's car and bundled him into the back seat.

The driver turned to look at him. 'You stupid English fool.'

Clocks settled himself into the seat and pulled the seat belt across him.

'Oh, look out, Ray. Kermit's little racist sister wants to 'ave a pop at me as well.'

CHAPTER FIFTY-FOUR

The evening sky had turned the colour of a blood orange as the vehicle containing Paterson, Clocks and Laurent pulled up at the end of one of the fanciest streets in Paris. All of the mansions were hidden behind fancy topiary and large gates, ensuring the residents the privacy they craved. Within hours of Paterson and Clocks's arrival, Laurent had received solid information that Alicia Warren had bypassed her offices in the centre of Paris and gone straight to the home of a powerful man for protection.

Behind them was a line of six police vans containing officers from the National Gendarmerie Intervention Group, the French equivalent of the Met's elite firearms unit, SCO19.

Footballers, politicians, popstars and criminals lived in peace behind the gates. Someone once joked that it was easy to tell the footballers' houses by the amount of Ferraris on the drive, the politicians by the amount of sex workers turning up at the gates, the popstars by the thumping party music coming from inside and the criminals by the number of alligators in the pool. Right now, sitting outside the home of Jacques Augustin, France's most feared criminal, Paterson figured that whoever said that had probably been right.

From his position, he could see that the property was heavily guarded. All were as tall as Clocks's sparring partner, Pierre, and as wide as Schwarzenegger in his glory days. Given the warmth of the evening, he almost felt sorry for them having to wear suits.

Paterson guessed there would be more inside. This wasn't going to be an easy hit. Laurent had warned him that Augustin would do everything he could to resist entry to his property, but even she looked shocked at the amount of men in sunglasses wandering around.

'Tell me more about this Augustin,' said Paterson.

'He is a vicious man. A psychopath. He controls many criminal enterprises in and around Paris.'

'Like what?'

'Prostitution, gambling, nightclubs . . .'

'Drugs?'

'Especially drugs.'

Paterson nodded slowly. 'Carfentanil?'

She shrugged. 'What is that?'

'I'll explain it to you later. Trust me when I say it's the bastard drug of all bastard drugs and, if I'm right, I think France is about to be the epicentre of a new wave of death that'll spread across Europe and then out across the globe.'

The car fell silent.

Paterson broke his own reverie. 'So, what's the plan?'

'I'm waiting to hear from Capitaine Babineaux.' Laurent tapped her radio. 'He will give us instructions.'

'Will 'e be long?' said Clocks. 'Only I'm bustin' for a wee. Me back teeth are floatin'.'

Laurent leaned forward slightly. 'Are you joking?'

'Nope. Shouldn't 'ave 'ad that last glass of snail wine or whatever it was on the plane.'

'Well, you will have to hold it like a big boy.'

Clocks pulled at his crotch. 'You'd think I could, wouldn't you? But I can't.'

'Tie a knot in it, Clocks.'

Clocks raised his eyebrows. 'I'm flattered you think it's big enough fer me *to* tie a knot in it, love, but if I don't go, I'll piss meself an' I ain't givin' you lot the satisfaction. Ta-ta.' He wrenched the door open and jumped out of the car.

'What is the matter with that man?' Laurent said to Paterson.

Paterson turned to look at her. 'Clocksy? Not a thing, love. He's as good as gold. Lairy. Fiery. A little bit ignorant in his world view and definitely old-school, but you'd be hard pressed to find anyone as solid as him.'

She chortled. 'I think he is an idiot.'

'Think what you like. I don't give a fuck.'

Laurent glared at him. 'Excuse me? How dare y—'

Capitaine Babineaux pushed his head through the open window of the car. 'Capitaine. Listen carefully. I shall say this only once. Our plan is simple. We will go through the gates without stopping. Once inside the property, we will deal with whatever is in there. Three of our vehicles will deploy and deal with the men outside. Once they are under control, we will enter the house. You will come behind us and take control of the prisoners. Is that clear?'

'Yes,' she said.

'Good. Follow us into the grounds after the last of my vehicles has entered. Is that also clear?'

'Yes, Capitaine Babineaux.'

'And, your Englishman . . . he was last seen running across the road to some bushes. We cannot wait for him.'

'Good,' said Laurent. 'We go when you go.'

Capitaine Babineaux walked back to his vehicle, a large armoured carrier. Laurent turned on the ignition and looked over her shoulder. Paterson yanked on the handbrake as she inched forward.

'What the hell are you doing?'

'We're not going anywhere until Clocksy gets back.'

Capitaine Laurent glared at him. 'Take your hand off the brake. You will do as we have been instructed.'

Paterson sniffed. 'Nope.'

'Paterson. You will go. I am in command here.'

He smirked. 'And yet, we're not going anywhere, are we?'

The first of the carriers passed them.

'Paterson! Let go! We have to go. Now!'

'When Clocksy gets back.'

The last carrier passed them.

'*Merde!*'

'I'm sure they can do without us for a minute longer. They all look a bit rufty-tufty.' Paterson looked out of the back window and saw Johnny Clocks running full pelt toward them. 'Actually, less than a minute.'

Clocks wrenched open the back door and threw himself across the back seat. 'Fuck me, Ray. They started a bit earlier than I thought. I pissed over two of me fingers in all the excitement.'

Laurent looked over her shoulder and wrinkled her nose at him.

'What? It's a drop of piss. Won't 'urt yer. 'Ave a little whiff.' He started to raise his arm.

'Fuck off, you filthy animal!' She stamped on the accelerator and shot off to catch the convoy. The lurch forward pinned Clocks back in his seat.

'What now?' said Clocks. 'Christ. A drop of the ol' yeller juice won't do you any 'arm. I mean, you lot still piss in an 'ole in the pavement, don't yer? So, you've probably pissed over yourself once or twice. Back of the legs an' all that. Must 'ave done.'

'Shut up! You are a filthy, vile, disgusting man!'

'Alright, love. Don't milk it. Any one of them would've done.'

'You ready, Clocksy?' said Paterson.

'Born ready, mate. Time for fisticuffs again, then?'

As the carriers smashed through the gates, the security guards panicked and pulled out their guns. Two of the guards opened up with a volley of shots as carriers two and three screeched to a halt.

Capitaine Babineaux drove straight at two men who were firing and too slow to move. The vehicle crashed into both men with a sickening thump, jumping slightly as it drove over their broken bodies. He slewed the van to a halt and debussed at the same time as his officers. Weapons drawn, they began returning fire at the remaining guards.

Carriers two and three slid in either side of Babineaux and their officers joined in the gunfight. Carrier four drove around the perimeter looking for strays.

Capitaine Laurent skidded, showering one security guard with gravel. The moment the car stopped, Paterson and Clocks were out, running toward the fight.

'Wait! Come back. It is not safe!' Laurent was in a sweat, her voice urgent. 'Come back. Fuck! Fuck! Fuck!' She drew her gun and threw it on the dashboard.

Paterson came up on his man. Intent on shooting the uniformed police, the guard never saw the neatly dressed policeman running at him, but he felt the powerful kick in the ribs that took him off his feet and sent him careening across the gravel. The guard, gun in hand, scrabbled to get to his feet. Paterson kicked him under the chin and snapped his head back, knocking him unconscious. Paterson turned.

Clocks was rolling around on the floor with a guard, and from where Paterson was standing it looked like he could use a hand. Even if he didn't want it, Paterson was going to give it.

Clocks, flat on his back, held his arms up across his face as the guard rained punches onto him. Paterson broke into a run. As he did, he heard a sharp crack. A bullet missed him by inches and tore a hole in his jacket as it flapped in the wind. He turned to see where the shot had come from — to his right. A guard had the drop on him. He stopped, hands held wide.

The guard moved forward then swivelled his hips and opened fire again as Capitaine Laurent sped toward him. The car hit him with such force that he was thrown backward a good twenty feet. Laurent slammed on the brakes and skidded to a halt.

Paterson could see she was bleeding from the face. Two of the guard's bullets had hit the windscreen. One had found its mark.

'Shit!' said Paterson. Forgetting about Clocks, he wrenched the car door open. 'Vivienne! Are you okay?'

Capitaine Laurent looked at him with glazed eyes. 'Yes. Yes, I think so. Yes.'

Paterson took it all in: fright, shock, a wound where the bullet had grazed her cheekbone. 'Lie down,' he said. 'I'll get help.'

He turned. The scene was carnage. At least four police were down and twice that amount of security. Clocks had let his man punch himself out and had now managed to get the better of him. He was busy kicking him in the ribs while verbally abusing the man's parentage and heritage.

'You finished, Clocksy?' Paterson said.

Clocks carried on kicking. 'Not yet,' he grunted.

'I think he's had enough.'

'Reckon?'

'I reckon.'

'Okay.' Clocks stopped kicking. 'How'd you like that, motherfucker? Eh? You've just met the Millwall Bushwackers, you knob!'

'Millwall Bushwackers?' said Paterson.

'Yep. Formerly known as F Troop.'

'Why the change of name?'

'People thought it sounded a bit violent.'

'And Bushwackers doesn't?'

'You know how it is.'

Paterson ignored him. 'Hey!' he shouted to Babineaux. 'Need some help here.'

'Do we?' said Clocks. 'Why?'

'Not us, you div. Capitaine Laurent has been shot.'

'Shit! Is it bad?'

Paterson shook his head. 'Nasty, but not fatal. Caught her on the cheekbone by the look of it. She's in shock.'

'Not surprised.'

'Me neither. Doubt she's been shot at before. At least not by a professional, anyway. More used to junkies and the like, I would think.'

'What 'appened to the bloke who shot at 'er?'

'Slumped up against the wall over there. She drove straight at him. Pretty sure she killed him.'

Clocks looked over Paterson's shoulder to where the man lay. 'Ooh. Good girl.'

Capitaine Babineaux joined them. Paterson quickly filled him in and told him to give medical aid to Laurent. He walked toward the building. Paterson could see the doors had been broken wide open and heard the sounds of tramping boots and loud shouts as the armed police officers searched the ground floor.

'Wait! Where are you two going?' said Babineaux.

'Us?' said Clocks. 'We're off to see the Wizard, Tin Man. Coming?'

'My officers are already inside, searching. Wait until they have secured the house.'

'Nah. Not doin' that, cockle. Gotta go find our lady and give 'er a piece of our mind before she legs it again. It's a bit overdue an' she's a slippery cow.'

Capitaine Babineaux eyed up the two men. 'I can see you are men of determination. Spirit.'

'And violence.' Clocks grinned at Babineaux.

'Do you have any weapons? Any identity on you?'

'There's a shitload of guns lying around on the ground,' said Paterson. 'And we'll wear our ID badges around our necks. Perhaps you could have a word on the radio and ask your men not to shoot the two very nice Englishmen who are about to enter.'

'I will ask them, but . . .' Babineaux shrugged. 'You know how it is — Frenchmen, Englishmen. Old rivalries.'

Paterson smiled. He knew the Capitaine was joking. Clocks didn't.

'Fair enough,' he said. 'Just let 'em know we bite back, fellah.' He crouched down to one of the dead security guards and relieved him of his pistol. He checked the clip for ammo before jamming it back into the gun. He spotted a wounded police officer and wandered over to him.

'Alright, son. Looks nasty, that. Bullet in the leg. That's your runnin' away days over.'

The policeman groaned and pressed on the bandage he had used to stem the bleeding.

'Seein' as 'ow you're out of the fight, I'm gonna borrow your machine gun 'ere an' go an' see if I can't avenge you an yer mates. Alright?'

'Capitaine?' the man groaned.

'It's okay, Jean. Let him take it.'

'Cheers, mate.' Clocks took the gun and looked around to see Paterson standing in the hallway. 'Oi, oi! Which gun you want, Ray? The big'un or the little'un?'

'Big'un for me, please.'

'Is that to make up for 'avin' a small knob?'

Paterson shook his head. 'Look . . . For the last time, I haven't got a small knob.'

'No?'

'No.'

'Big car. Big 'ouse. Big wallet. Now you want a big gun. Somethin's not right, is it?'

'Just give me a bloody gun. Either one. I don't fucking care anymore.'

'Cool. You 'ave the little'un, then. I wanted the big one all along.'

'Who knew?'

'We both did. C'mon. Let's go an' see who we can annoy.'

CHAPTER FIFTY-FIVE

Paterson and Clocks headed up the spiral staircase that sat in the middle of the hallway. Clocks held the machine gun close to his cheek, waving it from side to side.

'What are you doing?' said Paterson.

'What?'

'What are you doing?'

'What d'you mean, what am I doin'? I'm wavin' me gun around like they do on the telly.'

'Does it help?'

'It 'elps me. Makes me feel like I know what I'm doin'.'

'Then carry on.'

'I will. Thank you very much.'

Clocks reached the top of the stairs first. He crouched low and looked to his right, then to his left. There were several rooms in both directions.

'Which way d'you think we should go, Ray?'

'Left.'

Clocks stood up, tucked the gun into his chest and turned right. Paterson shook his head and sighed.

Ahead of them were three rooms: one to the right, two to the left. The furthest door on the left was half open. Clocks stopped and held his fist up.

'What're you doing, now?' Paterson whispered.

'Stopping. This is the sign to stop.'

'I know. But you don't have to do that. Just stop.'

'I 'ave. Obviously puttin' me 'and up works.'

Paterson wrinkled his brow. 'No. No. It's not bloody magic, John. It doesn't stop *you*. It's meant to stop the blokes behind you.'

'You've stopped too, ain'tcha?'

'Well . . . yes, but—'

'Then it's worked.'

Paterson nodded. 'Okay. It's worked. What you got?'

'Door up ahead. Half open.'

'Be careful.'

'I will, Mum. Promise.'

'I'll cover you.'

'What with?'

'Will you stop fucking about?'

'Very unlikely, mate.'

Clocks moved forward. Paterson followed, his back to the wall watching the one door to the right, gun held high. Clocks darted past the open door and put his back up against the wall by the doorway. He looked at Paterson and nodded.

Paterson hurried into the room and turned left, swinging the gun around in a wide arc. Clocks went right.

Standing with his arms folded, his back to them, a man looked through two large French windows and out over the grounds of the house. He was powerfully built and had thick, wavy hair that hung past his shoulders.

'Armed police!' Paterson shouted. 'Show me your hands!'

The man ignored him.

'I said, *Armed police! Show me your hands!* Do it! Do it now!'

The man carried on looking out of the window, completely ignoring him.

Clocks looked across at Paterson. 'Is 'e a bit mutton, d'yer think?'

'Mutton?'

'Mutt 'n' Jeff. Deaf.'

241

Paterson shrugged. 'Dunno. Might be all that hair. Maybe he's got some caught in his ears.'

Clocks gave a quick pull on the trigger, putting five rounds into the ceiling.

Paterson started.

'Oi, oi!' Clocks shouted. 'Goldilocks! Stick 'em up 'fore I put one in yer 'ead an' shoulders.' He grinned at Paterson. 'Geddit? Lots of 'air . . . 'Ead an' Shoulders shampoo.'

Slowly, the man turned around. Handsome in a bashed-up, scarred face sort of way, he looked up at the ceiling as wisps of dust and bits of plaster fell to the ground.

'Why did you do that?' he said in English, his French accent thick.

'To get yer attention,' said Clocks. ''Ave I got it?'

The man turned his gaze to Clocks, his dark eyes burning into him.

'You will pay for that.'

'No worries, Shirley Temple. Send me the bill. Mister J. Clocks. Number forty-seven, Don't Give a Fuck Avenue, London.'

Behind them, officers from Capitaine Babineaux's team poured into the room. Paterson knew the shots to the ceiling had drawn them in. He held one hand up.

'It's okay, boys. Stand down. He's unarmed.'

The French officers kept their weapons high. Paterson watched the erratic little cluster of red dots jiggle around on the man's white shirt.

'I'm guessing you're Jacques Augustin, owner of this dump,' said Paterson.

'Dump?' said the Frenchman. 'Oh, you wish you could afford something like this. Are you jealous?'

Clocks chuckled. ''E could buy an' sell you all day long, you big girly.'

Augustin turned to Clocks. 'I do not like you. At all.'

'Oh, no! That's me fucked with fright, then.'

Augustin frowned as he balled his fists.

Clocks smiled and handed his gun to Paterson. 'Aye up. 'Ere we go. Looks like Kermit's other sister fancies 'is chances with the Met's finest.' He waved him forward. 'C'mon then, Shirley Temple. Let's 'ave yer. No kissin' though. I don't do kissin'. Understood?'

The French police slightly lowered their guns and looked a bit bewildered.

'What's the matter?' Paterson said to the one nearest him.

'Can your man fight?'

Paterson grimaced. 'After a fashion, yes. Bit of a blunt instrument. No finesse.'

'Augustin is master boxer. It is rumoured he could have been a champion.'

Clocks looked at the officer. 'What?'

'He used to be a bare-knuckle champion too.'

Clocks sniffed. 'Did 'e?'

'Plus . . .' said the officer.

'Plus? There's a plus? Course there's a plus. Why wouldn't there be?'

'He has black belts in jiu-jitsu and karate . . . taekwondo . . . aikido.'

'Is that it? We done?'

'I think so. No! Wait!'

'What? There's nothing left, is there? Fucker does the lot.'

'Why do you think we are all pointing guns at him?'

'Funny fucker. Go on. What else?'

'Brazilian jiu-jitsu and mixed martial arts.'

Paterson grinned at Clocks. 'Want your gun back?'

'Might be an idea. I reckon 'e'd give *you* a run fer yer money by the sound of it, an' I know you're a bit tasty.'

Augustin just stared. Clocks seemed to comprehend the truth, that he'd be destroyed before he even raised his fist.

Paterson broke the tension. 'Listen, sir. Sorry about smashing your house up and shooting all your security, but we're looking for someone. Someone we know is here.'

Augustin smirked. 'Who is it you are looking for, police-man? Are you this one's keeper?'

Clocks grinned at him. 'Keeper? Why do I need a keeper? I'm lovely.'

'You are . . . how do you English say? . . . a retard. Yes. A retard. Fucking retard.'

Clocks frowned. 'Can he call me that?' he said to Paterson. 'Isn't that bit un-PC these days? Shouldn't he call me a person of mental bewilderment or something?'

'With his skills, John, he can call you whatever the fuck he wants.'

'You make a good point.'

'We're looking for Alicia Warren,' Paterson said to Augustin. 'Big-time villain herself. Deals in death. Organs, kids, that sort of thing. All-round scum of the earth.'

Augustin shook his head. 'Alicia? Yes, she was here.'

'Was?'

'*Oui*. We had sex and then she left. Back to her husband.'

'She has a husband?'

'So she says. Who cares?'

'I'd imagine 'er ol' man does,' said Clocks. 'An' 'ang on a minute . . . She's on the run an' she stops by for a leg-over? What's wrong with you French people? Can't you keep yer uglies tucked away in yer pants for more than twenny min-utes at a time? I know you've all got a reputation to keep up, but fuck me, catch yer breath once in a while.'

'How long ago did she leave?' said Paterson.

'A while ago.'

'Apart from yer little baguette, what else did she want with you?' said Clocks.

'Mind your own business, policeman.'

'You two fuckers cookin' up a little deal with the ol' carfunanil, carfennalil, carfen . . . fuck it. Drugs.'

Augustin's eyes narrowed.

'It's alright mate. No need fer the ol' evil eye, is there? I already know you're a scum-bucket, drug-dealin',' body-snatchin' tosswipe. I just figured you two were lookin' to join enterprises. Am I right?'

'No more questions. Now. All of you . . . Leave my home. You will be hearing from my lawyers for this intrusion. I am a peaceful businessman. Get out! All of you!'

'Have you boys searched this house properly?' Clocks said to the uniforms. 'From top to bottom?'

'Not yet, sir,' said one of them.

'Then we leave when we're done. Not before.'

Paterson heard something and turned his head toward a side door. 'What's in there?'

Augustin turned. 'Nothing. It's my writing room.' He licked his lips.

'Open it,' Paterson ordered.

Augustin looked around him at the officers present. 'I demand to see your warrant.'

'Warrant?' said Clocks. 'Here it is.'

He shot Augustin in the leg.

'There you go, son. Read it an' weep.'

The French police looked shocked. One of them grinned as Augustin rolled around the floor bleeding, cursing and groaning.

'John! The fuck?' Paterson was stunned.

'What?' said Clocks. 'It was an accident. I think I tripped on a snail and me gun went off. Total accident. Could've 'appened to any of us. Right, boys?'

The French police nodded.

Another small sound came from behind the door.

'The door, John.' Paterson nodded toward it.

Clocks moved forward, machine gun raised. 'Check that room, boys.'

Paterson heard a thump and ran to the window. Alicia Warren was on the move. 'Fuck it! She's here. On the roof! Move!'

One of the French police opened the door and two security guards burst out waving guns. Five seconds later, they lay dead, riddled with bullet holes from the French. From where Paterson stood, he could see an open window.

From somewhere outside, he heard the sound of a car's tyres spinning on gravel. 'Fuck!'

Clocks glanced on Augustin's desk. Car keys. He snatched them up and ran for the door.

'What are we looking for?' said Paterson.

'Dunno. A car of some sort.' Clocks ran outside and began pressing the key fob. An alarm chirped a hundred feet away. 'Ooh! Fuckin' bingo, dingo!'

'Shit!' said Paterson as they ran. 'You know what that is?'

'Looks like a fuckin' rocket.'

'It's a Bugatti Chiron Sport.'

'Is that a rocket?'

'Might as well be.'

Clocks wrenched the door open and jumped in. 'Fuck me! It is a rocket.' He looked around the interior. 'It's a bit cramped, ain't it? You think that's because the steering wheel's on the wrong side? This is a left-'ooker.'

'Nothing to do with the size of the cockpit,' said Paterson. He slid gracefully into the passenger seat and put on his seatbelt. 'Buckle up, John. Seriously.'

Clocks did as he was told. 'Is this as fast as it looks?'

Paterson nodded as he pressed the ignition switch for him. The car growled into life. 'It's known to have hit three hundred on the track.'

'Fuck off! Three hundred? That'll take us back to the future!'

'Three hundred. I shit you not. Be . . . fucking . . . careful.'

A big grin spread across Clocks's face. 'This is gonna be a hoot. Which way did bitch-tits go?'

Paterson pointed toward the smashed in main gate. 'Left out of here.' He closed his eyes, wishing to God he'd seen the keys first.

CHAPTER FIFTY-SIX

Clocks lost control before he'd even reached the gates. He pressed on the accelerator and pulled on the steering wheel at the same time. The car span in a half circle as the tyres struggled to get a grip on the gravel. The pressure of acceleration had pushed them both into their seats, and Clocks looked terrified as he managed to bring it under control.

'Fuck me! Don't fucking stamp on it, John. Tickle it. Jesus! You want me to drive?'

Clocks looked over at him. 'Nah. I'll get the 'ang of it. It's a car, right? Just need to remember that. We'll be fine.'

'Christ! Make sure you do. Last thing I want to do is die here.'

Clocks touched the accelerator gently, setting the car in motion. 'What's the matter with dyin' 'ere?'

'I always thought I'd get shot by some woman's husband after catching us doing the nasty in his bed. I really don't want to die in a . . . a . . . rocket with you somewhere in France.'

'You won't. Trust me.'

'Look . . . drive it like you were making love to a woman. To Lyndsey.'

'What? You want me to get all excited, 'ot an' sweaty an' then get out after five seconds?'

'Just drive, John.'

Clocks drove out of the gate and hung a left. The road was long and clear and, now that it was dark, he could see Warren's brake lights in the distance.

Clocks stopped the car, engine running.

'What are you doing?' said Paterson.

'Givin' 'er a decent 'ead start. I don't wanna get out of this too soon, do I?'

'Just fucking . . . drive! Go! Move!'

'You sound a bit exasperated, mate. You alright?'

Paterson rubbed his jaw. 'Jesus wept.'

'Oh, don't bring 'im into it. Always weepin' that Jesus fellah, accordin' to you.'

'Because he knows I have to put the fuck up with you every day.'

'Alright. Bit tetchy, Ray. What's crawled up your arse'ole an' died?'

'You. You crawled up my arsehole and died. You shot that fucker in the leg back there, you nearly killed us a second ago and now you're letting Warren get away. Just move, will you!'

Clocks sniffed. 'Now, 'old up a minute. Don't go on at me about what I've done. You burned down 'alf of Mumbai, didn't yer?'

Paterson watched Warren's taillights get smaller and smaller in the distance. 'What? No. Well, yes. Not that much. Just a bit. A little bit.'

'Well, there you go. No one's perfect.'

'Clocksy, she's almost out of sight.'

Clocks took a look. 'So she is. Now it's gonna be a chase.'

He pressed the accelerator and the car roared into life. They were thrown back in their seats again as the car shot forward and tore down the street. Clocks glanced at the digital readout: 93 kph.

'Fuck me blind!' he said. 'Jesus.'

'Told you it was fast,' said Paterson. 'This does zero to sixty in two point three seconds.'

'Is that miles or kilometres per hour?'

'Miles per hour.'

'That's alright, then. Looks faster in kilometres.'

Clocks gripped the wheel tightly as the speed rose: 145 . . . 162 . . . 170.

Ahead, a car pulled out from a side street, indicating. Clocks stamped on the accelerator. 206. He shot past the car before it had time to half complete its manoeuvre. Paterson's eyes were wide. *He sped up. Who the fuck does that?*

Clocks's face took on a serious look. 'Got her,' he said and brought the car down to 130 kph. 'Ray . . .'

'What?'

'I wanna flash me 'eadlights. How'd I do that?'

'I don't know. Get in front of her and force her to stop.'

'What? What if she don't? What if she rams us?'

'You better hope she don't. You're not insured and this is worth a bundle.'

'Yeah? 'Ow big a bundle?'

'Ticket price is two point seven million.'

'Fuck off! Three million quid for a fuckin' jam jar? What sort of fuckin' arse'ole pays three million quid for a car?'

Warren's car hung a sharp left. Clocks braked, skidded slightly and got back behind her. She accelerated.

'Oh, you sure, love? What's she doin' now?'

'Probably still trying to escape, John. That's what villains do when the Old Bill come calling.'

'Alright! Don't get out yer pram.'

'To be honest, I'd rather be in a pram right now than locked in here with you. You've got no idea what you're doing, have you?'

'What? I took the same advanced driving test you did.'

'I know, but it wasn't in one of these things, was it?'

'Nope. S'pose you're a racing car driver too?'

'I've done a bit.'

'Yeah, course you 'ave. Shoulda known, really.'

'Look, why don't you pull over and let me drive.'

'Yeah, right. On yer bike, mate. I'm enjoyin' meol' self. You want one, go buy one when we get 'ome.'

'And that's the problem. *If* we get home.'

'Oh, shut up moanin', you big ol' tart! Look, we've got her. Watch this!'

Clocks drew closer . . . closer.

'John . . .'

Closer.

'John. If she brakes, we'll end up wearing her!'

'Just gonna give 'er a little nudge. How much do you think that'll cost in damages?'

There was a sudden bump as Clocks touched the bumper of Warren's Mercedes. It swerved violently. Clocks pulled to the right. Warren straightened up her car and accelerated.

'Bollocks! I thought she'd take the 'int and call it a day.'

Parked in an alleyway, a pair of French policemen looked bewildered as the two cars flashed past them and kissed each other at 135 kph. It was an ambitious move on the part of the French police, but the driver started up his car and gunned the engine. The passenger hit the siren and they took off in pursuit. Paterson caught the flashing lights in his wing mirror. 'The frog plods are behind us.'

'Good luck to 'em,' said Clocks. 'What's that funny little noise?'

'Noise?'

'Yeah. Some sort of siren.'

'That's because they're police.'

'Stupid little sound, innit? Sounds like we're being chased by Mr Whippy.'

A bright red glow lit up the cockpit of the Bugatti as Warren braked hard. Clocks, too close and with nowhere to go, stood on the brake but still slammed into the back of her. Mercedes and Bugatti spun away from each other in a shower of twisted metal and glass. The Bugatti's safety features kicked in. The airbags deployed, punching them back into their seats. The car spun around violently before the back end mounted the kerb, took out a couple of overnight market stalls and slammed to a juddering halt after hitting the corner of a building and turning sideways.

Paterson and Clocks sat in silence in the cockpit, both shocked and bewildered.

'Happy?' said Paterson after a few seconds.

Clocks sniffed. 'Not overly.'

'Are you okay?'

'I think so. You?'

'I think so.'

Clocks pushed against his door. It made a rasping sound and he had to shoulder it a few times before it opened. Paterson clambered out and surveyed the damage. It was going to be expensive.

He looked up to see the French police closing in on them in one direction and Alicia Warren going the other. The back of her car was badly damaged. The boot was buckled and nodding up and down as she tore away, dragging the bumper and other various bits along the road in a shower of sparks.

'Shit in an 'at an' punch it!' Clocks smacked the roof of the car. 'Fuck!'

The French police car skidded to a halt and both officers bailed out of the car, guns drawn and pointed at them. They screamed at them in French. Paterson and Clocks got the gist.

'*Bonjour*, officer,' said Paterson. He raised his hands.

'Alright, cockle?' Clocks raised his hands too.

One of the French police shouted to them in English. 'Hands up!'

'They are up,' said Clocks. 'They won't go any 'igher!'

'English?' snapped the officer.

'Yep,' said Clocks.

'On your knees.'

Clocks eyed the man. 'No chance, mate. I only get on my knees for two people . . . the queen and me missus.'

'On your knees.'

'John . . .' said Paterson. 'Just play the game. He looks like he's got the needle. No point getting shot now.'

Clocks sighed and slowly got down on his knees. The officer handcuffed them both.

'You are both under arrest. What were you doing? Racing?'

'*Non*,' said Paterson. 'We are police officers. I'm Superintendent Paterson and he's Inspector Clocks. We're from the Metropolitan Police in London. We're working on an Anglo–French case together with Capitaines Laurent and Babineaux. We were chasing a suspect, a wanted criminal, when we lost control of the car.'

The French officer holstered his gun. 'Babineaux, eh?'

Paterson nodded. 'You know him?'

'I know *of* him. And where is Capitaine Babineaux now?'

'He's at the scene of a serious incident. The woman we were chasing was the cause of it. My warrant card is in my pocket. Take it and check us out.'

'I will. Wait there and do not try anything.' The policeman took Paterson's ID and walked back to his car. In the distance, the wail of sirens coming their way pierced the night air.

'Lost 'er again,' said Clocks.

'Yep. Getting fucking tedious.'

'Doubt we'll pick 'er up now. Long gone by the time we get sorted out 'ere.'

Paterson sighed. 'She's a slippery one. She'll pop up somewhere, mate. They all do eventually.'

'I know, but I *really* wanted to nick this bitch.'

'Yeah. We will. Just not tonight.'

The French policeman came back. 'Their story checks out,' he said to his colleague. 'Let them go.'

Free from their handcuffs, Clocks rubbed his wrist. 'Bit tight that, mate,' he said to the officer.

The officer shrugged. 'How did you lose control? Can you not drive?'

Clocks nodded. 'I can drive, mate, 'course I can.'

'Then what happened?'

'Dunno, mate. I think I must 'ave skidded on a big snail back there somewhere. The bloody things are everywhere.'

CHAPTER FIFTY-SEVEN

'Capitaine Laurent . . .' said Paterson. 'I didn't expect to see you here. Come to see us off?' He couldn't take his eyes from the stitches that took the place of the dimple on her cheek where the gunman's bullet had grazed her. The wound wasn't deep but it had caught her jaw bone as it passed by.

Vivienne Laurent looked at him. She looked strained and weary and she obviously was in no mood for the pair of them. Moreover, the stitches were making it difficult for her to talk.

'I've come to mae soor you both lea,' she mumbled and drooled at the same time. 'An to mae soor you ne'er ome back.'

Clocks wrinkled his nose. 'What'd she say?'

'I think she said she's here to make sure we never come back,' Paterson said.

''Ello? We . . .' Clocks gestured to himself and Paterson. 'We . . . cannot . . . understand . . . you. Do . . . you . . . speak . . . English?' He gave Laurent a thumbs up.

Laurent rolled her eyes.

'Do . . . you . . . not . . . want . . . us . . . here? No?'

Laurent turned away from Clocks.

Paterson frowned. 'Is he right? I thought you liked us. Me especially.'

'You thor . . . wrong.' She winced and gingerly touched her jaw gingerly. 'All I wan . . . is for you and *l'animal* to geh on the plan and retur . . . return France to us.'

'I take it you mean me, treacle?' said Clocks. 'It's me again, innit? I'm the animal, yes?'

She nodded.

'Look. We got off on the wrong foot, babe. I'm a lovely chap once you get to know me. Salt of the earth. Ask anyone.'

Capitaine Laurent snorted. 'I doud it.'

He stepped closer and had his path blocked by Pierre. 'Oh, leave off, Kermie. What d'you think I'm gonna do? Stand down, big boy.'

Refusing to move, Pierre bunched his fists and glared at him.

'Iss okay.' Laurent wiped her mouth. 'Step aside.'

Reluctantly, Pierre did as he was told.

'Seriously, what did we do that you're chuckin' us out of France for?'

Laurent's eyes widened. She winced again. 'Tell him, Pierre. Ma heh aches when . . . e'er he speaks.'

Pierre sniffed. 'Where do I start, little man? You assaulted a number of innocent people.'

'Not innocent, were they?'

'You assaulted me.'

'After you assaulted me.'

'You bit Claude's finger.'

'I told 'im to stop wavin' it at me.'

'You shot an unarmed suspect.'

'Not on purpose. I tripped on a snail in the room. Accident.'

'There were no snails in the room.'

'They're everywhere, mate. You're probably so used to 'em that you don't notice 'em anymore.'

'You stole a luxury sports car—'

'Borrowed. I borrowed it.'

'And wrote it off.'

'Snail in the road. Just jumped out in front of me. Accident. I did report it.'

'You were not insured to drive it.'

'Didn't know I needed it. I've seen the way you lot drive over 'ere. Fuckin' atrocious. I'm surprised you 'ave insurance firms willin' to insure yer.'

'You implied French people are all cowards.'

'Wasn't implying anything, mate.'

'You verbally abused a number of people, including me.'

'What? Abused yer? What're you talkin' about?'

'You called me Kermit the Frog.'

Clocks cocked his head to one side. 'Oh, get over yerself. That's not abusive. I'll fuckin' show you verbal abuse if you want some.'

'John! No!' said Paterson. 'Enough, now. Let's just get ourselves home. We're not wanted, so let's go.' He said a final goodbye to Capitaine Laurent and headed toward the steps of the plane.

Clocks grinned up at Pierre. 'I'll miss you, yer big ol' lump of soap-dodgin' snail juice, you. C'mon, out the way. Let's say ta-ta to the Queen of France.'

He held his arms out to Laurent. 'C'mon, love. Bring it in. Gis a squidge. You know you want to.'

Capitaine Laurent squinted. 'I 'ould . . . rather kill myself . . .'

'Oh, don't be like that. C'mon. Just a little squidge. It's not like I'm gonna 'ave a good feel of yer tits when yer pressed up against me or anythin'. Just a cuddle.'

She turned sharply on her heel and stormed off.

'John!' Paterson shouted. 'Stop fucking about and get on this plane.'

'Comin' boss! Just sayin' goodbye to all my fans.' He joined Paterson on the plane and took his seat. 'They're a right miserable lot, ain't they?'

Paterson chortled. 'Certainly no sense of humour, that's for sure.'

'Right. Ol' Kermie got the right needle when I asked if he could score me mates' rates on tickets to Disneyland.'

CHAPTER FIFTY-EIGHT

'Welcome home, gentlemen. I understand you've both been extremely busy while you were out globe-trotting.' Commissioner Morne sat behind his desk, his hands resting on his stomach.

'Thank you, sir,' said Paterson. 'It was, shall we say, eventful.'

'Indeed it was.' Morne sat forward and opened a brown folder on his desk. He picked up the top sheet of paper. 'Let's see what's happened while you've been gone, shall we? What have we got? Let's start . . . here. The UK. Criminal damage . . . assault . . . several people dead, maimed or otherwise injured . . . London's senior pathologist arrested for murder — who, by the way, was found hanging by a belt in his cell this morning. What can you tell me about that?'

Paterson and Clocks looked at each other and shrugged.

'I've got a formal complaint from two undercover officers who say that you were both fraternising with your criminal targets in a direct breach of policy and that you both told one of the officers in question to "fuck off".'

'Sir,' said Clocks, 'if we're gonna be 'ere for a while, any chance I could trouble you for a cuppa tea? My mouth's as dry as a camels flip-flop.'

Morne stared at him. '*Really?*'

'Really.'

'Would you like biscuits as well, perhaps? Maybe a slice of cake, or what about a blueberry muffin? They always go nice with tea, I find.'

'Nah. I'm alright for the ol' biscuits an' cake, guv, thank you. I'm not 'ungry. Just thirsty.'

Paterson spoke out of the corner of his mouth. 'He's being sarcastic, John.'

Clocks nodded. 'Don't worry about it, guv. I can 'ang on.'

'That's good of you.' Morne sat back in his chair. 'You two clowns are here for a massive bollocking. Not to drink tea and eat biscuits.'

'Sorry, guv,' said Clocks. 'Carry on.'

'Thank you, John. I will. In Mumbai, the commissioner — after you allegedly threatened to beat the shit out of him — was then arrested by the assistant commissioner. Well done. Sounds like a coup of some kind. I understand that just prior to his arrest, the commissioner was shot in the leg by persons unknown. I don't suppose we have any information on the sniper that shot him, do we?'

Both men shook their heads.

'I thought not. Let's move on.' He looked back down at his piece of paper. 'Hotel staff assaulted . . . several police officers assaulted . . . clinic staff assaulted. Oh, a few more people dead. Several medical centres burned to the ground. Roughly twenty million pounds' worth of damage caused. Anybody know anything about that?'

Paterson and Clocks looked anywhere but at Commissioner Morne. 'No sir,' they said in unison.

'Hm, Hm. Turning to France now . . . two French police officers assaulted — one of them had his finger bitten.' Morne looked at Clocks, who shrugged. 'The house of a notorious criminal raided . . . bullet damage to the ceiling and said notorious criminal received a gunshot wound to the leg . . . a multi-million-pound car written off. Anybody know anything about *that?*'

Both men shook their heads again.

'I see,' said Morne. 'Well, it's bloody obvious you two have been up to your old tricks and kept yourselves busy, but you've now caused me about six months' worth of paperwork and heavy damage to relationships with two countries. Thank you for that.'

Clocks sniffed.

'How's the wound, John?'

He shrugged. 'Yeah. Not too bad. I've had worse.'

'No, you haven't,' said Morne.

'No, I haven't,' Clocks parroted.

'I see that one half of the notorious grave robbers, Burkhan and Dare, was killed.'

Paterson looked over at Clocks. He looked just as puzzled as he was.

'Grave robbers?' said Paterson.

'Yes. Well, not really grave robbers, but the names. Burkhan and Dare. Burkhan. Dare. Burke and Hare. Scottish grave robbers back in the eighteen hundreds.'

Clocks looked up at the ceiling and sighed.

'What?' said Morne. 'Don't tell me you missed that? That's not like you, John.'

Clocks nodded. 'Fuckin' 'ell, guv. Don't. It's bleedin' obvious now, innit? I could kick meself. I've probably done meself out of hours of quality jokes there. Think of the piss-taking I coulda done. Fuck!'

'Don't be too hard on yourself Clocksy,' said Paterson. 'I'm sure you're not the only person to have missed it.'

'Yeah, I know, but I'm s'posed to notice stuff like that. It's what I do. I must be slippin' in me old age. I've got the right 'ump now, so don't talk to me until I get over it.'

Paterson smiled. 'So, what happened to this Alicia Warren woman?' said Morne.

'She got away from us, I'm afraid,' said Paterson.

'Was that anything to do with the wrecked car? I understand you hit a snail, John. Is that correct?'

A smile spread over Clocks's face. 'Yes, guv. Bastard thing jumped out of nowhere. Nothing I could do.'

Paterson chuckled.

'And what can you tell me about the fires in Mumbai, Ray?'

'They're hot, sir. Like everywhere else.'

Clocks stifled a laugh.

Commissioner Morne sighed. 'You're supposed to be the sensible one, Paterson.'

'Sorry, sir.'

'Publicly, the Home Office are jumping up and down again. They want you gone. They say you've embarrassed the whole country with your antics and that you are, and I quote, "nothing short of criminals", unquote.'

Neither man spoke.

'Relax. You won't be going anywhere. Privately, the HO is pleased with what you've done. So am I. On the plus side, you severely dented a worldwide organ-harvesting trade and completely interrupted the chain of supply of this carfentanil drug. You've set them back at least a year. The organ racket will take longer to recover. You've saved countless lives. The French have lots of evidence against Augustin and he'll not see the light of day again for at least thirty years.

'All in all, gentlemen, bloody good work. What's next? Warren? Are you going to go and find her?'

'Dunno where to start, guv,' said Clocks. 'She's ducked right under the duvet. If she sticks 'er 'ead up anytime soon, we'll 'ave 'er. Don't worry about that.'

Morne smiled. 'Oh, I'm not worried, John. Not worried at all.'

CHAPTER FIFTY-NINE

Johnny Clocks tucked himself away at the back of his favourite little café in Greenwich Park. Strictly speaking it was off his manor, but he knew that he would be less likely to run into anybody who knew him.

He took a swig of his tea from a mug that looked as though it had been through the dishwasher far too many times and then a bite of his London cheesecake. This was one of the few places that still sold them. He wiped some crumbs of pastry from the table onto the floor and glanced at his watch: 11.03 a.m. He turned to look at the main entrance to the café. Outside he could see someone coming along the pathway and he took a deep breath.

Seconds later the door opened and a young man in his mid-twenties strolled in. Clocks eyed him up quickly: tallish — five foot eleven maybe, broad shoulders, same colour hair as himself, decent-looking but nothing to write home about. He was smartly dressed in designer shorts and a bright white linen shirt that was clearly on the large side. It was blazing hot outside, so Clocks figured that the extra room was to help him cool down a bit.

The young man looked around the café, spotted Clocks tucked away and raised his hand in greeting.

'Over 'ere, mate,' said Clocks.

The young man made his way over and dragged out a chair opposite Clocks, scraping it along the floor and annoying all the other customers. He plonked himself down. 'Alright?' His accent was old-school South East London.

'Yeah. You?'

'Yeah. Good, good.'

Clocks pointed to the cup of tea he'd purchased for him. 'Might be a bit on the cool side now. If it is, I'll get yer another.'

The young man picked it up and took a quick sip. 'Nah, you're alright. Cheers.'

'Got you a London cheesecake if you're 'ungry. You 'ungry?'

'Never say no to one of these buggers. Ta very much.'

Clocks took a deep breath. 'So, word is that you're me son? That right?'

The young man nodded as he bit into the cake. 'Yep.'

'Ronnie, right?'

'Yep,' he said again.

'I see what yer mum did there. Very good. Johnny Clocks, Ronnie Clocks. What was 'er name?'

'Karen. Karen Rodmell.'

Clocks searched his memory until his face lit up.

'You remember 'er?'

'Yeah. Course I do. Well, not very well. We were both young. Kids ourselves, really.'

'Yeah, she said that. Said I was the result of a knee-trembler behind the bike sheds. That's always been nice to know.'

Clocks chuckled. 'See? Sense of humour. 'Ow she doin' these days?'

'Alright, I guess. Not livin' fancy. Makin' 'er way, y'know?'

'Got any pictures of 'er with yer?'

Ronnie pressed a button on his mobile phone. A few swipes and he found some photographs of his mum and showed them to Clocks.

'Christ, yeah. I *do* remember her now. She was a cracker, yer mum.' He smiled as a few memories came creeping back.

Ronnie frowned.

Clocks's smile faded. 'Yeah. Well. So look, seein' as we're not gonna be 'uggin' each other or nothin', 'ow come you've decided to rock up now, after all these years?'

Ronnie took a swig of his lukewarm tea and shrugged. 'Thought it would be good if we connected.'

'After what? Twenny-four, twenny-five years?'

'I'm twenny-eight, an' better late than never.'

'Twenny-eight! So me an' yer mum were what . . .'

'She was sixteen.'

Clocks wrinkled his nose. 'Ouch! That was close.'

Ronnie shook his head.

'So why'd you pop up on me weddin' day? What was that all about?'

'Mum heard through the drums that you were gettin' married an' thought it'd be nice if I went along.'

'That's good of 'er. Gotta be honest, though. It was shit timin'. Me missus is ravin' about it.'

'Why?'

'I told 'er I never 'ad any kids.'

'Why'd you tell 'er that?'

Clocks looked at him, slightly dumbfounded. 'Because I never knew about you. I thought we'd already established that.'

'Oh, yeah. Sorry 'bout that. What's she like, me stepmum?'

Clocks looked mortified. 'What? What'd you say?'

'What's she like?'

'No, no, no. You said *stepmum*, didn't you?'

'Yeah.' He shrugged.

'Oh, fuck me. If you want to see twenny-nine, don't you ever call 'er that. She'll kill you where you stand. Understand me?'

Ronnie's eyebrows went up. 'What? Yeah, alright. Bit much though, innit? She seemed a nice enough lady at yer weddin'.'

'She is. She's fantastic. But she'll still kill you if you call 'er that. An' then she'll kill me.'

Ronnie smiled. 'Fair enough. I'll give it a swerve, then.'

Clocks calmed down a bit at that. 'Good.'

'Where is she?'

'Out an' about. She's lookin' at a new job. Dunno whether she'll take it.'

'What's it doin'?'

'This an' that. You don't need to know.'

Ronnie swallowed the last of his London cheesecake and wiped his mouth. 'Ah, that's the Ol' Bill comin' out. If I tell yer, I'll 'ave to kill yer.'

'Somethin' like that.' Clocks held his hand up until he caught the waitress's eye. 'Another tea, Ron?'

'Go on, then.'

'Two teas when you've got a minute, sweet'eart.' The young waitress nodded and wandered off toward the counter.

'So, look,' said Clocks. 'This 'as all been nice, but what is it you want from me after all these years?' said Clocks.

'I was thinkin' twenny-eight years of back Christmas an' birthday presents to start with.'

Clocks chuckled. 'Oh, yeah? Dream on. Anythin' else?'

Ronnie nodded.

'Oh, 'ere we go,' said Clocks. 'Let's 'ave it then? What d'you want?'

Ronnie grimaced. 'You're really not gonna like it, Dad.'

CHAPTER SIXTY

'You better be fuckin' pullin' me plonker, you little prick!'
Clocks banged his hands on the table as rage exploded inside
him. The waitress, carrying two teas and halfway toward his
table, jumped in surprise and threw the teas up in the air. She
yelped as some of the hot liquid caught her leg.

He looked over at her. 'You alright, babe?' He could
see she was shaken as she looked back at him, eyes wide. She
nodded several times.

'Sorry. My bad. Sure you're okay?'

She held her hand up. 'It's okay. Just made me jump.'

'Yeah. I'm really sorry. Sorry.'

She headed back toward the counter. 'I'll get you
another two.'

'It's alright, babe. Scrub it. He'll pay for those two,
though.' Clocks turned his attention back to Ronnie. '*Are*
you pullin' me plonker? You fuckin' better be, boy!'

Ronnie shook his head. 'Look, calm down a minu—'

'Calm down? Calm the fuck down? The fuck you think
you're talkin' to, boy? You tell me you robbed a post office
and then tell me to calm down 'cos I'm not 'appy about it?
You've got some front.'

'Look . . . I didn't know who else to turn to. Mum said to come an' talk to you. Thought maybe you could 'elp.'

'Did she? Well, fuck 'er an' all.'

Ronnie looked at him, his face serious. 'Don't talk about my mum like that.'

'Or what? What you gonna do about it?'

'Just don't push me. You can 'ave a go at me, fair enough. But not me mum. Alright?'

Clocks noticed Ronnie's body language. Leaning forward, face reddening, fists bunched. He was gearing up. Clocks was already there. He stared at Ronnie, willing him to lash out. He didn't.

'Look. I'm sorry. It was a mistake. I was out of order. Shouldn't 'ave asked yer.'

'No. You shouldn't 'ave, you fuckwit knob-jockey!'

Ronnie pushed his chair back and stood up. 'Okay. I'm leavin'. It was nice meetin' yer . . . *Dad.*'

'Where you think you're goin?' Sit yer arse back down, boy, before I sit you down meself. You're goin' nowhere until I say you are.'

Ronnie stared at Clocks. 'Am I under arrest, *Dad*?'

'Not yet, but if you keep on with the *dad* shit, you will be. Now, siddown!'

Ronnie sat himself back down and dragged his chair nearer the table. 'What?'

'Don't *what* me, boy. I ain't seen 'ide nor 'air of you since I rattled yer mum behind the bike sheds twenny odd years ago, an' you suddenly show up out the blue *claimin'* to be me son, *wantin'* to connect an' all that bollocks, but it turns out all you really want is for me to bail you out of the shit.'

'Said I was sorry. Let's leave it at that.'

'No. We ain't leavin' it at that. You sit down 'ere, drink the tea and eat the fuckin' cake I bought you then calmly tell me you're wanted for a blag on a post office. I mean . . . who blags a post office in this day an' age? That went out in the seventies fer Chrissakes. What'd you get? Fifteen quid an' a book of second-class stamps? I mean, I know they're expensive these days but . . . c'mon.'

'It was stupid. I know it was. Said I'm sorry.'

'*Stupid?* This? Oh no, mate, this was next-level stupid. If they 'ad your sort of stupidity as an Olympic event — never mind a gold medal, they'd 'ave to knock you up one made of platinum encrusted with diamonds. Blaggin' a post office. Jesus. You been in trouble before?'

'Yeah. A bit.'

'Like what?'

'Mostly robberies.'

'What *sort* of robberies? C'mon. Don't make me pull it out of you.'

Ronnie shrugged. 'Bit of street. Odd warehouse job.'

Clocks shook his head. 'Anyone 'urt?'

'Couple of people. Some of 'em thought they'd be a hero. Not bad though. Just slapped about a bit. Y'know how it is.'

'Yeah I do, you little shit. How'd you get into all that?'

'Got in with the wrong crowd.'

'That was clever.'

'Well, not like I 'ad a dad to keep me on the straight an' narrow, was it?'

Clocks reared up on him. 'Don't come it, boy. I knew nothin' about you. You gotta a problem with that, take it up with yer mother. She should have told me. This is not on me.'

Ronnie kept silent.

'Let me just double-check somethin' . . . You're wanted for an armed robbery on a post office, right?'

'Actually, a few.'

'What? 'Ow many?'

'Five.'

'*Five?*'

'Yeah.'

'So, you want a bit of 'elp an' you think I'm the one to do it?'

'Yeah.'

'An' in order to ask for me 'elp, you decide to show up at me weddin'?'

'Yeah.'

'Which is full to the brim with coppers?'

Ronnie nodded. 'Yeah.'

'In 'indsight, it wasn't the best plan, was it?'

'No. Not in 'indsight.'

'An' yer mum thought it was a good idea?'

'Hm-hm.'

'An' that little sort you were with. Who's she?'

'Me fiancée.'

'You're gettin' married?'

'Yeah. Later in the year.'

'An' she didn't think it was a bad idea either?'

'Not really.'

'Jesus wept. Not a brain cell between the lot of yer.'

'Oh. I meant to tell you. She's 'avin our kid.'

For the second time that morning, Clocks looked mortified. 'What's that now? What did you say?'

'I said—'

'I know what you said. You sayin' I'm gonna be a granddad?'

'Yeah. You are. I s'pose that makes your Lyndsey a gr—'

Clocks held his hand up. 'Don't say it. Don't say another word. Oh, you little prick. I am so fucked. So very fucked.' He closed his eyes and pressed the balls of his hands into them for a few seconds before rubbing his face and the back of his neck.

'Alright, leavin' that to one side, tell me this . . . Why didn't you show up on the PNC? Our database.'

Ronnie smiled at him. 'You looked me up?'

'Course I did. You think I'm not gonna dig around into a bloke that *claims* 'e's me son? What was I? Born yesterday?'

'Fair enough. Me real name is Reggie.'

'What? Reggie?'

'Yeah, but I fuckin' hate it, so I told everyone me name was Ronnie.'

'So, I've got a son, *alleged* son, called Ronnie *and* Reggie? Oh, *ding, ding.* That's a fuckin' prize-winner right there, innit, son? Guess the name of Johnny Clocks's boy? *What's that madam, Ronnie an' Reggie? Correct. You win a teddy bear.* Fuck me sideways with a baseball bat. Couldn't make it up if yer tried.'

'I must admit, it is a bit funny.'

'Yeah, well laugh this off. You're fuckin' nicked.'

Ronnie stared at him. 'What?'

'You 'eard. Get yer coat.'

'I ain't got one. It's boilin' outside.'

'Figure of speech.'

'You serious?'

'Too right I am. A couple of years in Brixton might straighten you out. At the least, they might 'ave some sort of brain-growin' course on the curriculum. That might 'elp you out. Post offices . . . soppy bastard.'

'But you're my dad.'

'So you say. I don't know you from Jack Shit, matey boy.'

'I am. I swear. An' I'm 'avin' a baby. Your grandson.'

'Again, so you say. Anyway, poor little fucker'll 'ave a bit more of a chance if one of you doom-brains is out of the picture.'

'I don't believe you. What sort of a fucker are you that you'd nick yer own kid?'

Clocks leaned across the table. 'I'm the sort of fucker that needs a lot more proof that you are who you say you are, an' I'm also the sort of fucker that ain't gonna let an armed robber go when 'e's dumb enough to put his 'ands up to it. Now, up! We're goin'.'

Ronnie suddenly shoved the table into Clocks and then upended it, sending the cups and plates sliding to the floor and pushing Clocks over with them. He turned and ran, shouldering the waitress as he went past her.

'You little fuck!' Clocks pushed the table off of himself and scrambled to get to his feet amid various curses and threats of death to the running man.

He ran at the door and tried to shoulder it open. It didn't budge and he grunted as his body collapsed against the metal frame. He looked through one of the glass panes and saw that Ronnie had stopped to lift a bench and jam it under the handle. He could see the boy in the distance, running down the hill. He wouldn't catch him now.

But he'd got what he came for. He had Ronnie's DNA on a cup.

CHAPTER SIXTY-ONE

ONE WEEK LATER

Paterson and Clocks sat opposite each other in Clocks's large living room. Paterson was sprawled out on the large white sofa while Clocks leaned back in a matching chair, one leg dangling over the arm. Both had full glasses of vodka and both were a little bit the worse for wear. The TV was showing some minor celebrity cook demonstrating how to cook a sausage pie.

'John, I was thinking . . .'

'Steady yerself.'

Paterson chuckled.

'Go on. What about?'

'The boy . . . your son.'

'Yeah? What about 'im?'

'Have you had a sit-down with him yet? Got to know him a bit better?'

'Still dunno if 'e is me boy. I got some DNA off of him for a test.'

Paterson's eyes widened. 'Really? He consented to that, did he?'

'Dunno. I didn't ask for it.'

'What? How'd you get it?'

'Mug. I bought him a tea. Dunno if it'll work, but it's worth a shot.'

Paterson shook his head and sighed. 'I guess it's the sensible thing to do, I'll give you that. Although, having spoken to him at your wedding, it's obvious he's as thick as you, so you won't be accepting that as proof?'

'Nah. Loads of people are as thick as me. Some even worse. So, no, that won't cut it.' Clocks took a large swig of his vodka, spilling some on his chin. He wiped it off with a muttered curse. 'Fuckin' more of a shock to me than anythin'.'

'Do you remember his mum?'

'Yeah. Boy showed me a picture.'

Paterson looked at him. 'And?'

'She's still got a crackin' pair of tits.'

'That's it, is it? That's all you can say about the mother of your child.'

'Tch. Alright. She's got a nice arse too. 'Appy?'

Paterson sipped at his drink. 'Has Lyndsey met her?'

Clocks stopped the glass halfway to his lips. 'You off yer nut? No, she ain't, an' it's best it bleedin' stays that way. You know what she's like.'

'She'll be alright, mate. She'll get over it. She looked like she'd forgiven you over in India.'

'Yeah, I know. I did feel better about things. Plus, I 'ope you're right, 'cos I really don't wanna 'ave to give back this 'ouse you got for our wedding present.'

Paterson chuckled again.

'Ray.'

'What, mate?'

'Somethin' I need to tell you about this kid.'

Paterson took another sip of his vodka. 'Like what?'

Clocks squirmed in his chair, swung his leg back down and sat forward, a serious expression on his face. 'Well . . .'

'What is it? What's the matter?'

'Well, when I met up with 'im, 'e told me a coupla things. Things that are quite . . .'

'What? Quite what? Spit it out, John.'

'Jesus, Ray, I . . .'

'Let me guess. You're gonna be a granddad?'

Clocks's eyes widened and his mouth fell open. 'The fuck did you know that?'

'Fuck off! I was joking. You serious? A granddad?'

'Yeah . . .'

'No!'

'That's what I said. Yep. If 'e is me son, an' we still don't know yet, I'm gonna be a granddad, and you know what that means?'

'It means I get to call you Grandpa John. Or Granddad Clocksy.'

'You fuckin' don't wanna. I'll pull your face right off if you do. No. It means—'

'Lyndsey's a stepnan. Oh . . . my . . . God. You are dead, man. Dead.'

'This is my worst fuckin' nightmare come true.'

'Yeah, I can see that. You might as well get the divorce papers drawn up now and give her the house and half the money. I knew you wouldn't have it for long anyway.'

Clocks sighed. 'It gets worse.'

Paterson chuckled. 'Next you'll be telling me he's . . . what? An armed robber?'

Clocks cleared his throat. 'You're a bit too fuckin' good at this. We need to talk.'

On the table next to his chair, Paterson's mobile phone rang. He looked over to see who the caller was. 'It's Wol. What's he want?'

'Answer it an' then you'll know, won't you, bullet? That's 'ow these things work.'

Paterson smiled and tapped the screen. 'Wol! How are you?'

'Put him on speaker,' Clocks said.

Paterson held the phone away from his ears and tried to focus on the speaker icon. He tapped it.

'. . . doing alright, thanks. Everyone's fine.'

'Alright Wol?' Clocks shouted.

'Ah. We're on speaker. Hi, John.'

'Is my missus with you, by any chance? Not 'eard from 'er in a while.'

'She is. She's fine, but we've been a bit busy.'

'What you up to?' said Clocks.

'Where are you both?'

'At John's. Why?'

'Is the telly working?'

'Yeah,' said Paterson.

'Good. Do yourselves a favour and go into set-up mode and then autotune.'

Clocks frowned. 'Why?'

'Just do it, John. Trust me.'

Clocks picked up the remote control and did as Wol asked.

The TV screen went blank as it ran through the tuner, stopping every few seconds as it picked up a terrestrial channel before setting off in search of another.

'What are we looking for?' said Paterson.

'You'll know it when you see it. I've got you that present you wanted.'

The TV searched on until the screen showed a split-screen picture, one from a slightly different angle, of five people sitting at a desk. The screen showed the faces of Tony Dare, Jacques Augustin and Alicia Warren. Opposite them sat two men in suits. Clocks pressed a button to hold the channel in place.

'How's it going?' said Wol. 'Got it yet?'

'Oh, yeah,' said Paterson. 'We've got it.'

'Took us a while to track down all three. We've been following them separately. Augustin was the really tricky one to find. Seems the van taking him to court was attacked and came under heavy fire. He got away and went into hiding. He has both the money and the resources. We picked up chatter that confirmed that he and Warren were going into business together, with him relocating to a country with no extradition orders. Although he makes money from a number of enterprises, he was more interested in the supply of carfentanil and intends to push it out beyond France and into Europe. From there, America and Russia. Lucrative markets.

'As for Warren, seems you boys gave her such a wallop — particularly you, Ray — when you burned down her clinics, that it gave her a wake-up call.

'The loss of the money hurt, of course, but she realised she needed to invest in security and Augustin had the muscle — a virtual army of naughty people. So he offered to help her out with much, much better protection this time around if she agreed to a partnership. What you're looking at now is the signing of the business agreements. The other men are lawyers to witness the signatures.'

'Business agreements?' said Clocks. 'That's a bit odd, surely? Villains don't normally sign anything when they go into business together. I'm pretty sure the 'atton Garden gang didn't draw up paperwork.'

'Shell companies, John. They're setting up shell companies. Legit on the outside, dodgy on the inside. The bent money will be washed through the legit companies and come out clean.'

'I can see that,' said Clocks.

'What's Tony Dare doing there, then? He's small-fry, surely?' said Paterson.

'Not so much,' said Wol. 'Seems he and Burkhan were running operations globally on the ground, so to speak. They were the ones who ran the camps and they were the ones who chose victims for their organ- and drug-smuggling operations. Again, chatter suggests that he's to become a partner, albeit a minor one in this little unholy enterprise.'

Clocks shook his head. 'Bastard. Shoulda killed 'im too.'

'Yeah, well. Shit happens, John. But, no worries. We're about to do that for you.'

Clocks almost dropped his drink. Paterson smirked.

'What?' said Clocks.

'Yes. Happy to. Thanks to Alice, our resident tech genius, what you're looking at is live through the sights of two very high-powered rifles. When you got chucked out of Fra—'

'We didn't get chucked out,' said Clocks. 'We were politely asked to leave. So we did. Not stayin' where we're not wanted.'

'Whatever. Ray asked us to stay on for a week or so to see if we could track them down and finish the job. As you can see, we did and we're about to.'

Clocks looked across to Paterson, who raised his glass. Clocks did the same as they watched the screen.

'Who're the shooters, Wol?' said Clocks.

'Hi, John.' Lyndsey's voice sounded over the speaker system.

'Lynds! The fuck?'

'How are you?'

'Er . . . er, yeah, alright. You?'

Paterson looked at his partner. *Silly thing to say.*

'I'm fine, my darling,' she said. Clocks brightened instantly. 'Sorry I haven't been in touch, but we've been keeping this building under surveillance for some time now. Had to go comms blind. You know how it is, waiting for it all to come together. Thought it wouldn't happen, then lo and behold . . .'

'Lynds,' said Clocks, 'are you sure about this?'

'Of course. This ain't my first rodeo.'

'I know. But the other times were in service of the job. Not fer fun.'

'I'll be fine, hun. A head's a head. And this isn't for fun. This is a good deed. These three are pure fucking evil. Topping this lot will save hundreds, if not thousands of lives in the long run.'

'If you do this, you can't come back to the police. Your career's over.'

'I don't think I want to go back. This is much more satisfying for the soul.'

'I take it the Ghost is the other shooter?' said Paterson.

'Hello Mr P.,' Bailey answered.

'Liam. Which one is yours?'

'I'm taking out Dare. Lyndsey'll do Augustin and, just for target practice, we'll both do Warren.'

Paterson winced at the thought. He'd considered Warren good-looking and now . . . well, she'd have to be buried without a head.

Augustin picked up a pen and began signing the papers in front of him.

'What about the lawyers, Ray?' said Wol. 'Them too?'

Paterson didn't answer for a moment. Clocks looked at him, a pensive expression on his face.

'Leave them,' said Paterson.

'Understood,' said Bailey. 'Standby.'

The TV showed crosshairs form on the heads of Dare and Augustin.

'Three. Two. One.'

The last thing Augustin did in this life was to push the sheaf of papers toward Warren. With his fingers still on the papers, his head disappeared in a small explosion of red, showering Alicia Warren in blood and gore.

'Target neutralised.' The White Ghost's voice was calm.

Tony Dare's head went a moment later and added to Warren's bad day.

'Target neutralised,' said Lyndsey.

Alicia Warren, rooted to her seat, her face dripping with the blood and bone of her fellow villains, looked up at the window from where the shots had come. Less than a second later her head disappeared like some kind of freaky magic trick. Her torso remained where it sat, pen still in her hand.

Clocks let out a huge sigh as he watched the spectacle unfold in front of his eyes. Three seconds . . . three dead. 'Jesus,' he whispered.

For a second, everything was quiet. Then the lawyers bolted.

Wol's voice broke in. 'Job done. Good shooting, team. Alice? Thank you for your help. We'll see you soon. Ray? Happy?'

'Ecstatic,' said Paterson.

'John?' said Lyndsey. 'I'll be home soon. Make sure you get some shopping in before I get there.'

The screen went dead.

Clocks looked over at his friend. 'Jesus, Ray. You *paid* for this?'

Paterson took a sip of his drink before answering. 'Hm-hm. Thought it was only right. These bastards don't deserve to live.'

Clocks nodded slowly. 'I know, but . . .'

'Are you upset? I thought you'd enjoy this. Justice. That's what we both stand for, right?'

'I'm not upset about dishin' out a bit of justice, rough or otherwise. I'm just a bit worried about you. I know we've both pulled some strokes before, but this all seems a bit . . . I dunno. Callous in the extreme. I mean, it's not the first time we've been 'ere, is it?'

'How d'you mean?'

'General Abrafo. His missus. The ex-naval officer woman. Can't think of 'er name. All of 'em killed on your say-so.'

'And?'

'And I'm worried about you.'

'Why?'

'Honestly?'

'Go on.'

'I sometimes wonder if you enjoy 'avin' them done.'

'Well, I don't cry myself to sleep, if that's what you're worried about.'

'I'm not worried about that and I'm well aware you're not cryin' yerself to sleep. That ain't what I mean.'

Paterson shrugged. 'Do we have a problem, Clocksy? If we do, now's the time to spit it out.'

Clocks shook his head. 'No, we don't, Ray. We don't. I'm not criticisin' an' I'm not looking for a ruck. I just know you've 'ad a few problems in the ol' mental department — like me, before you say anythin' — so I'm concerned that maybe, *maybe* you're losin' yer humanity a bit. That's all.'

'My humanity? I'm doing this *out* of humanity. *For* humanity, if you like. These. . . *creatures* don't deserve to live after the things they've done. They're no good to anyone, are they? All they do is bring pain and misery to untold numbers of victims and their families. Fuck 'em all, Clocksy. No regrets.'

Clocks sighed then gave a sharp nod.

'Look. You don't need to worry about me, Clocksy. I know exactly what I'm doing.'

'And what *exactly* is it you're doin', Ray?'

'Told you. Nothing complicated. Just trying to make the world that little bit safer from the bad people.'

'Yeah,' said Clocks. 'I can see that, mate. And it is safer now, I'll give yer that. But what worries me is that now you've got yer own little killin' squad on tap, is the world safe from you?'

THE END

ALSO BY STEVE PARKER

DETECTIVE RAY PATERSON
Book 1: THEIR LAST WORDS
Book 2: THE LOST CHILDREN
Book 3: THE BURNING MEN
Book 4: YOU CAN'T HIDE
Book 5: THEIR DYING BREATH
Book 6: CHILD BEHIND THE WALL
Book 7: HIS MOTHER'S BONES
Book 8: DEAD ON DELIVERY

Thank you for reading this book.

If you enjoyed it please leave feedback on Amazon or Goodreads, and if there is anything we missed or you have a question about, then please get in touch. We appreciate you choosing our book.

Founded in 2014 in Shoreditch, London, we at Joffe Books pride ourselves on our history of innovative publishing. We were thrilled to be shortlisted for Independent Publisher of the Year at the British Book Awards.

www.joffebooks.com

We're very grateful to eagle-eyed readers who take the time to contact us. Please send any errors you find to corrections@joffebooks.com. We'll get them fixed ASAP.